J.T. Brannan trained as a British Army officer at Sandhurst, before deciding to pursue a writing career. A former national Karate champion, he now teaches Karate, MMA, and his own system of reality-based self-defence. He lives near Harrogate with his wife and two young children. EXTINCTION is his second novel.

Praise for J.T. Brannan:

'What an absorbing, rollercoaster of a read' Elly Griffiths

'Origin is a truly original novel, seamlessly meshing a modern high-tech chase thriller, stuffed full of guns and gadgets, with elements of ancient history to produce a book that's both thought-provoking and relentlessly exciting' James Becker, bestselling author of THE FIRST APOSTLE

'Hugely authentic … unpredictable' *SciFiNow*

'There are shades of Dan Brown in this impressive debut novel' *Choice Magazine*

'A high-octane cross genre thriller' *Living North*

By J.T. Brannan and available from Headline

Origin
Extinction

EXTINCTION
J. T. BRANNAN

headline

First published in Great Britain in 2014 by
HEADLINE PUBLISHING GROUP

1

Cataloguing in Publication Data is available from the British Library

ISBN 978 1 4722 0680 0

Typeset in Granjon 12.5/14.75 pt by
Palimpsest Book Production Limited, Falkirk, Stirlingshire

Printed and bound in Great Britain by
Clays Ltd, St Ives plc

Headline's policy is to use papers that are natural, renewable and recyclable
products and made from wood grown in sustainable forests. The logging and
manufacturing processes are expected to conform to the environmental
regulations of the country of origin.

HEADLINE PUBLISHING GROUP
An Hachette UK Company
338 Euston Road
London NW1 3BH

www.headline.co.uk
www.hachette.co.uk

For Justyna, Jakub and Mia

Acknowledgements

I WOULD LIKE to express my heartfelt thanks to my terrific agent Luigi Bonomi and everyone at LBA; my fantastic editor Alexander Hope, along with editorial assistant Darcy Nicholson, my publicist Ben Willis and the rest of the team at Headline Publishing; my parents for their continued support and help with last-minute baby-sitting; my children for letting me write, and for telling everyone they meet that their daddy is an author; my good friend Tom Chantler for his excellent eye for detail and his scientific expertise; and most importantly, thank you to my wonderful wife Justyna, who does . . . well, almost everything, really! You're the best.

'Extinction is the rule. Survival is the exception.'

Carl Sagan
The Varieties of Scientific Experience:
A Personal View of the Search for God

Prologue

'READY?' CLIVE BURNETT asked, excitement written across his weather-beaten features, clear in the intense midday sun of the unforgiving Egyptian desert.

'Ready,' Tom Bowers answered, barely suppressing his own excitement. He was the archaeological team's demolitions expert and he had rigged forty pounds of plastic explosive to a natural rock formation nestled within the country's fabled Valley of the Kings.

Burnett had been a field archaeologist for over three decades, and he was convinced this barren desert location was hiding what he had been searching for all these years – the legendary 'Hall of Records'. The Hall was one of those common myths of Egyptology that might just be true – a huge repository of ancient texts, including those from the Library of Alexandria, which were thought to have been secreted away in Egypt before that city had been razed to the ground thousands of years before.

Years of painstaking, meticulous research had led Burnett to believe that he had at last found the location, and high-altitude X-ray tomography had recently shown a very large structure under these sands. The only trouble was, the fifty thousand tons of granite which covered it precluded a dig further into the sand beneath.

But Burnett had presented his evidence, and Egypt's Supreme Council of Antiquities had finally relented and authorized the use of explosives to clear the site. As Burnett watched Bowers make his final preparations, he felt a trickle of sweat slide down his face – caused by anticipation, not the fiery heat of the desert sun.

Bowers nodded to Burnett as the rest of the team stood watching behind the safety markers. Bowers smiled, one friend to another, and pushed the plunger of the demolitions box.

At first there was nothing – no sound, no explosive concussion – and Burnett feared that the charges had failed to go off. But moments later he felt the ground shake beneath his feet, and grinned as clusters of debris shot high into the pure blue sky above them, shattering the foundations of the rock formation which hid his prize.

He could see the rock shivering, resisting the power of the linked explosives, putting up one last fight, before it forever relinquished its hold on the sands and shattered.

Burnett watched as dust and debris was thrown hundreds of feet into the air and the solid rock seemed to literally disintegrate before him.

He turned to Bowers, ten feet ahead of him at the limits of the safety zone, and gave him a gleeful thumbs-up.

But something was wrong; Bowers wasn't smiling. Instead he seemed alert, confused, scared even.

Then he turned fully to Burnett and the rest of the team. 'Get back!' he yelled at the top of his voice, struggling to be heard over the falling rock. 'It's going down!'

Burnett only had moments to consider what his friend meant. Surely the rock was supposed to be going down, wasn't it? But then he saw what the demolitions expert meant as the remnants of the vast granite rock slipped beneath the rapidly opening ground and millions of tons of sand were pulled towards what was now a gigantic sinkhole.

Burnett saw Bowers' legs go from under him as he was pulled inexorably towards the ravenous mouth in the middle of the valley. He instinctively made a move forwards to help his friend but then felt the ground moving once more beneath his feet, rooting him to the spot. His legs seemed useless, turned to stone by the shock of the event, and then arms grabbed him, hauling him further behind the safety lines. His breath ragged, adrenalin coursing through him, he turned and looked one last time at the place where the rock had once stood, and saw his friend's hands disappearing over the edge, pulled deep into the sinkhole in the desert floor.

He struggled against the hands of his colleagues, straining to get to his friend, but eventually relaxed, head bowed, resignation taking him.

It was too late. Tom Bowers was gone.

It was over twelve hours later that the site was deemed secure enough to venture close to it and the first order Burnett gave was to retrieve the body.

He and his team stood at the edge of the sinkhole, which seemed to drop far, far down into the valley floor, straining their eyes to find Tom Bowers. It took several minutes, but the battered form was eventually spotted, half buried in the sand about thirty feet down, one broken arm and two-thirds of his mangled face sticking out grotesquely from the caved-in wall.

Burnett was issuing instructions to the retrieval team when he heard a cry from Claire Goodwin, a senior member of the team. 'Get over here!' There was a beat pause, and then she repeated the call with increased urgency. 'Get over here! Everybody! Now!'

Burnett was the first one there. He peered down into the chasm, in the direction Goodwin's finger pointed. 'What?' he asked, irritated by the interruption. 'I don't see any . . .'

Burnett's voice caught in his throat as he saw what Goodwin was pointing at, and it didn't take long for everyone else on the team to spot it too.

Metal, glinting dully in the glare of the sun, perhaps one hundred feet down.

There was no ancient stonework here, only a long, curved piece of metal – the outer edge of something far larger, still buried.

The discovery excited Burnett but he put aside the archaeological purpose of the mission until the body of Bowers had been retrieved, his family had been – painfully, but necessarily – informed, and repatriation arrangements had been made.

The funeral was to be held back in the US in ten days' time, and Burnett decided to postpone his grief and concentrate on the mission at hand, determined that his friend should not have died in vain.

Some members of his team suggested the metal structure

buried deep beneath the sands might be some sort of war bunker, or research facility left over from the Nazis. Hitler was known to have been interested in archaeology, looking for historical evidence in support of his 'master race' theories. He had authorized many digs throughout North Africa and the Middle East, and it was possible that the structure was in some way related to this.

But, Burnett argued, how would they have buried it in one hundred feet of sand – over the entire valley, he added, and not just in this one area – and then topped it off with a fifty-thousand-ton geological formation?

It was possible that seismic activity might have shifted the sand, but the granite suggested something else.

Two days later, the site had been cleared up and the walls of the sinkhole shored up and secured, enabling members of the team to descend on to the top of the structure and start clearing away more of the sand and debris.

'What's it made of?' Burnett asked the team's chief metallurgist, John Jackson.

'I'm not exactly sure,' Jackson replied. 'Seems to be some sort of variant of titanium, but nothing I'm familiar with.'

'Can we get through it?'

Jackson thought for a moment, then nodded his head. 'We can, yes. It'll just take some time.'

'Get started now then. We don't know when the locals will turn up, and I want to be inside before they get here.'

Jackson announced that he was through more than six hours later. Word quickly spread to other parts of the camp, and within minutes all thirty members of the crew were there.

The curved metal object was an access hatch, much like a submarine hatch, and was located on what appeared to be the roof of a building still buried underground.

The hatch opened to reveal a metallic access tunnel, with a ladder leading down into the dark.

Burnett stepped forward and turned on the torch secured to his helmet. 'I'll go first,' he announced with authority, and as he placed his feet on the metal rungs, he only knew one thing – this wasn't the Hall of Records.

He hoped that whatever it was would be worth his friend's sacrifice.

Claire Goodwin and two other members of the team accompanied Burnett, while the others listened to the radio sets connected to their chief's communication system.

There were long pauses as the four archaeologists descended the ladder, Burnett commenting every now and then on the structure of the tunnel, and their current depth.

'We're at the bottom,' Burnett eventually announced. 'We're leaving the access hatch and entering the structure itself.'

There was another pause as the team dismounted the ladder, and then everyone still on the surface heard a sharp intake of breath, loud over the radio.

'I . . . I . . .' Burnett seemed lost for words. The team members still on the surface heard him breathe deeply several times, trying to collect himself. 'I . . .' he continued eventually, 'I don't believe it.' Another pause. 'I've never seen anything like this before in my entire life.'

PART ONE

PART ONE

1

THE COLOSSAL STATUE could be seen from miles away by anyone approaching the city on the main freeway that crossed through the rainforest until it broke out on to the coastal plain. The statue loomed over the city from its position over two thousand feet high on the mountain, a robed, bearded figure with its arms outstretched towards the ocean beyond.

Made out of concrete and soapstone, the forty-metre-high statue had been a symbol of the city for over ninety years, a focal point for the nation's devout religious fervour. Weighing in excess of seven hundred tons, it was one of the world's largest statues, visited by millions of tourists each year, many of whom made the pilgrimage all the way up to the top of the mountain to stand at the huge pedestal upon which the statue rested. There they stood, craning their necks and looking up in awe at the image of the prophet above them.

One such group of pilgrims stood there now, squinting tired eyes into the sun to see their redeemer in all his glory.

And despite the strength of their religion and the passion of their beliefs, nothing in their experience had prepared them for what they saw next.

* * *

It was early in the morning, a time many people made the pilgrimage to the top of the mountain, to watch the sun rise over the horizon. It bathed the statue in an otherworldly glow, making it seem even more impressive, as if the statue and the sun were somehow connected. But this morning was different. As the tourists looked on, believers and non-believers alike, they saw the statue *move*.

The movement of the statue was no mere tilt, as if with the wind, or wobble, as if disturbed at its base; incredibly, the entire statue leaned backwards and raised its enormous head to look at the rising sun, lifting its gigantic stone arms high above its head.

It stopped then, leaning backwards slightly and gazing at the sky between upstretched arms, as if this was how it had stood for almost a century. But the people there knew that this was not the case; they had watched for two whole minutes as the statue had moved ever so slowly to reach for the sky, as if asking the Heavens themselves for help. But help for what?

Soon, it wasn't just those who were there who were asking the question. The first footage went out over the social media networks just seconds after it happened; within ten minutes, everyone who had filmed it or taken pictures had sent them over the airwaves to family and friends across the globe. And within thirty minutes the entire world knew, and had seen it.

The statue – this seven-hundred-ton block of concrete and soapstone – had *moved*.

And the world wanted to know why.

2

JOYCE GREENFIELD FELT the bracing morning air and smiled. Another beautiful day, she thought as she skipped lightly down the steps of her brownstone apartment, holding the lead of Sebastian, her pedigree hunting dog.

Sebastian was the pride of her life, at least ever since her boyfriend Adam had left her for another woman late last year. You couldn't trust men, she'd learnt that the hard way. But dogs you could trust. Especially Sebastian, whom she'd had since a puppy, a wonderful little thing who had been her constant companion in both the good times and the bad.

It had happened late last year, the same old clichéd story heard a million times before, except this time it had happened to her: she had come home from work early one afternoon to find Adam – her beloved, the man whom she had hoped to one day marry – in bed with another woman. In *their* bed – an even worse betrayal. It was where they had discussed their hopes, their dreams, their ideas of what living a life together would be like; it was where Joyce had told him the little things, the secret things which made a person unique, and which she had shared with no one else.

And the woman wasn't even just *another woman*, it was

Georgina Wilcock; maybe not her *best* friend, but a friend nevertheless. How could a friend do that? Joyce supposed she should have known – she'd seen Georgina do the same to other women's boyfriends, even other women's husbands, but she had never suspected it would happen to her. Stupid. You couldn't trust men, and it turned out you couldn't trust women either.

But, she repeated to herself as Sebastian trotted along obediently at her side, you *could* trust dogs. You could *always* trust dogs. Cats were nice too, she thought, but not like dogs. She had always agreed with the idea that there were dog people and cat people. You could like both, sure, but not equally – you had to decide one way or the other which you preferred, and she was definitely a dog person.

She had lived with dogs all her life – her parents were dog people too – and had even found a way to smuggle Francis, her pet from the age of six, into her college dorms for the whole three years she was there; she just couldn't live without dogs.

She had had others over the years, often fostering dogs for animal shelters before they found permanent homes, and the stories of their lives more often than not reduced her to tears. How could people be so cruel? It never ceased to amaze her. Malnutrition and neglect were the least of the dogs' problems – some had been forced into fights, resulting in horrific wounds, another had been set on fire for making too much noise during the night, one more had had all her teeth pulled out with pliers for chewing the leg of a kitchen chair.

But with Sebastian, it was a clean slate. She had always loved the breed, long and sleek but well-muscled, a ridge of hair rising along the length of its back giving it a unique look. And some of the things it was bred to hunt! But Sebastian was a pure pet dog, bred for health and appearance, and Joyce felt herself admiring his perfect form, his long, easy gait, the way he carried his large, heavy head proudly, chest out, chin up.

Being a pedigree – descended from champions, no less – he hadn't been cheap. But she had always wanted one, she earned good money, and the opportunity was there – why not take it? And so she had paid her five hundred deposit – the balance of fifteen hundred would be paid when a new litter was born and she had made her selection – and put her name on the waiting list.

She had never regretted the decision once, and it made her feel good to walk with him through the city streets, as she felt eyes turning towards them, admiring Sebastian; and in that admiration she felt mutual acclaim, the fact that she was with him making *her* someone to be admired – *look at how that lady walks that beautiful dog*, people would say, *she must really have something about her*.

And that was how she felt that morning, a deep glow of satisfaction within her, making up for all the other problems in her life. She would walk down the street, across the junction and then into the park, where Sebastian would have a good half-hour runaround, and Joyce Greenfield felt good. Sure, she worked long hours and hadn't had a proper relationship since Adam, but with the sky blue and full of promise, and Sebastian at her side, her worries faded into the background.

*　*　*

She first felt the difference as they waited to cross the road to the park. Sebastian would normally wait patiently by her side, in a perfect 'sit' position, but this morning he seemed agitated by something. He started to fidget as they waited for the lights to change, then stood up and pulled forward, yanking her arm.

Surprised, she nevertheless managed to rein him back in; and then the lights changed and they crossed for the park, although Sebastian kept on pulling her. What was wrong with him? Could he smell something? she wondered. Maybe a girl doggy over in the park? She'd been meaning to have him 'done' for a couple of years now – after all, it was supposed to help prevent serious disease and all sort of other things – but she still thought she might breed from him one day and so had never made the appointment.

Sebastian calmed as they entered the park, and she momentarily forgot about it as they walked down the tree-lined paths towards the playing fields where she would throw the ball for him.

But then she noticed that other people walking their dogs were being jerked along by their agitated canines. As she started to pay more attention, it seemed everyone was having some problems with their dogs.

And then Sebastian pulled her again, harder this time, and she fought to correct him, but he fought back and pulled her forwards, faster and faster, towards the playing fields, and now she had no control, she was just being pulled along behind him, stumbling over herself in an effort to keep up. What the hell had gotten into him?

They were in the playing fields just moments later, and Sebastian paused, tense, as if sensing something beyond Joyce's comprehension.

Her head snapped round at the screams that broke out seconds later, and she saw the huge dog just two hundred yards away with its jaws wrapped round its owner's arm, blood gushing.

Over to the other side, a pair of old ladies screamed as their little toy dogs began to snap and bite at their heels, continuing their attack as the women fell to the ground, claws and teeth going for their faces with savage ferocity.

Everywhere she looked, dogs were attacking their owners, biting legs, arms, faces, necks. The green grass of the fields was stained red with fresh blood everywhere she looked.

And then Sebastian turned towards her, lips pulled back in a feral snarl. No, surely not her own dog as well, surely not Sebastian, her faithful companion?

But in the blink of an eye Sebastian launched himself at Joyce, forcing her to the ground. She cried out as in a frenzy his claws and teeth ripped her to pieces.

3

Hans Glauber looked out of the little window of the huge aircraft and stifled a yawn. Four hours already, and only halfway there.

He loved his job as head of international sales for a distinguished yacht firm, but the travel could be a real killer, hopping from one continent to the next, sometimes more than four times in a single week. He'd grown accustomed to it now of course but it hardly made it any easier.

He'd arrive at his hotel at about eight in the morning and, although the temptation would be to simply crash out and get some sleep, he knew the best thing to do would be to follow his daily routine and go to bed that night at the normal time. His body would adjust to the time difference naturally this way, and he'd be absolutely fine by the following morning, which was when the big meeting was scheduled for.

'What's that?' he heard himself ask, almost without realizing.

The middle-aged lady in the seat next to him leant across to have a look. 'What's what?' she asked.

Glauber wasn't sure. He peered out of the window, looking harder.

'There!' he exclaimed, prodding at the glass with a pudgy finger.

The woman looked in the direction of Glauber's finger, towards the front of the aircraft. There was movement in the sky ahead but she couldn't make out what it was.

Glauber stared. It looked like lots and lots of tiny specks criss-crossing the sky, a long way away. Like grains of sand, moving independently of one another, coming together in small groups, then separating again. How many were there? A thousand? A million?

'Are they birds?' the lady asked him, and he realized she was right; they were birds, circling the sky maybe dozens of miles away, vast numbers of birds, swarming together, separating, and then swarming again.

But why?

In the cockpit, Flight Navigator Lao Che Huan turned to the pilot, Hoa Man. 'They're on the radar now,' he announced, voice calm and professional. 'They must be converging.'

Huan and Man had been observing the birds for some time; they were following the same course as the airplane. At first the men had had no idea what the specks in the distance were, but after a while it became clear that they were birds. But they behaved in a way neither man had seen before, flying apart and then coming together in larger groups. And now it seemed that they had formed one enormous supergroup.

'How large?' Man asked.

'I've got no idea,' Huan said, now struggling to contain himself. 'There must be millions of them.'

'But they're still some way ahead of us,' Man said hopefully.

'Yes, sir,' Huan answered immediately. 'They're about twelve . . . Oh no,' he gasped.

'What?' Man questioned.

Huan swallowed hard. 'They're turning.'

In the cabin, Glauber felt the woman beside him shudder. He'd seen it too, the birds coming together into one huge group, bigger than anything he'd thought possible.

And it wasn't just Glauber and the woman – other passengers had also noticed now. There was a collective gasp as the birds all came together, and then there were cries of alarm when the birds turned, and started flying towards the aircraft.

The pilot and navigator tensed as the flock swooped and turned, until it was flying directly towards them, less than a mile away now.

Hoa Man tried to take evasive action, but the birds turned with him, getting closer, ever closer, until they were all he could see, all that anyone could see; the cockpit window was filled with the birds, coming relentlessly towards them, a huge black cloud of birds that seemed to fill the whole sky.

Glauber watched as the birds soared towards the aircraft. The woman next to him gripped his arm reflexively, her fingers tight with anxiety.

The birds swarmed from all sides, all over the aircraft, and the plane lurched up and down as if hitting turbulence.

Glauber heard the woman next to him scream, heard others scream all through the cabin; and then the birds were gone, the sky outside clear once more.

'What the hell is going on?' the woman asked breathlessly. 'What do they want?'

Glauber's brow furrowed, as he searched the sky for the birds. What do they *want*? He had never considered the idea. What *do* animals want? Food, shelter, to reproduce; Glauber knew that, as far as an animal could *want* anything, it wanted to survive. But how was this behaviour accomplishing anything? Flying towards the plane in a group of thousands, maybe millions, then breaking away and flying off? It seemed that the purpose was merely to frighten the people in the aircraft, but that was clearly ridiculous. Why would any animal want to do that?

'I don't know,' he admitted.

There were cries from around the cabin – *There! – Over on the right! – There they are!* – and Glauber saw them again, circling in smaller groups, swarming and then breaking away as they had before. But he realized moments later that this was another group entirely. Surely it must be. The aircraft would be travelling at well over five hundred miles per hour, an impossible speed for birds to keep pace with.

This realization filled him with even greater horror. It was as if nature was rebelling. It seemed utterly impossible for there to be another group of these birds; but there they were, as before, coalescing into a huge, living, pulsating mass.

* * *

'They're coming again,' Flight Navigator Huan said, his voice urgent, panic creeping in. Their flight training was rigorous – what to do in case of mechanical malfunction, terrorist attack, even how to keep control in the face of a hurricane – but nothing had prepared him for this.

'A different flock,' Man said, his tone uneven, disbelieving.

Huan nodded his head; he could see the two separate groups on his radar system, the first group left far behind. Two separate groups of birds, both acting in a way which seemed to contradict the very laws of nature. What did it mean?

But then this group of birds was on them also, and he heard Man grunting with the effort of keeping the plane stable as it was rocked up and down, side to side, by the army – for that was surely the word for it – of winged creatures, no longer the benign little angels that Huan had once believed them to be, but savage beasts, cruel and vindictive.

The plane was rocked harder this time, for longer, but the army finally passed again, flying away to swarm and regroup. Huan breathed a sigh of relief.

'Damage report?' Man demanded, doing his best to retain his professionalism, although the sweat that dripped down his face revealed the pressure he was under.

Huan's keen eyes swept the instruments, trying to identify any irregularities – altitude, oil pressure, fuel, engine temperature, bearing, rudder adjustment – but miraculously everything was still fine, all as it should be.

'Nothing,' he reported, regaining some of his own composure.

* * *

Glauber wasn't sure which was more frightening – the third group of birds, massing again in their millions underneath the dark, ominous clouds, creating a huge, even more menacing cloud of their own – or the scene inside the aircraft, where fear and panic were starting to take hold.

Some people merely stared out of the tiny windows in open-mouthed disbelief, whilst others screamed, screams of a sort that Glauber had never before heard in his life – screams of pure terror. Children sobbed gently or cried hysterically; actually, not just the children, Glauber realized, but men and women too. Most people who weren't screaming were crying.

Others, however, were more active. Some were hammering on the cockpit door, demanding answers from the flight crew, and Glauber was disgusted as he saw a big, bearded man grab a stewardess by the front of her dress and slam her into the toilet door, yelling in her face. He was tackled to the floor by other passengers.

Another man had begun to talk loudly, preaching to the passengers – *this is it, it's finally time, better repent now, Judgement Day has come, it's the time of the Apocalypse*.

Further along, one family was taking down their luggage from the overhead racks, almost as if they expected to be getting off the plane at any moment, forgetting they were still thirty-eight thousand feet in the air. Shock, Glauber thought.

Glauber glanced to his side, saw the woman bent with her head between her knees, muttering prayers to herself – actually, Glauber realized, it was the same prayer, repeated over and over and over again. He himself wasn't in shock. He felt something different. Disbelief perhaps? Disbelief that something like this was happening?

No. As the third group of birds began to converge on the aircraft, starting their final approach in one huge amorphous mass, moving with seemingly demonic intent, Glauber realized what he felt was acceptance.

He knew he was going to die.

In the cockpit, Man was the first to scream, just half a second before Huan.

The third attack had started the same way as the first two. Anticipating the move, Man had violently turned the aircraft, cutting across the line of attacking birds, avoiding them entirely.

Man had taken a short breath, allowed himself a brief glimmer of hope, but then he saw the birds ahead had been a decoy. His evasive action had taken his airplane, his crew, and his three hundred and fifty-six passengers directly into the path of another flock, this one even bigger, a fact neither man thought possible but which was undeniable. *There must be tens of millions of them*, Man thought with a shudder, just before they reached the plane.

The first line of birds hit the cockpit window, bodies breaking across the glass, bones, feathers and blood smeared and splattered everywhere. Then the next wave hit, then the next, wave after wave after wave of broken and smashed bodies, until the window started to break, to cave inwards.

Huan, despite his fear and panic, still managed to notice the warning lights go on for the engines, first one, then two, then three, then four, until all engines were out, and his mind was still able to process the fact that the birds had flown straight into the huge, churning jet engines, sacrificing themselves to destroy the aircraft, just as the birds were doing against the windscreen in front of him. He noticed the altitude start to drop, saw how cabin pressure was being lost in the main passenger area, realized that the birds must have broken through the cabin windows.

And then the reinforced glass of the cockpit finally gave way, and Huan's screams were forever silenced by a crushing mass of feathers, blood and bone.

Glauber could now hear nothing – not the prayers of the woman next to him, nor the cries of the children, nor the screams of everyone else.

Vision was his only sense, and he looked on in mute amazement as the birds flew into the jet engines mounted on the wings, hundreds upon hundreds, until the engines blew, flames and charred feathers bursting across the sky. But still the birds didn't stop, and Glauber watched with an almost fascinated terror – not even feeling the drop in altitude, the ferocious rocking of the plane's fuselage – as the broiling, seething mass succeeded in ripping the entire wing off, sending it spinning away across the sky in an almost balletic display.

Glauber was still watching the wing spiralling down to earth when the first of the birds smashed through into the cabin, the pressure reducing, anything unsecured – luggage, food, drink, magazines, bodies – being sucked out by the vacuum. But then more birds entered, and nothing else could be sucked out, and Glauber felt the entire aircraft start to spin and understood that the other engines were lost, maybe the entire wing too.

His attention was now focused inside the aircraft, and he saw, through the incredible shaking and spinning of the fuselage interior, how the passengers were entirely covered in birds, little broken bodies smeared over people's features, and he couldn't recognize anyone any more, there were just hundreds of people covered in *bird* – terrible, bloody, greasy, broken *bird*.

And then Glauber's window broke open, and he too was covered in *bird*, a terrible mass of tiny bodies breaking across his face, and he realized – too late – that more than anything else in the world, he finally wanted to scream.

4

Sirens blared in the background, almost deafening James Carter as he addressed the television camera, which picked up the scenes of chaos surrounding him – storefronts smashed and broken, people still escaping with clothes and sneakers from the sports store behind, and with wide-screen TVs and computers from the electronics store to the side. One of the buildings was on fire, along with several of the cars which lined the normally peaceful street, the flames licking perilously close to Carter as he gave his report.

'I'm here on Hudson Boulevard,' he announced over the din of rioters and looters, 'where chaos is running rampant. After the giant statue was seen to move last week, there have been more strange incidents all over the world – domestic pets have attacked their owners, birds have destroyed large passenger airplanes by flying into them in huge numbers, zoo animals have gone on the rampage, fish have been dying in their millions. And some people believe that these unexplained incidents are heralding the end of the world, the Apocalypse.'

Carter flinched instinctively as one of the cars behind him erupted in a huge fireball, then continued, 'Already, apocalyptic cults are emerging, driving people into a frenzy, claiming all sorts of things – but the bottom line is that we are all doomed.'

Carter looked around to survey the carnage behind him, then turned back to the camera. 'Whether that is true or not,' he went on, gesturing to the destruction of the neighbourhood, 'it is clear that their words are having an effect. Earlier this evening the first riot broke out, here on these streets. The police managed to arrest the main offenders but now the looters have moved in.

'It starts here, but mark my words,' Carter said gravely, 'it will spread. This is only the beginning.'

PART TWO

1

'THEY'RE BEHIND US,' Leanne Harnas whispered urgently across the cabin of the fast-moving SUV, almost as if she expected her pursuers to be able to hear her.

Karl Janklow could see the headlights in his rear-view mirror. Three vehicles, approaching fast. Gaining on them. His nerves threatened to get the better of him as he manoeuvred the vehicle down the treacherous, snow-covered mountain road. Huge trees veered up on either side of him, cutting out all natural light from the stars and moon and making the route seem all but impassable. And yet he knew the road was just fine; indeed, he'd driven this way home for the past three years. He tried to rein in his paranoia. So there were vehicles behind them; so what? Plenty of other people lived off base, many of them in the same small town as Janklow did.

But this time, Janklow had no intention of ever going back; he and Leanne had discussed the matter at length, and both had decided that they needed to go public with what was going on at the base. And now that they had made that decision, and acted upon it, the fear that they had been discovered was running cold through both of them.

'If they knew,' Leanne said, 'why didn't they stop us at the gate?'

Janklow increased speed, the big SUV threatening to tilt over and go spinning into the trees at every turn. He shook his head. 'I don't know,' he answered, knowing it was a lie. He knew the reason. Colonel Anderson had let them leave the base so that they could be killed out here, in the wilderness. Away from prying eyes.

His foot pressed the accelerator harder, and the wide tyres struggled to keep a grip on the icy forest road. He saw the headlights fall away behind him and allowed himself a grin of triumph.

It was short-lived; the lights were back again just moments later, closing the gap even further. Should he risk turning off into the treeline? If he could just get round the next bend fast enough, break through a gap into the trees and turn his lights off, Anderson and his men might go shooting straight past them.

It was worth a try, he decided, increasing his speed even more as they shot towards another corner.

'Slow down!' Leanne screamed at him, as she felt the tyres giving way under the heavy vehicle. 'We're going to—'

The sound of automatic gunfire drowned her words. In the mirrors, Janklow saw flashes of light erupting from the vehicles behind him. He felt the impact of bullets hitting his car, heard the windows shatter. He struggled to control the car as one of the tyres was blown out.

He turned to Leanne to tell her to hang on but saw only her lifeless body sagging in the seat next to him, head lolling uselessly on her chest, a round having blasted straight through the back of her seat into her body. Only then did he realize that the windscreen was covered in blood, pierced and webbed where the bullet had passed out of her body and carried on forwards.

He felt instantly nauseous, and vomited over the steering wheel and dashboard even as another tyre was blasted out and his car finally, spectacularly, went spinning off the mountain road into the trees beyond.

Colonel Easton Anderson stepped out of his jeep and smelt the air, picking up the scents of gun smoke and leaking gasoline. *Good*. This business would finally be put to rest.

Not so very long ago, Karl Janklow had seen the computer of a technician who had been working on the base's covert sub-programme. The technician had gone straight to Anderson to tell him. Anderson had chastized him for his lack of attention to security but was happy the man had had the balls to admit he had messed up. They had put surveillance on Janklow straight away, and Anderson was perturbed, although not entirely surprised, when the computer expert had started to hack the internal system. Anderson had ordered some files to be moved, others to be changed, but there was still enough to alarm anyone looking.

Anderson had allowed Janklow to probe, all the while monitoring his every step. Although it appeared that he had stumbled upon the covert project by accident, there was always the possibility that he was working for someone else – the police, the government, a foreign government. Anderson was responsible for the programme's security, and he had to know if there was someone behind Janklow.

It soon became apparent that there wasn't, but then the man had confided in one of his colleagues, Leanne Harnas – a woman Janklow was having some sort of on-again, off-again romance with – and Anderson knew the moment was coming when he would have to act.

The very next day, Janklow and Harnas had announced their intention to take a weekend trip together. It was a trip Anderson could never allow to happen, and yet he didn't want to take care of the pair back at the base; there were too many people, too many questions that would be asked.

And so here he was now, having followed them from the base and gunned them down. He would have liked a cleaner method, but Janklow had to be stopped in the woods, in the middle of nowhere. Things would be much easier to tidy up this way, arranged to look like some sort of unfortunate car crash.

His attention was caught by one of his men, waving from the wreckage of Janklow's SUV.

'What is it?' Anderson called over.

'Janklow's not here, sir!' came the immediate reply.

Anderson sprinted towards the car until he could see the bloody remains of Leanne Harnas, half thrown through the bloody windscreen.

'Check the area! Maybe he was thrown clear.'

Men moved off, torches up to illuminate the snow-filled woods. If Janklow had been thrown through the windscreen, there was no way he would have survived at that speed, and yet . . .

'Sir!' came another cry, over towards the other side of the road.

Anderson went over, saw the tracks the soldier was pointing at with his torch. They were the tracks made by a man on skis, and led downhill, away from the mountaintop and down to the small civilian town at the bottom.

Damn it! Anderson restrained the urge to punch the trunk of the nearest tree. He called over to the crew of one of the vehicles which had come with them, a big ten-ton truck.

'OK,' he shouted, 'get the snowmobiles deployed, right now!'

As Janklow veered in and out of the trees, the pitch dark was almost all-enveloping, causing him on more than one occasion to nearly ski straight into one of the huge trees that made up this sub-arctic forest. He managed to adjust his course every time, at just the right moment; the darkness wasn't quite complete, sufficient light filtered down from the moon to aid his progress.

His head throbbed from the crash, but the airbag had deployed and probably saved his life. He had known there was no point in checking but he had felt for Leanne's pulse nevertheless, having to suppress the urge to vomit again as he held back the mop of bloody hair to feel for the carotid artery at the neck. There had been nothing.

He choked back his tears, bitterly regretting that he had got her into this situation in the first place.

Janklow kept skis in the back of the SUV. Shorter than conventional skis, they were designed for cross-country use, a sport he enjoyed and one of the reasons why he had chosen this remote posting. He'd made it across the road with his skis and boots just seconds before Anderson's team had arrived on the scene, and was off down the mountain before Anderson reached the annihilated SUV.

But now, with the cold wind whipping against his face as he shot down the mountain, weaving in and out of the trees, he heard the sound of engines behind him, high-pitched, straining. *Snowmobiles.*

He knew they would be able to catch him but he would not give up. The will to survive, to *live*, overrode his fear, adrenalin pushing him further and faster than he would have thought possible. Part of his mind wanted to give up, to just sit down in the snow and wait for the killers to finish him off. But a deeper part, one he never knew existed within him, spurred him on. And so he continued his run for freedom.

Colonel Anderson piloted the lead snowmobile, leading a squad of four vehicles down the mountain, powerful headlights letting him see all obstacles long before he reached them.

He knew Janklow had a head start, but against engine power, the man had no chance. And the tracks in the snow were as clear as day.

Anderson admired the man for his efforts, and the evening's action was certainly a diverting change from the normal routine, but it would soon be at an end.

The sound of the snowmobiles was louder now, and the snow around Janklow was lit up by the snowmobiles' headlights.

And then the terrifying sound of gunfire penetrated the

still air once more, and Janklow watched in terror as the soft snow was ploughed up around him, missing his skis by inches.

He swerved in and out of the trees faster, cutting down at an angle across the mountain to a narrow pass that he thought the larger vehicles might not get through.

He saw the lights turn to follow him, bullets ripping up more of the snow. He hit a shelf and jumped, flying through the cold air for what seemed an eternity before landing, taking the shock through his knees and hips, careening up on to a single leg before regaining his balance and carrying on down the steep slope.

He heard gunfire again, felt something hit the back of his arm. Looking down, he saw a gaping wound in his coat at the bicep, and realized he'd been shot, the bullet passing straight through his arm. He felt dizzy, started to lose balance, but then his peripheral vision caught movement, and he momentarily forgot about the pain and shock and turned to see what it was.

His eyes went wide as he saw two small bear cubs. They stopped playing and watched him. Even as he carried on down the hill, his mind processed the information that the bear cubs were scared. And that would mean—

The adult bear came charging towards him, snow churning up behind it, teeth bared and reflecting dimly in the faint moonlight. Janklow's heart almost stopped, but he aimed himself towards a log with a drift of snow lying up its side. He sailed up it just as the huge animal reached out for him. He flew off the other side in a high arc, hit the ground and stumbled, blood loss from his arm making his coordination suffer, and then he was rolling, the skis striking the ground and flying off into the trees beyond, his body curling into a pain-filled ball as it shot down the mountainside.

Anderson recognized the sound and knew he should avoid the area but he simply didn't have the time, and before he knew it his headlights picked up the ferocious image of a bear charging through the snow towards him. He pulled off left at the last minute and his snowmobile slammed straight into a tree and sent him sailing through the air.

The bear brought its great paws crashing down on to the front of the second snowmobile, crushing it instantly and sending the pilot tumbling across the snow. The huge beast ignored the man, now curled into a ball on the ground in a last-ditch effort to protect himself, and launched herself at the last two snowmobiles which were trying to take evasive action. One swipe of the bear's huge paw sent one driver flying into the trunk of a nearby tree. Directly behind, the driver of the fourth snowmobile piloted the craft straight into the animal. The driver was thrown from the snowmobile, but the bear was propelled backwards, letting out a roar of pain and anger as she came down on to all fours.

Anderson, covered in snow, used the momentary distraction to get to his knees. Using the broken snowmobile as a rest, he laid his rifle on the top and aimed at the bear through the weapon's night sight.

The bear, recovering and still protecting her cubs from

the perceived threat, reared back once more on to her hind legs, raising her arms above her head, ready to smash them down into the body of the driver which had hit her. And then her chest erupted in a spray of blood as Anderson opened fire, peppering the thousand-pound mammal with an entire magazine of high-velocity ammunition.

Anderson watched in wonder as the bear stood still for several moments, as if contemplating her injuries. Anderson was halfway through reloading his rifle when finally, with a deep, rumbling groan, the huge animal fell to the ground, dead.

Moments later, ignorant of the danger, the two cubs came bounding over, nuzzling the dead bear and emitting wailing cries.

Anderson ignored them, anger taking over. The snow-mobiles were out of action, and who knew what state his men were in.

With a sigh of resignation, he accepted that Karl Janklow had escaped.

Janklow finally came to rest at the bottom of the mountain. Even though the snow was thick and deep, he had still smashed into fallen branches, rocks and stones on his way down. He was badly battered and barely conscious. He staggered to his feet, half falling through the last of the trees, and stumbled out of the forest on to the dark grey asphalt of a road.

He turned one way, then the other, and saw lights heading towards him.

He held back, worried it might be more soldiers from

the base, but then he saw the multi-levelled lights and realized it was a commercial truck. Almost delirious with the joy of a survivor, he stepped out into the road, waving his good arm frantically.

The truck sounded its horn, and Janklow wondered if it was going to hit him and end everything right there and then; but then the brakes were applied, and the huge truck started to slow down.

By the time the truck driver got out of the cab to help him, Janklow had passed out and lay unconscious on the icy road, his head filled with a single thought before oblivion.

I've made it.

2

ALYSSA DURHAM'S FINGERS pinched the tiny outcrop of rock with a vice-like grip, the sides of her painfully tight climbing shoes pressed against the almost sheer surface for added traction.

She was free-climbing a one-hundred-foot granite cliff face, a short climb for her but made difficult due to the low temperature, which ensured the wall was covered in a thin layer of ice.

In earlier years, she would have done the climb as a free solo, without ropes for protection, but now, as the lone parent of a beautiful eight-year-old daughter, she was not willing to risk making that child an orphan. And so she used ropes, but only to save her if she fell – she wouldn't use them as an aid in her climbing.

Her daughter, Anna, was higher up the mountain, skiing. Alyssa was a good skier herself, but Anna was something else – she'd started at the age of five and shown a natural aptitude for it. They went to the mountains every opportunity they got, which wasn't as much as Alyssa would have liked. Her job was demanding, and there was only one of her, after all, but it was enough for Anna to have become pretty incredible for an eight-year-old.

The trips had started after the death of her husband, Patrick. He had contracted a rare form of degenerative disease at a shockingly young age, and Alyssa had nursed him for twelve painful months before – mercifully for him, agonizingly for her and Anna – he had quietly passed away one night. She had cried for hours – helpless tears, hopeless tears – but had gathered herself before Anna woke. She needed to be strong for her, and although both Alyssa's parents and Patrick's parents were a huge help, the fact of the matter – at least as Alyssa saw it – was that Anna was her responsibility, and nobody else's. And she was now all that remained of Patrick.

Anna herself had found it hard to deal with her father's death. He had been ill for some time and had not been involved in her upbringing during that final, painful year, but the gap that he left was difficult for a young girl to deal with. *Where's Daddy?* she would ask incessantly, especially before bedtime, when he used to read stories to her before kissing her goodnight. *When's Daddy coming home?* It was hard for Alyssa to explain, and Anna had cried for days, for weeks, and Alyssa had cried along with her.

It wasn't until their first trip into the mountains, a few months after Patrick's death, that Anna had started to come round. The magical quality of the snow, the serene peace of the valleys, the majesty of the mountains themselves had shown Anna another view of the world, perhaps of something beyond it, and given her hope; and Alyssa had felt it too, the pull of something beyond, the first faint rays of a life beyond the one that had been wrenched so terribly from them.

Alyssa and Patrick had been winter sports addicts – skiing, snowboarding, ice climbing; anything that could be done, they would do it. They had even met on a mountain, thousands of miles from home, and when holiday romance had bloomed they were delighted to find they lived only a hundred miles from one another back home. Alyssa's first love was climbing, and had been since she was a little girl, but Patrick's was snowboarding, and he had shown her everything he knew. They were wonderful years, those early years, getting away whenever work let them. She was an up-and-coming journalist, cutting her teeth on the local papers but determined to break into the nationals; he was an up-and-coming public prosecutor, destined for the DA's office. But then Anna had come along, and it wasn't so easy to get away any more. They hadn't regretted it, not for a second; on the contrary, their years of adventure were simply put aside as other priorities took hold.

But when Patrick died, the first place Alyssa had thought to take Anna – after the worst of the grieving was over and behind them – was the mountains. If Patrick had loved them, she thought, maybe Anna would too. And she had, with a wild abandon, and for the first time in as long as she could remember Alyssa had felt free, the strains of her life miraculously lifted.

Anna had wanted to ski. She was adamant about that, having watched as people shot down the slopes, leaning first one way and then the other, slicing through the snow in graceful arcs.

Alyssa had taught her at first, and the first season had

just been the basics – how to put on the equipment, how to stand, how to move, and then the first few tentative movements down the training slopes – and Anna had loved it. Alyssa had seen the excitement in her eyes, the joy of being a little girl that had been absent for so long, and had almost wept with happiness herself.

Further visits to the slopes had shown that Anna was moving beyond her mother's teaching limits, and so Alyssa started to arrange more expert instruction. This was what had led them here, to the special training centre in the heart of the western mountains, where Anna was undergoing the first stage of selection for the national team. Alyssa was probably even more nervous than Anna was, but however Anna did, it didn't matter. The girl was perfect whatever happened.

Alyssa, at a loose end for a couple of hours at the foot of the mountain, had decided to get a little exercise of her own, and the pull of climbing – the sharp surge of adrenalin flooding her bloodstream, the overcoming of physical barriers, the feeling of accomplishment when a wall, a rock-face, a *mountain*, had been conquered – had been too much to resist.

The wall was a real battle, full of tiny holds that required all sorts of gymnastic contortions to reach; hard enough without the ice, nearly impossible with it. But she perse-vered, gaining an inch here, an inch there, pulling herself up the cliff face through sheer determination.

And finally she was there, levering herself on to the top shelf of rock where she sat for several moments to gather

her breath. Then she got to her feet and gazed out across the glorious scenery around, above and below her.

She shielded her eyes from the sun, and could see the ski school on one of the slopes in the distance. Squinting hard, she could make out twelve kids, two assessors. She could even make out Anna in her bright orange parka, waiting at the top, listening to the instructions of the experts, and then she was off, skiing down the mountainside, and Alyssa's heart filled with pride as she watched.

Anna was at the bottom of the slope just a few minutes later, an instructor was talking to her; Alyssa guessed – hoped – he was telling her how well she had done.

And then Anna and another little girl waddled away to the side, and waited for the chair lift to take them back to the top. Alyssa watched as the tiny chairs scooped them both off the ground, the lift operator closing the T-bar over them as it went on its way.

She stamped her feet and rubbed her arms; she was dressed for climbing, not for standing around watching, and her jacket and boots were back down at the bottom. She checked her watch. Just after half past one. Anna's lesson was scheduled to finish at two, so she knew she'd have to start making a move.

She was considering whether she had time to climb down or whether just to abseil with the rope, when she heard it. The horrifying screech of tortured metal, then a gut-wrenching snapping sound that could only be . . .

Her eyes found the chair lift immediately, and she felt as if she'd been slammed in the stomach with a baseball bat. The chairs had stopped moving upwards, the cables immobile as the seats swung backwards and forwards underneath.

There was a double cable arrangement, and as Alyssa's eyes scoured the length of the lift, she saw that one of the cables was broken, the snapping sound she had heard echoing across the valley. The chair next to the break hung precariously, sixty feet over the rocky mountainside. She stared more intently, shielding her eyes against the crystal-clear winter sun, and almost fell to her knees as she saw the little girl in the orange parka screaming as the chair started to tilt and slip from the cable.

Alyssa was at the training centre within minutes, having instantly launched herself from the cliff top, taking the hundred feet in just three bounds with the rope.

She now stood in a crowd of dozens, all looking up at the single chair as it moved further and further to one side, tilting towards the vertical, the two little girls screaming as they struggled to hold on.

'That's my baby!' a woman to her left shrieked, hysterical. 'That's my baby!' the woman kept on repeating, louder and louder, as her husband pulled her close, a look of terror on his own face.

The other chairs looked stable, not yet under threat from the broken cable, but the children were all crying, shouting and screaming nevertheless, their parents back on the ground shouting up at them, telling them to stay calm, help would come.

Alyssa told herself the same thing. *Keep calm. Don't panic.* She knew shouting up to Anna would be useless.

Even if she heard her mother over all the other noise, the blood rushing through her ears from the intensity of the terror would almost deafen her anyway.

Alyssa spotted the operator who had secured her daughter with the T-bar. 'Hey!' she called to him, pushing through the crowd towards him. 'Hey!' She grabbed hold of his thick jacket, turned him towards her. 'What's happening?'

He looked just as frightened as everyone else. 'The . . . the cable's broken!' he stammered.

'I can see that!' Alyssa exclaimed, even as she heard the tearing of more metal, and turned to see the chair turn fully on its side now, the girls pulling themselves hard against the T-bar. Alyssa knew they wouldn't be able to do it for long. 'What are you doing to help them?' she cried.

'Mountain rescue are on their way,' the operator managed, regaining some semblance of composure.

'How far?' Alyssa asked urgently. 'How long until they get here?'

The man looked down at his feet nervously as the screams continued to echo across the valley. 'An hour,' he said finally.

Alyssa looked up at Anna in her bright orange parka, struggling to keep hold, to save herself from the sixty-foot plummet to what would undoubtedly be her death, and made a decision.

Just under two minutes later, Alyssa was halfway up one of the support posts that suspended the cables at regular intervals up the mountainside. It was an easy climb, as the posts had rungs for maintenance access, but Alyssa struggled to control her breathing, her heart rate skyrocketing as she kept the two little girls in her sights, gripping hard to the metal T-bar of the ski chair.

Down on the ground, she had announced what she was going to do – climb the support post, then pull herself along the intact cable until she reached the chair, secure her daughter to her, and then pull them both back to the post, where they would climb back down, but to her disgust nobody was willing to help. Not the chair-lift operator, not the instructors, not even the parents of the other little girl. All they wanted to do was hug each other, cry and moan, and hope a miracle would come along.

But Alyssa didn't believe in miracles. A miracle hadn't saved her husband from the disease that claimed him at the age of twenty-eight, and a miracle wouldn't save her daughter now. She would have to do it herself. And she knew she would have to try and save the other girl too. She only hoped that the remaining cable wouldn't break, and the girls would be able to hold on for long enough.

Alyssa was just securing herself to the cable at the top of the support post when it happened. There was another screech of metal and one of the chair's attachments broke free from the stress of the twisted, unnatural position. The whole chair sagged and then jerked down, falling a few inches before stopping, the other attachments holding tight.

But the other little girl lost her grip and started the inexorable, fatal, slide down the chair seat, tiny hands scrabbling for something – anything – to hold on to, and then there was nothing, only sky. Alyssa closed her eyes as the girl's scream pierced the cold mountain air, the crowd below too shocked now to make any noise at all, and then Alyssa heard a sickening *crump*, and the little girl was gone, quiet now, forever.

Alyssa opened her eyes and focused on Anna, who had instinctively reached out for the other girl, and Alyssa's heart leapt into her throat as Anna, too, started to slide down the seat, towards oblivion.

Alyssa pulled herself on to the cable, upside down, her head towards her daughter, her legs wrapped tightly round the thick metal cable, and she started to pull herself along. She couldn't fail. She *couldn't*. Not after everything that had happened. It simply couldn't happen.

From her position under the cable, she saw as Anna managed to grasp hold of the edge of the T-bar, her little body suspended now beneath the chair, legs kicking out over the empty expanse, tears streaming down her face.

'Mommy,' she cried in a scared whisper. 'Mommy, please . . .'

Alyssa pulled herself along faster, the cable cutting through her trouser legs, blistering the skin. Just fifteen feet left . . . ten . . . five . . . She could almost reach her . . .

'Mommy, please . . .' her daughter begged, eyes going wide as her grip finally gave way, her little hands unable to hold on any longer, and the breath caught in her throat as she, too, fell from the chair, down into the freezing air, into nothing at all.

No! Alyssa reached out one hand, both hands, just inches

away as she swung down, supported by a single belt clip and the strength of her legs.

But it was too late, and she watched, sick and helpless, as her daughter, beautiful little Anna, whom she had promised to look after forever, fell sixty feet through the cold, empty sky.

Alyssa shot bolt upright in her bed, screaming, sweat covering every part of her body, shivering as if she was back there in the snow, the ice, the cold. The terror.

But it was just another dream, a nightmare, the same as she'd had ever since the death of her daughter three years before. They came less frequently now, but when they came, they were no less devastating.

She shook her head, and took a drink of water from the glass on her bedside table.

She jumped as the phone next to her started ringing, water spilling in her lap. She looked at the clock; it was just gone three in the morning. Who the hell could it be at this time?

Reluctantly, she picked up. 'Yes?'

'Alyssa? Is that you?'

The voice on the other end of the line was urgent, frantic, and the tone made Alyssa immediately alert. 'Who is this?' she asked.

'You know who it is. Your old climbing buddy,' the voice said nervously, and Alyssa knew not to say the name out loud. Whatever the problem was, it was obvious that Karl Janklow didn't want his name spoken on an open line.

'What's wrong?' she asked, puzzled. She hadn't heard from Karl in years.

'Are you still working for the *Post*?' came the nervous reply.

'Yes,' Alyssa confirmed. 'I'm a senior investigative reporter on staff.' What was it Karl did? Alyssa thought it had something to do with computers but couldn't remember exactly.

'I need to talk to you about those things going on. You know, planes crashing, animals going crazy. You know what I mean?'

'Yes,' Alyssa said. Everyone in the world would know what he meant, it was all anyone was talking about. She wasn't on the story herself, as she was in the middle of a piece on tax evasion by the country's biggest companies, but she had read all about it in the past few days. 'What about them?'

There was a pause before Karl spoke again, as if he was summoning the courage to go on. 'I think they're being caused by something connected to where I work.'

Alyssa was momentarily at a loss for words. Birds attacking airplanes, millions of fish dying, a massive stone statue moving, and Karl, the friend she had not seen in years but who had something to do with computers, was suggesting that the events were not just linked but actually caused by something at his workplace?

Her years in the field had taught her to be sceptical and this sounded fantastical, but she couldn't ignore it. 'Where do you work?' she asked him cautiously.

'Not over an open line,' he answered quickly. 'We have to meet.'

3

ALYSSA NEGOTIATED THE crowds as she headed for the subway, amazed by the density of human traffic on the city streets. And everywhere she looked there were people with replicas, models – even blown-up photographs – of the great statue which had moved, the glorious 'miracle statue', which everyone seemed to think was heralding something.

The fact that the statue was a religious icon only helped to confirm people's feelings. And it wasn't just the crazed mutterings of a few hard-to-believe fanatics who might have dreamt the whole thing, either; the entire incident – Alyssa still wasn't sure if she could use the term *miracle* – had been filmed by several people, and had now been seen by an estimated two-thirds of the planet's population. Lapsed members of the faith were suddenly finding their faith renewed, and all sorts of other groups had sprung up, preaching messages far removed from the mainstream. Some were cults of the statue itself, proclaiming that it had always been divine, although Alyssa suspected that most of these cults had been around less than a week. But the ones that caught her attention as she was jostled by the crowd were the so-called 'apocalyptic' cults. For every ten members of the recognized religions, she suspected there must be at least two or three from these new 'end of the world' sects, and there were more with every passing day.

Her attention was drawn to a group over on her left, not the closest, but with the most people crowded round the speaker. The man who was addressing the crowd was tall, muscular and dark-skinned. It was hard to estimate his age – he could have been anywhere from his late twenties to his early forties, his skin young but his eyes old. But it was not his physical characteristics that drew her gaze, nor his dress – shamanic white robes with gold bracelets along his arms and a gold headband pushing back his thick, wiry hair. Instead, it was something more, an energy that radiated from him and seemed to draw people to him. She felt it herself, pulling her towards the crowd to listen.

'My brothers and sisters,' he intoned in a deep, melodious voice that seemed vaguely hypnotic, 'we stand today at a crossroads. Believe me, it is the crossroads between life and death.' He opened his hands wide above him. 'The time is coming, the great change is upon us. The world needs to refresh itself, to cast us out and start anew. The earth needs to be reborn. Believe!'

Those gathered closest round him dropped to their knees and bowed down; then they looked up at the sky and bowed down again, and continued to repeat the action, whispering prayers of a type Alyssa had never heard before.

As they did so, the man spoke once more. 'The governments of the world are trying to control the natural order of things but nature is more powerful than the government. Nature is more powerful than Man. It will not be tricked, it will not be stopped. The time is coming! Our time is at an end, and there is nothing we can do about it except embrace it. Yes! We must embrace our fate. The earth must cleanse itself, so that life can start anew. We must die to ensure our survival. Believe! Believe! Believe!'

Alyssa had heard enough. It was similar to the other groups, nothing she hadn't heard before. It was common enough when anything strange happened, when something couldn't be explained, or it seemed that the world was threatened. Cults and sects would always emerge, claiming that the world would indeed end, nothing could be done to stop it, so followers might as well forsake their worldly possessions and wait, unencumbered, for the end. The cults would typically take responsibility for those possessions – money, cars, houses, shares, anything that was 'unnecessary' to face the coming apocalypse – and get rich overnight in the process.

The dark-skinned man was impressive certainly, a master of his craft, no doubt, but Alyssa was under no illusions about his real profession. He was a con man, plain and simple.

Turning away, she continued on her way towards the subway, wondering what light Karl Janklow would be able to shed on such strange events.

For his part, the dark-skinned man also saw Alyssa Durham. Oswald Umbebe had never seen her before in his life but he knew the type. *Damn reporters*. They were a cynical bunch, he knew that from experience. She probably thought that the Order of Planetary Renewal was just one more made-up sect cashing in on the current situation. She probably had no idea that the Order had been around for a long time. A *long* time; much longer than anybody realized. And she probably had no idea that his prophecies about the end of the world were not simply empty words designed to separate the gullible from their hard-earned money.

No, his words were far from empty; what he prophesied, however hard it was for people to accept, was the truth.

4

ALYSSA COULD HEAR the excited chatter of teenagers behind her as she sat next to Karl Janklow on the comfortable leather bench seat. Giggles erupted as the rollercoaster started to move slowly forward and upward.

Alyssa had been surprised when Karl had suggested the amusement park as a meeting place, but on reflection she could see the logic of it. The area, a seaside resort on a peninsula just outside the city, had three such amusement parks, and Karl had chosen the oldest and, in Alyssa's opinion, most charming.

She'd spent many happy hours with her family and friends on the rides here. It all came back to her in vivid, living colour – the roar of the coasters, the screams of the thrill seekers; the smell of candyfloss and hot dogs; the glare of the neon lights; the carousels and the big wheel delivering thrills and excitement to the hundreds of people who visited the huge pleasure ground.

Karl Janklow had been a friend of both her and her husband, many years ago. He was a systems engineer, Alyssa remembered now, and Patrick had told her how good he was. A good climber too, he had accompanied them on several trips. But then Alyssa had become pregnant, her and Patrick's priorities had changed, and despite a couple of attempts to meet up, they had finally lost touch with their old friend.

They'd been here once before, she remembered, the three of them. Before Anna, before Patrick's illness, before the accident that had changed Alyssa's life forever. It had been a summer's day, and the three of them were young, carefree, just enjoying the pleasure of life as it came. Those had been good days, Alyssa thought, and the throng of visitors here today seemed completely unaffected by the growing chaos back on the streets of the city beyond. Yes, it was a good place to meet, and more importantly, perhaps, it was noisy and crowded, an ideal place to lose anyone who might be following you. It wasn't likely they'd be overheard, either.

But when they met, Karl seemed nervous, jittery, and even more paranoid than he had sounded on the phone; he wanted to ride the rollercoaster, claiming that he feared their conversation might still be monitored despite the noise from the rest of the park. His paranoia made her feel a little bit better about the fact that she'd disguised herself for the meeting, a longstanding tactic she always used when meeting sources.

Karl even remained silent as the rollercoaster train started to move, pulling them inexorably upwards to start the ride. She let him be, patiently waiting for him to tell her what he knew.

They reached the top of the first peak and, despite herself, Alyssa felt the excitement rise within her. It was a combination of the physical thrill of the old wooden rollercoaster and the anticipation of the secrets Karl had to tell her.

As the train started to tip over the peak to its stomach-churning first descent, Karl finally turned to Alyssa. As the teens behind them let out unbridled screams and the train shot down the coaster at a speed which rippled the skin, he gestured with his head, beckoning Alyssa to come closer.

She leant in, but even with his mouth at her ear, she still had to strain to hear.

'Alyssa,' Karl shouted above the roar of the tracks and the screams, 'the things that are happening, they are *not* natural. They—'

Alyssa didn't catch the next words, Karl's head had moved away. She leant in even closer and felt the weight of his head resting on her cheek.

She pulled back to look at him, and her stomach lurched violently, independently of the motion of the rollercoaster. Karl's eyes were still open, staring straight ahead, his mouth agape. And, to Alyssa's horror, there was a neat hole in the centre of his forehead and blood was dripping over his disbelieving face.

And then, for the first time during the ride, she screamed.

'Good shot,' Colonel Anderson announced over the radio headset worn by the sniper. The professional soldier was lying comfortably on a shooting rug, positioned strategically on the roof of a building over half a mile away. 'Now take out the woman,' Anderson ordered.

The sniper followed the path of the coaster with his

optical sight, tracking the unknown woman as she turned, realized what had happened, and started to scream. The angle wasn't quite right yet, but down the next hill, up and round a bend, would be just perfect.

'Yes, sir,' he responded confidently.

He would be putting away his equipment and high-tailing it out of there within thirty seconds.

Alyssa could feel herself starting to hyperventilate. As she hunched reflexively down in the train, trying to minimize her target profile, she tried to get control of her breathing, her years in the mountains having instilled in her the knowledge that panic would be her worst enemy.

Where had the shot come from? A sniper could be literally anywhere. Was she a target too? Of course she was, she quickly realized; if they had killed Karl to keep him quiet, they would kill her too in case he had already told her anything.

She knew nobody else would have any idea what was going on – the people behind her would be too wrapped up in the rollercoaster ride to notice, everyone was screaming anyway, the ride was too far away and going too fast for anyone on the ground to realize what had happened. She was on her own.

The speed of the coaster wasn't helping her think, but she knew immediately what she had to do. In the train, she was a sitting duck. Karl had been hit right in the middle of the forehead, so whoever was out there, they weren't amateurs. She couldn't stay on the rollercoaster. She was going to have to get off while it was still moving.

* * *

What the hell is she doing? the sniper wondered, watching as his second target started squirming in her seat.

She had previously ducked down as far as she could, which he had anticipated – it still wouldn't stop him making the fatal shot in just ten seconds' time – but now she was twisting, wrenching, and—

She's trying to escape! The sniper couldn't help but admire her. Most people would have just capitulated entirely, fear overcoming their faculties of reason. But not this woman. Oh no, she was going to get out of the train and then – what? Jump?

Knowing the futility of her actions, the sniper settled down and waited to take the shot.

The lap bar that secured Alyssa had also secured Karl, and because he had significantly larger legs than she had, there was a gap of at least an inch between the bar and her own thighs. Space enough to move; space enough to escape.

Alyssa had no idea what she was going to do when free, but she knew it was first things first. She had to take things one at a time, and her primary task was to get out of the confinement of the coaster train.

She shifted in her seat, trying to slide through and across. Ideally, she would have just pushed down on the bar and levered herself out upwards, but the acceleration of the coaster prevented this; even if it hadn't, her instinct for self-preservation made her want to get down low, not make more of a target of herself.

She lay down across the seat, her head in her dead friend's lap as she tried desperately to manoeuvre her legs out of the narrow opening. She clawed herself across, straining to release her lower body from the safety bar.

She gasped as one knee popped out, and quickly extended her leg out over the seat and then shifted her hips, pulling free the other leg as the coaster got to the top of another rise and started to slow down.

Her legs free, she pulled her head away from Karl's lap and risked a glance at the track. There was a bend up ahead, which meant the coaster would be slowing down even more before accelerating down the next peak.

If she was going to make her move, it would have to be soon.

'Target's moving,' the sniper reported, his voice cold and professional.

'What do you mean?' Anderson asked from his mobile command centre in a converted motorhome just outside the amusement park.

'She's trying to get out of the car.'

'Can you take a shot yet?' Anderson asked quickly.

'Negative,' the sniper replied. 'Not yet. After this bend. She . . .'

There was a pause, and Anderson knew his man would be watching the woman's actions carefully. Then muffled thumps came over the connection; the sniper was firing. But there were too many shots.

'What the hell is going on?' Anderson demanded.

'I've missed,' the sniper replied. 'She got out over the

other side, used the train for cover. She's in the tunnel scaffolding, heading down to the ground.'

'Dammit!' Anderson cursed. 'Keep watching. If you get another shot, take it.' Cutting the connection, Anderson changed channels to link with the other members of his team. 'All units, converge on the rollercoaster. The woman has escaped. Don't let her leave this park alive.'

The 'slow' section of the roller coaster was still terrifyingly fast. But fearing a bullet even more, Alyssa finally took a deep breath, steadied herself, and swung her body right out of the car.

She saw chips of wood flying inches from her hands, and some small part of her mind processed the information, realized the sniper was shooting at her. The car was blocking the shots and she gripped the side for dear life, timing her next action carefully.

One . . . two . . . now!

Alyssa let go of the coaster and stepped out on to the side of the wooden tracks. The speed left her stumbling, falling, about to go right over the edge and plummet forty feet to the ground below. But then she managed to grab a metal strut in the tunnel scaffolding and steadied herself.

She could hear screams from below now as people realized what she had done, vaguely saw people pointing up at her. But then one of her hands spun off the scaffold as something hit the metal strut, the sound of the ricochet coming moments later, and she knew the sniper was firing at her again, and the cars of the rollercoaster were no longer there to protect her.

Gasping, she stepped off the side of the track and dropped straight down, catching hold of the metal struts underneath, steadying herself once more in the scaffold, hoping the wooden tracks would give her cover.

Breathing out slowly, gathering herself, Alyssa looked down; a crowd was gathering beneath, and she felt safer knowing that there were people there. Surely nobody would risk killing her once she was among them.

She hadn't climbed since that fateful day in the mountains, when she had failed her daughter so badly. She hadn't visited so much as an indoor climbing wall since. She just hadn't been able to bring herself to do it. But now she barely gave those fears a thought. With the adrenalin surging into her system, for the first time in years the desire to climb became as powerful – as natural – as the urge to breathe.

Steeling herself, she started to carefully climb down the scaffold.

'There are a lot of people here,' Anderson heard one of his men say as they approached the coaster. 'Too many people.'

Anderson understood. Other information coming from the park indicated that the ride was being stopped; too many people had seen the woman climb out on to the scaffolding. And when the ride stopped and Karl Janklow's body was discovered . . .

A thought struck him suddenly, and he thumbed the microphone. 'Use your police IDs,' he ordered his team. 'Clear the area beneath the scaffold. When she gets down, arrest her.'

The original plan was for his men to pretend to be with federal law enforcement, telling the park authorities that they'd had the area under surveillance and removing the two dead bodies from the coaster before the real cops could move in. But for the time being, there was only one dead body, which put something of a spanner in the works.

Still, Anderson knew that plans rarely survived contact with the enemy. Flexibility was the key, and Anderson issued his new orders. They would claim that the woman killed Janklow – it wouldn't be immediately obvious that the shot had been long-range – and then some of his men could take Janklow's body whilst others could move in to 'arrest' the woman, and kill her someplace away from the park; away from prying eyes.

Halfway down, Alyssa saw the crowd dispersing and wondered what was happening. And then six suited men arrived, looking up at her. They had handguns drawn and what looked like badges pulled out. Cops?

Alyssa allowed herself to relax ever so slightly. It was OK. She was going to be OK. The police were here, and they would handle it. She looked further across to where the six-car train had come to a halt, saw other men extracting Karl's dead body and restraining the shocked and screaming teenagers. Park security were erecting a cordon around the area, sealing the ride off from the rest of the park, ushering the other riders out of the way. Yes, she thought, it would be all right.

But then she paused, going no further, her mind racing furiously. Why were they moving the body? It was a murder scene, wasn't it? And she'd covered enough of those in her time to know that the body shouldn't be moved. The cops should be leaving it for the forensics people and other members of the crime scene investigation team. And come to think of it, what the hell were non-uniform police doing here anyway? There were six below her, another six taking care of the body. How could they have got here so quickly?

Something wasn't right, and Alyssa knew immediately what it was: the twelve suits weren't the police at all. They were here because they wanted to kill her. It was the only explanation that made sense; they were clearing the body before Karl could be identified, and they were waiting for her so that they could finish the job.

She checked around her, looking for avenues of escape. The faces on the 'cops' below her changed from expressions of welcoming helpfulness to ones of concern as she stopped moving towards them. She watched as they spoke into lapel microphones, listened to their earpieces, looked up at her again with even greater concern as she still refused to move.

Anxious, she scanned the area. The scaffold she was on was wrapped round one section of track and led all the way down to the ground. She was on the internal side of the scaffold but she noticed that the bare metal structure went further out into the park. She peered between the thick metal struts and saw that there were stalls below on the other side, the scaffold just feet away from the rear of their canvas coverings.

Without a second thought, she turned her body, twisting through the metal to head towards the outside of the structure. Gripping the metal tightly, she manoeuvred past the track and out into the abyss, nothing below her for thirty feet except exposed metal bars and the solid, unforgiving concrete of the park floor.

She heard the fake cops shouting to her from below, bellowing instructions for her to come back, but she ignored them and headed quickly for the other side of the scaffold. The people below her would have to head back out of the entrance and race all the way round the structure to get to her. She turned to look at them, saw that they were already setting off at a run. Trying to keep calm, she knew she would have less than a minute to escape.

Slipping her lithe body through the bars, she quickly got through to the outside of the ride, clinging tight to the struts as she looked at the small stalls beneath her. She knew she could climb down in a couple of minutes, but she also knew that this would be far too long; she only had about thirty seconds left before the killers would be there.

The sound of a ricochet and the hot spark of damaged metal jolted her, adrenalin flooding her system once more, rocketing her heart rate and making her palms instantly slick with sweat. She almost lost her grip and went sailing to the ground below, but just held on, years of climbing instinct hard-wired into her.

Sniper, she thought, and knew the people after her must be getting desperate. The shooter must have been positioned to fire at the inside of the tracks, and the shot had come through the scaffold at her, which explained how he'd missed. The guy must be an incredible shot just to get close under such conditions. Then there were more shots, sparks from the metal struts hitting her skin and burning her face.

Her reaction was instantaneous, and utterly unexpected to her pursuers. Taking one single, deep breath, she crouched down and jumped from the scaffolding towards the park below.

The sniper watched as his target jumped from thirty feet. What was she thinking?

His view wasn't ideal, the heavy metal of the scaffold obscuring much of it, but he could see that the woman hadn't fallen. No, she had bent at the legs and intention-ally *jumped*. Had the shots scared her into trying a suicidal escape?

Despite the extremely demanding conditions, he had still been disappointed to have missed. Anderson had ordered him to take the shot as soon as he knew the woman was heading away from the other agents, and he had done so, knowing that hitting her would be a miracle but wanting to do so all the same. It was not in his nature to accept missing his target.

But perhaps he hadn't had to hit her anyway; she would be stone-cold dead as soon as she hit the concrete even without a bullet inside her.

Alyssa had purposefully propelled herself forwards, away from the scaffold, hoping to make several feet of distance as she plummeted earthwards.

As she sailed through the air, she prayed she'd jumped far enough; and then she was there, her feet reaching the stretched canvas roof of one of the amusement stalls on this side of the ride.

The fabric bent, and Alyssa's heart dipped as she thought it would tear; but then she used the stored energy in her legs to jump again, pushing down against the taut canvas to dispel the force of gravity, and managed to somersault forwards, turning in mid-air to grab hold of the edge of the roof and swing her body round and down until she let go and dropped to the ground amidst a group of startled onlookers.

She saw the crowds parting beyond her and realized that the killers would be on her in seconds. Ignoring the offers of help from those around her, she turned to face the opposite direction and ran, pushing through the mass of people, desperate to get away, her heart pumping so violently she thought it was going to explode right out of her chest.

'Status?' Anderson asked twenty minutes later, every nerve shredded.

He knew the answer before it came through to him. 'Negative,' the reply came. 'We lost her, sir. She's nowhere to be found.'

Anderson didn't even bother to reply, just thumbed off the radio and sat back in his chair. How had the operation gone so badly wrong? Picking off two defenceless subjects while both were strapped in place should have been child's play. Who could have predicted that the woman would have jumped off the damned ride?

But he should have predicted it; that was his job, after all. It didn't matter in the slightest that it was a rushed operation, set up in only a matter of hours; Anderson knew he could have handled it better.

After Janklow went missing, he had requested authorization to use every tool available to catch him, but the computer specialist had proven a crafty opponent. He had avoided detection at every transport hub he must have used, and Anderson feared that he might have disappeared from the grid entirely.

But then fate had intervened, voice recognition software capturing a call from a payphone to the amusement park, Janklow's voice requesting details of the opening times.

Anderson had reacted instantly, setting up observation posts around the park and putting it under constant surveillance. It had taken time, though, and Anderson had worried that Janklow might already have visited the park and left, to be lost once more. It also occurred to him that it was a red herring, Janklow's idea of a joke to waste his pursuers' time.

But then his men had seen him, first entering the park and then meeting up with the woman. It was obvious she was a contact, someone he had arranged to meet. But who the hell was she, and why was Janklow meeting her? Was she a girlfriend? Someone in law enforcement or government? Or even – and this would probably be the worst outcome – a reporter of some sort?

Anderson had ordered high-definition pictures taken, and government supercomputers were hard at work trying to identify her. But Anderson had ordered her death anyway, along with Janklow; he couldn't take the risk of the information getting out.

But now she had escaped, this mysterious woman, and she carried who only knew what information from Janklow, with which she was going to do who knew what. And he still didn't even know who she was.

But he did know one thing, he told himself as he leant back in his chair, stretching his aching body. Whoever she was, he was going to find her.

5

General David Tomkin stretched out in his seat as he took the call, trying to get some life back into his tired limbs. He had spent a lifetime in the military, and had fought on every front his country had been involved in for the past thirty years, first as an infantry officer, then in Special Forces, and later in intelligence. He was an active man, even now in his late fifties, and the sheer inactivity of his latest job was enough to make him scream.

He was, admittedly, the highest-ranking military officer in his nation's esteemed armed forces, a position he was proud to have been granted, and one he took very seriously indeed. But despite the important and highly prestigious office that he held, the fact remained that he no longer actually had any operational command over combatant forces; the role of Chairman of the Joint Chiefs was advisory only, and as such Tomkin spent far more time than he would have liked behind a desk.

But the job meant that he was enormously influential; he had command over personnel and budgets, and had control over the structure and utilization of the world's most powerful military force. His ability to work the budgets was one he had never foreseen being so expert at.

Back when he had been leading platoon attacks against hostile militias down in the world's worst hellholes, fiscal policy was the very last thing on his mind. But over the years, as he had progressed through the ranks, he had realized the importance of correctly organized budgets; correctly organized in the sense that certain 'black' projects could be lost, forever beyond political scrutiny. He had developed a certain skill at manipulating military budgets over the years, and was now able to hide such programmes – weapons research, illegal prisons for terrorist suspects, covert 'snatch squads', paramilitary hit teams – in places that would never be found by prying eyes.

It was this skill that had brought John Jeffries, the Secretary of Defence, to call him that morning. 'John,' Tomkin said warmly as he picked up the secure line, 'how are you doing?'

'Good, David,' Jeffries responded with equal warmth. 'How's the family?'

'Can't complain. Got us another grandson on the way, Maggie this time, her first.'

'Congratulations, that's terrific. How many's that now? Six?'

'Seven,' Tomkin corrected. He had four children, three of whom were married with kids of their own, one who had just finally got engaged. He'd been married himself for nearly forty years – something of a success story for a career military man – and he was enormously proud of his family. 'It's gonna make Christmas expensive, that's for sure,' he joked.

'That's true, my man. I've got six of my own, I know just how it is.' There was a chuckle on the other end of the line, then a pause. Tomkin realized that the small talk was over, and Jeffries was about to get down to business. 'So how's Spectrum Nine advancing?'

Tomkin cracked his neck from one side to the other and straightened in his chair, pain running through each vertebra of his spine. 'Tests are going well,' he answered. 'The system should be ready soon.'

'Is anybody else aware of the project?' Jeffries asked nervously.

'No,' Tomkin answered immediately. 'That would be impossible. Funding for the project has been buried so deep that even *I* don't know the full details any more.'

'But the human element?' Jeffries persisted. 'Could anyone talk?'

'Nobody that's connected to the programme will talk. They're all patriots, vetted beyond all normal classification. Besides which, Colonel Anderson is there to keep an eye on things.'

Tomkin could hear Jeffries grunt on the other end of the line, and wasn't surprised by the reaction. Colonel Anderson had a reputation.

Tomkin decided not to trouble Jeffries with the recent business about Karl Janklow, even though the latest news from Anderson was not exactly what he'd been hoping for. Janklow was dead – that was the good news – but there was now a new troublemaker, as yet unidentified. Tomkin had recently ordered a full-scale identity search for the woman based on the pictures Anderson had sent over, but the situation was still unresolved. It was a major concern, but it was too early to brief Jeffries on the matter. It was an operational concern, not a strategic one, after all.

'Glad to hear it,' Jeffries replied finally.

There was another pause, and Tomkin could sense that Jeffries was about to address the real reason for the call. 'But,' he ventured gingerly, 'might there be any possible ramifications from recent incidents?'

It was Tomkin's turn to pause as he considered the matter. He had given it a great deal of thought already, and still couldn't be entirely sure. Anything was possible, after all. But he would not be telling Jeffries that. 'None, John, you can be sure of that,' he answered confidently. 'There is absolutely nothing, and I mean *nothing*, that could lead anyone to us. Believe me.'

'I believe you,' Jeffries said quickly. 'I just want to be sure, that's all. If we go to the President with a finished project, something that works, something that's guaranteed, that's one thing. He'll listen to us, maybe even use it like we want. If he finds out some other way, though, somebody lets something slip, somebody discovers what we've been up to, then that's it – we're talking jail, plain and simple.'

'I know that, John,' Tomkin said soothingly. 'I do. But trust me. He won't find out until it's ready. Nobody will.' *And*, Tomkin thought silently, *he won't even find out until it's already been used in anger, maybe not even then, maybe not ever*. Because General Tomkin knew what John Jeffries didn't: there was no way in hell that the President would ever authorize the use of Spectrum Nine. You'd have to be crazy to even consider it.

Tomkin smiled to himself. What the President didn't know wouldn't hurt him, Tomkin was sure. It never had before.

6

JACK MURRAY RECLINED and stretched out, balancing precariously on the swivel chair beneath him as he made a straight line with his body from his toes to his fingertips.

How long had he been here? As he settled back into the uncomfortable chair behind his workstation, Murray did the calculation. *Fourteen hours*. Fourteen hours behind this damned desk, crunching numbers.

It wasn't that he didn't have any other option; he could have signed off six hours ago. But where was there to go? The research base was in the middle of absolutely nowhere, and there was a blizzard coming down outside that was ferocious. All personnel had been confined to base for their own safety for the duration of the storm. Murray's apartment in the small town of Allenburg was more than a forty-minute drive away, and he resigned himself to the fact that he wouldn't be seeing it again for some time. Not that it was anything special anyway.

Accommodation was laid on for them at the base – bunkhouse dorms like you'd get in an army barracks – but he wanted to avoid going there until the last possible minute. And so he had volunteered for overtime, and was going to put in another two hours before he'd head off to the bunkhouse. As he stretched out again, he wasn't sure which was worse – the swivel chair here, or the iron cot in the staff dormitory.

At least there was work to be done. Ever since Karl Janklow had been lost in an avalanche a few days ago, there had been two jobs to be getting on with. In fact, Karl's tragic death was one of the reasons the staff were now confined to base. The weather had been bad then too, and poor visibility was the probable reason for Karl losing control of his car. It was too short notice to get a replacement, and Murray had therefore been doing Karl's job as well as his own ever since.

It upset Murray to think of Karl. They'd been sitting across from one another for over a year now, trading jokes and banter. Karl lived – had lived, Murray corrected himself sadly – in Allenburg too, and the pair had regularly met up for nights on the town. Allenburg wasn't exactly the most exciting town on earth, but the nights had been good, and more often than not had ended in female company. At least they had for Murray, blessed as he was with his rough good looks, lilting baritone voice, and an ability to charm anyone he met. Karl, smart and funny though he was, had never had the same kind of appeal. Whereas people were always surprised that Murray was a computer technician – with a doctorate from the country's leading technical university, no less – somehow they would always be able to guess what Karl did for a living.

Damn, Murray thought as he looked over at the empty workstation opposite him. *I miss him*. Good ol' Karl, computer geek extraordinaire. *My friend*.

Murray pushed Karl from his mind, telling himself that these things happened. People died. The world went on. It was the nature of things, and the world couldn't be any other way. What had his father said when he'd asked him, all those years ago, why people died?

'Jack,' his father had said, placing both of his big workman's hands on his five-year-old son's shoulders, 'if we all lived forever, how would we find the space? The food? The world's only so big. That's just the way it is.'

It was logical really, and he'd never asked again. Not when his mother had been taken from him two years later, when a car had hit her at sixty miles per hour and shattered every bone in her body. Not when his sister had drowned whilst trying to save her dog when she was just twelve years old. And not when his father was on his own deathbed, dying of blood poisoning from unregulated chemical leakages at the factory he had worked at his entire life. He had cried, he had grieved, he had felt all the things a normal person would, but that was life. There was no other way.

When he'd applied for the job here, the location had not bothered him in the slightest – it wasn't as if he had anyone to leave behind. Run as it was by the military, he had undergone thorough vetting and security checks. He was not surprised when there had been questions asked about some of his political ideas – college friends must have talked about some of his campus activities, although they had been harmless enough. It meant, however, that he was employed lower down the food chain than his academic achievements might have warranted, but that was OK. He was here, and that was the main thing.

Unfortunately, nobody at the base would even understand the real reason he was there. It was a shame, he reflected as he looked around the large room, filled with technicians behind workstations, a hundred feet under the huge radar array on the snow-covered surface. He would have liked to be able to talk about it with at least one of his friends or colleagues here. But he knew what response he'd get; everyone was too conditioned – by society, by religion, by all sorts of constraints and controls meant to keep the status quo – to accept his true aim in life.

Because Jack Murray knew that this project had the capability to save the world; and his aim in life was to make that happen.

7

It was late afternoon by the time Alyssa Durham got back to the city. A thousand questions were racing around her brain, but there were no answers. What had Karl wanted to tell her? Who had killed him? Who were the people who were now trying to kill her?

She knew the key to the answer would be finding out where Karl had been working, and so despite still feeling badly shaken by the day's events, she had decided to head straight for the office. Her editor, James Rushton, would support her, offer her all the help he could. She wondered if he would recommend going to the authorities, and realized that of course he would. But she would try and convince him otherwise. How did she know they could trust the authorities? Instead, she would convince him to let her investigate. She would use the newspaper's resources to find out where Karl had been working, and then take it from there.

Another question that plagued her was whether the enemy – for that was surely what they were – knew who she was. The wig and glasses she'd been wearing weren't the most sophisticated of disguises, but they might be enough to give her some time. Besides which, she'd find out soon enough. If they knew who she was, they'd be waiting outside the office to put a bullet in her head.

Before she went to work, she was curious to see what was going on in the city square but the taxi driver hadn't been able to get close; traffic was backed up for miles all around the city. And so she had got out, paid the driver, and set off on foot, keen to see if the stories she had been hearing on the radio on the way back to the city were true.

Walking had proved equally difficult, the streets more and more crowded the closer she got to the square. It was clear that everyone in the city wanted to see it with their own eyes too, with the result that pedestrian movement was as restricted as the traffic.

But slowly, ever so slowly, she did move forwards, until finally she was at the square itself, at a barricade erected by the police. A barrier built to separate people from bats. *Millions* of bats.

Alyssa had never seen anything like it. The square was literally crawling with them, piled on top of each other, covering every square inch of the city centre meeting spot, horizontal and vertical. The radio reports had estimated the numbers to be upwards of twelve million, all coming to roost in the square over the past few hours, utterly unprecedented behaviour that only served to encourage those predicting the end of the world.

She looked around the crowd and noticed that the preachers were already here, some from the regular religions, some from the cults of the statue, and even more from apocalyptic sects. Down the line from her she saw people gathered round a man wearing a white robe and gold arm- and headbands. He was dressed like the man who had caught her attention earlier, on her way to meet Karl. Those guys were everywhere. There'd probably be a story in that, she considered, as she started to make her way slowly round the barriers.

Unfortunately, her office was on the far side. She checked her watch. Half past four. She sighed, hoping that Rushton wouldn't have left for home by the time she got there.

Almost an hour later, she was in Rushton's office, looking out over the square from the plate-glass windows of the twenty-first floor of the newspaper building. Even from up here, the sight was incredible.

'And in the daytime too,' she said in wonder.

'I know,' Rushton said, handing her a steaming cup, which she took gratefully. 'Bats just don't behave like this. And where in the hell are they from, anyway? We don't have that many bats in the state, never mind the city. At least, I don't think we do. But they must have come from somewhere.' He shook his head, then looked up. 'But first things first. I think it's time to call the police.'

'No,' Alyssa said immediately, shaking her head.

'Alyssa, these people are dangerous,' Rushton said. 'Snipers? People impersonating the police? And from what I can find out, there's no evidence of your friend's body whatsoever. Whoever is behind this, they're professional. And if they don't know who you are already, they will soon enough.'

'James, who can we trust? For all I know, those people

were the police; maybe corrupt, maybe working for someone else. I'm only assuming they were impersonating cops.'

'I have friends in the Bureau.'

'But they'd have to tell someone, wouldn't they? And then what?' She shook her head once more. 'I want to do some digging first. Find out where Karl was working, what sort of things he was involved in. We might have a better handle then on who's involved, who we can contact.'

Rushton took a sip of his drink, obviously uncomfortable. 'You really think there's some connection between where your friend Karl worked and these weird things that are happening?'

'Someone sure as hell thinks he knew *something* important. Whatever it was, it's worth killing for.'

'That's just what I'm afraid of,' Rushton answered.

The computer screen bathed Alyssa's tired, drawn face in a pale blue light as she accessed database after database. It was getting late now, and there was only one other journalist left in the research room. Eduardo Lubeck covered vice stories, and was well known as a night owl.

Not for the first time, she was grateful for the paper's vast investigative resources; within minutes, she had found evidence of Karl's transfer papers from his previous job, setting up anti-hacking programmes for several blue-chip firms in the capital. That was just under three years ago, but finding out where he'd gone next was more challenging.

She quickly found out that he had been headhunted by the Department of Defence for some contract work, but she was struggling to find out exactly where he'd been posted.

She decided to try a different tack, searching the vehicle registration database for a match. She wasn't exactly authorized to do such a search, but her years in the field had taught her the rudiments of cyber hacking, and the vehicle database was one of the easiest government sites to strong-arm.

Her eyes lit up as she found an SUV registered to Karlssen D. Janklow – thank heaven for unusual names, she thought – and she quickly took note of the address.

It was a rented apartment in Allenburg, a small town way up north. Pretty much in the middle of nowhere, pure wilderness territory. What was he doing there?

As she took a sip of coffee, she entered a new key phrase into the computer's online search engine – 'computer systems Allenburg'.

The hits came back soon after, dozens relating to local businesses, everything from laptop repairs to bespoke software programs. None of it sounded like anything he'd need a DoD clearance for.

She tried again – 'military research Allenburg'.

She drank more coffee as the page loaded, then glanced down at the results. This time, each site seemed to list the same four-letter acronym – HIRP.

It seemed oddly familiar to Alyssa but—

Without warning, she felt her chair suddenly move beneath her. Her coffee spilled on to her leg, burning her, and then her chair moved again. She planted her feet more firmly on the floor to keep her balance.

Opposite her, she saw Lubeck rocked backwards in his own chair, his eyes going wide. 'Earthquake!' he shouted at her, even as the entire room started to shake, the desk moving across the floor, the walls rippling with the shock.

Alyssa screamed briefly as the lights went out, then gathered herself and grabbed Lubeck, pulling him underneath the desk. If the ceiling collapsed, it might provide some protection. That was what people did, wasn't it? But she didn't know for sure; earthquakes didn't happen here!

The room continued to shake, pictures vibrating and falling off the walls, glass shattering on the floor. Alyssa heard Lubeck whimper next to her.

And then, as soon as it had started, it was over. In the dark, Alyssa was surprised that Lubeck was hugging her. Seconds later, the lights came back on.

Under the table, Lubeck and Alyssa just sat there staring at each other, their faces white with shock.

Alyssa glanced up at the computer. It was back on now and reloaded, the strangely familiar acronym HIRP challenging her to press on with her investigation.

8

'ARE YOU OK?' Rushton asked Alyssa as they stood in the crowded city street, watching as firefighters and paramedics entered the building, along with a team of structural engineers. It was late, but some of the buildings here were residential units which also had to be evacuated.

Alyssa was surprised that Rushton had still been in the building, but perhaps she shouldn't have been; with millions of bats in the square outside his office, and strange things happening not just across the country but across the world, he would have a caseload of literally hundreds of stories to manage. It would be a miracle if he ever found the time to go home again.

'I'm fine, James, thanks. More surprised than anything, I guess.' It wasn't entirely true; she was still a little shaken by the quake, 'minor' or not. Added to which, her nerves were still shredded from watching her friend get shot right next to her, and then the subsequent attempt on her own life. But, she decided, the best way to cope with it was the method she always chose: ignore her tangled emotions and concentrate on work. Psychologists would probably give her hell for it but it seemed to work for her.

She wanted to get back to the research room right away

but all the buildings in the city had been evacuated whilst the damage was assessed, and each building had to be judged safe before anyone could return. As Alyssa looked around, she could tell that the quake had indeed been minor – everything was still standing, after all. But there was smoke pouring out of more than a few nearby windows, and she realized that it made sense to be careful.

Rushton seemed to be having the same thoughts. 'Pain in the ass, right?' he said. 'We're probably not going to get back in for hours. Still, I don't suppose they can take any chances.' He studied her again. 'You sure you're OK?'

Alyssa nodded. 'Just thinking.' She paused, then turned to him. 'Have you ever heard of a government research programme called the HIRP?' she asked, initializing the word.

Rushton's eyes narrowed briefly, then he nodded his head. 'Yes, I think I have. Is that where Karl was working?'

'I think so, yes. He was working for the DoD some place, and HIRP is the only base near to the town his vehicle's registered to. When I can get back in there,' she said, gesturing to their offices, 'I'll try and confirm it. But what is it?'

'If my memory serves,' Rushton began, 'it stands for the High-frequency Ionospheric Research Project.'

'And what the hell is that?'

Rushton smiled. 'I know about the project because Jamie Price was going to do a piece on it last year.'

'Going to?' Alyssa prodded.

Rushton nodded. 'I had to pull it in the end,' he admitted. 'It was good, but it was a bit too inflammatory, without the evidence to back it up. It was intriguing, but in the end it was just based on hearsay and circumstantial evidence.'

The pair had to move as a stretcher was raced past them towards one of the buildings which still had smoke coming out of the windows, and Alyssa felt slightly perturbed as she saw people readying their cameras to get shots of the victim when he or she was trundled back to the ambulance. It didn't help that she knew some of the photographers.

'OK,' Alyssa said, turning back to her editor, 'tell me about it.'

'HIRP was designed over twenty years ago to investigate atmospheric data. Apparently the ionosphere is a great conductor of radio signals, and what started out as a purely scientific project caught the interest of the military when they realized that they could improve their communication and navigation technology by exploiting the ionosphere in line with this research. Secure comms with the submarine fleet and ground-penetrating radar – you know, the kind that could investigate, say, a cave system in the Middle East, see if any terrorists are living there – are just some of the things the DoD are interested in.'

'Sounds like there's nothing too out of the ordinary there,' Alyssa commented. 'So what was Jamie's story about?'

'Well, it all started when the residents of a small village near the base started to suffer from headaches. And I don't mean just your average little headache, I'm talking about really debilitating migraines, suffered by pretty much everyone in that village, over a hundred people.'

'And?' Alyssa asked. 'What did he find out?'

'Well, he did some digging, turned up a few rumours

about the place; I mean, just the average, what you'd expect when the military takes on scientific research and sets up a covert, secretive base around it. You know the sort of thing, they're building some sort of new weapon of mass destruction there, something worse than nuclear, maybe biological or chemical. Another theory was that they were experimenting with mind control, beaming out special radio waves to subdue the population, make us all into government lapdogs.'

Alyssa nodded, aware how it all worked. Anything labelled 'covert' was an immediate target for the lunatic fringe, who seemed to compete to come up with the most imaginative – crazy – purpose for the project concerned. But the fact that a seasoned reporter like Jamie would launch an investigation was interesting. 'So what was Jamie's take on it?'

'Well, by the time he got up there to interview the people, lawyers from HIRP had already been there to apologize and negotiate a payoff. They accepted and just clammed up, wouldn't speak to Jamie at all. Apparently HIRP admitted that a recent test might have been to blame, I think they said it was just a five-second burst from the radar field to do a live check on submarine communications. Anyway, that was that – nobody would say anything, and all Jamie could get was an interview with a HIRP spokesperson, and that wasn't even on the base itself.'

'So he never even got to see the base?'

'He took some long-distance shots but nothing we could use; he was too far away, and the location is protected and remote.'

'So have outsiders never been there?' Alyssa asked, her curiosity piqued further.

'Well, I wouldn't say that. Every year they actually have a public open day, even people from the press can attend. It's all very sanitized of course, and you aren't allowed to roam free, but they show you some of what they do there, and they publish a lot of their research online too.'

'I suppose it's too much to hope that they've got one of these open days coming up.'

'The last one was just two months ago, so there won't be another until next year. And they don't let the press in at any other time. So what are you going to do?'

Alyssa thought about it for several moments, not even noticing when the body was stretchered past her, camera lights flashing all around. Finally, her mind made up, she said, 'First of all, I'm going to confirm that Karl was working there. Then I'm going to go and see Jamie, look at what he found out. And then I'm going to go and have a look at the base.'

'And just how are you going to do that? No press, no outsiders, remember?'

Alyssa looked at him, her features set, determined. 'I'll find a way,' she said.

9

It was almost midnight by the time the newspaper offices were cleared ready for use again, but the late hour didn't deter Alyssa. As soon as she was able, she was back in the research room, behind the same computer; the only difference was that while Lubeck had decided not to return, the room was now much busier than it had been before. An earthquake was a big story, after all, especially here in the city, and her paper's reporters were some of the best in the world, hard-working and dedicated. But, she soon found out, they weren't here just for the earth-quake story; things had been happening elsewhere too.

In fact, it turned out that small-scale natural disasters had occurred over a significant portion of the globe. Checking the online news stations, Alyssa saw floodwaters crashing over fishing villages, sandstorms sweeping over desert cities, a volcano that had spewed out a gigantic ash cloud; image after image of devastation.

Tyler Bradshaw, a local reporter sitting at the desk next to Alyssa, turned to her. 'It's probably not as bad as it looks,' he said, in a tone that was less than confident. 'Like what we just had, these things are all classified as low-level events. What's of more concern,' he continued, 'is that there have been so many, spread over such a vast area of the planet. There have been fourteen of these low-level disasters around the world in the last few hours. It's just unbelievable,' he said, shaking his head.

Two hours later, Alyssa had found clear evidence that Karl had indeed been working at the High-frequency Ionospheric Research Project.

The task had been made easier by knowing where to look; concentrating only on HIRP focused the search and enabled her to spend her time a lot more efficiently.

As Rushton had pointed out, several facets of HIRP's activities were available on the web for scrutiny. On an open data research site, she finally found Karl's name on two separate papers, labelled as a consultant on computer network security at HIRP. The trouble was, these papers had been published two years before, so all it proved was that Karl had worked there at that time; it didn't necessarily mean he had still been employed there.

She also found him in a group photo taken at one of the base's 'open days', which appeared on numerous websites. This was more recent but still over a year old.

She used some of the open data sites to delve further into the web, until she found the archives of the internal staff newsletters. These weren't exactly public access, but they had been easy enough to find. Nothing secret was likely to appear in a newsletter, after all. She scrolled through endless notices about bake sales and softball games, and at last found what she was looking for, in a newsletter just two weeks old: '*HIRP Adventure Club will be meeting at the Bear Tavern in Allenburg at 7 p.m. this Tuesday to discuss provision of a new hangar for the club glider. HAC president Karl Janklow requests that all members attend.'* This was confirmation that Karl was still working at the base when he was killed.

Thinking back, Alyssa recalled that he had always been fond of clubs and meetings; indeed, he had been president of the Ski Association back when she'd first met him. The memories of those times flashed before her, events, parties, faces . . .

Why didn't I think of this before?

She almost cursed as she reached for the telephone. It was late, but she had to know. And if she played it right, then perhaps gaining access to the base might not prove as impossible as Rushton feared.

Despite the lateness of the hour, the phone rang only twice before a nervous, tearful voice answered, 'Hello?'

'Is that Elizabeth Gatsby?' Alyssa asked, sure from the reaction that it must be. Liz Gatsby was Karl Janklow's younger sister, and the tearful voice answered one of the questions she'd had – Karl's death must have been reported already.

'Yes,' Liz answered. 'Who is this?'

'I don't know if you remember me, but I'm Alyssa Durham. We met a couple of times at parties a few years ago. I was a friend of Karl's.'

The tears started again, but Liz managed to control them. 'Yes . . . Yes, I remember you.'

'I just wanted to tell you how sorry I am to hear about your brother. We were good friends.'

'Yes, I remember . . . How did you hear?'

'I'm a reporter,' Alyssa replied. 'I saw the name over one of the wires, and just wanted to get in touch, offer my condolences. Do you know what happened?' she probed, wary of being too interrogative but at the same time needing some quick answers.

'Yes . . . The local police, well, local to where Karl was living, called to say that he'd been involved in an accident. An avalanche while he was driving . . .' The voice started to crack again, and Alyssa let her cry, just waited until she was capable of going on. 'They say they can't find the body . . . They might never find it. Oh!' And the tears began once more, and Alyssa felt her heart go out to the woman.

Karl had always been close to his sister, Alyssa knew; he had looked after her in the way typical of an older brother, and she had looked up to him in turn. Alyssa was no stranger to loss, and knew exactly what she must be going through.

Eventually, Liz managed to carry on. 'And there was someone else too, a lady I think Karl was seeing, Leanne . . . somebody. I don't know . . . Karl and I hadn't seen each other since he moved away. I don't think he was allowed to get away much.'

Alyssa made a note to check out the name. An avalanche was clever, she thought. In that part of the world it could well hide a body indefinitely. And who was going to investigate that far north anyway?

'Has HIRP been in touch with you at all?' Alyssa asked next, fishing for information.

'You . . . know he worked there?' Liz asked, her surprise evident.

'A guess,' Alyssa replied evenly. 'It was about the only place up there he could be working.'

Liz seemed to be thinking on the other end of the line. 'Yes,' she answered finally. 'With Mom and Dad gone, and Karl unmarried, I'm the next of kin. They rang a few hours ago, to express their sympathies, ask if I wanted to go up there, collect his personal effects, you know.'

Alyssa's heart leaped, her unvoiced hopes confirmed, but she managed to contain her sudden excitement. 'So will you be going?'

'I really want to,' Liz replied, 'but I can't afford to go up there. And with two kids at school and my own work, I just don't have the time anyway. I asked them to pack up his things and send them down to me.' She paused. 'Even though they've not found the body, we're going to have a memorial service for Karl at our church. I need to speak to the priest but I think it will be early next week. It would be nice if you could be there.'

Alyssa forced back her own tears, the reality of Karl's death coming violently back to her. 'I will.' She sniffed. 'Thank you, Liz.'

Over three thousand miles away, Professor Niall Breisner waited in the secure communications room for the call to be patched through. He was sweating, and it wasn't from the heat generated by the large banks of electrical equipment that filled the room. This wasn't a conversation he was looking forward to having.

Moments later, the image of General David Tomkin appeared on the screen in front of him, the large high-definition picture making it appear that the man was in the room with him, an impression that did nothing to calm his nerves.

'Professor,' Tomkin said in greeting.

'Good evening, General. How are you?' Breisner winced at the banality of his words even as they left his mouth.

'Not happy, so let's skip the pleasantries,' Tomkin said plainly. 'What the hell is going on up there?'

'We always knew there would be indicators,' Breisner offered. In fact he remembered quite clearly that he had briefed Tomkin in precise detail as to how these sorts of things were more than likely to happen.

'Indicators are one thing,' Tomkin said impatiently. 'The events we've just seen are like a big flashing neon sign. It's unacceptable, Professor.'

Breisner nodded. 'You're right. It is unfortunate. But I'm afraid such exposure is very much part of the deal. We cannot test the device without ramifications of some kind. You must surely realize that.' Breisner wondered if he'd overstepped the mark by addressing the general in this way, but the man merely paused, head bowed.

'OK. What's done is done, we can't change that now. Just tell me that it was worth it. Is the device operational?'

Breisner shook his head very slightly. 'Effective, yes. Obviously. But not yet fully operational. There are some details that need to be ironed out. Questions of control and direction. Obviously, the device needs to be fully accurate, and I cannot guarantee that at the moment. But we

94

are close,' he said with pride. 'We are very close.'

Tomkin grunted. 'Close doesn't cut it with me, Professor. I want results; that's what you're paid for.'

'We are on schedule,' Breisner countered.

Tomkin stared at him through the computer screen, his blue eyes piercing. 'Good,' he said firmly. 'Make sure you don't fall behind.'

Breisner nodded. He knew what would happen to him if he let the general down.

Moments after the connection was severed, Breisner's head snapped round as his landline desk telephone started to ring. He picked it up instantly. 'Yes?'

'Is that Professor Breisner?' the voice on the other end asked; a tearful female voice, and Breisner knew instantly who it was.

'Yes. Is that Liz?' he asked, his voice sympathetic. He knew what Anderson had done, and that Janklow's sister had been given the party line about the 'accident'. He thought it had all been dealt with, and wondered what she wanted.

'Yes,' the voice came back. 'I'm sorry to call so late, but I've changed my mind.'

'Oh? Changed your mind about what?'

'About collecting Karl's personal effects. I've decided to come. I . . . I need closure, I think. I hope it's still OK.'

OK? Damn, it sure as hell *wasn't* OK, but Breisner knew he had to keep up the pretence of normalcy; he mustn't arouse the woman's suspicions. They would just have to escort her in, show her Janklow's workstation; maybe he'd even have a word with her himself, offer his condolences personally; and then she would be escorted off again, and the whole sorry incident could be forgotten.

'Of course it's still OK,' he answered. 'When do you want to come?'

Alyssa smiled as she cradled the telephone next to her ear. She checked her watch; it was still before midnight up at the base. 'There's a flight that will get me there by tomorrow evening.'

10

'Have we identified the woman yet?' Anderson asked as the private jet carried him back towards the frozen wastelands which sheltered the HIRP base.

'Negative,' the answer came back over the satellite phone. Anderson had left some agents behind to investigate the scene – physically check CCTV footage, interview witnesses, and so on; he had also been in contact with the experts back at the base, ordering them to make an immediate electronic search for the woman. The computing power at HIRP was enormous, and Anderson had instructed the CCTV footage of the mystery woman to be plugged into the system for a facial match to be run. The woman may have been in disguise, but the dimensions and contours of the face would be unchanged.

He had also ordered a thorough background check on Janklow, including finding all the interviews done during his security vetting checks when he had applied for the post at HIRP. The woman was probably known to Janklow, and looking back at his past might well provide them with the answer.

The woman obviously wasn't Janklow's girlfriend;

Leanne Harnas was already dead. Unless he had another? Anderson thought this unlikely, but you never knew. The man's mother was dead, and his only living female relative was his sister, Elizabeth Gatsby. His agents had already established that she was at work teaching grade school over five hundred miles away when Janklow had met the woman at the park.

It was possible, of course, that the woman was genuinely unknown to Janklow; perhaps he had been approached by someone, forced to work for them.

The intelligence analyst back at the base went on, 'We have, however, highlighted evidence of a detailed web search about HIRP performed very recently.'

Anderson considered the matter. It could be nothing; HIRP was always the target of conspiracy theorists, and so web searches were nothing to get excited about. However, the timing seemed just a little too coincidental. 'Where did the search originate?'

'We're still working on that, sir,' the man answered. 'But it might take some time – the search was initiated by a secure system, on a protected network.'

This started alarm bells ringing for Anderson; the crazies didn't normally have access to such technology. It indicated that the investigator was professional, and Anderson again considered the possibilities – another government department, a foreign intelligence agency, or the press. Any of them spelt trouble.

'Concentrate on that,' Anderson ordered. 'By the time I get there, I want to know where that search originated.'

* * *

Alyssa was glad to be able to go home at last, for one night at least. Get some proper sleep, in her own bed. The next few days promised to be busy.

She had reported in to Rushton, who had been amazed by her gall. He had at first refused to countenance the idea of her getting on to the base by pretending to be Elizabeth Gatsby, but she had finally won him round and he was now in the process of lining up some false identification papers for her. He could sense a big story and although he acknowledged the danger to Alyssa, the reward might just be worth the risk.

The task of impersonating Liz should not be too difficult, Alyssa reasoned. By her own admission, Karl's sister had never visited him at the base, and nobody there was ever likely to have met her in person. She realized that the security personnel might have pictures of Liz, but she knew she would be able to make herself look sufficiently like the woman to pass muster. Their body proportions were very similar, they were the same age, and Liz wore glasses – a great accessory to mask the face. The only major change would be hair colour – Alyssa's was dark brown, whilst Liz was a redhead.

She was going to have to get some hair dye, several bottles of the best, and so she headed across town for the minimart just a few blocks from her apartment building. It was the middle of the night but the store was open twenty-four hours a day.

She would get the things she needed, sort her hair out back at her apartment, get some much-needed sleep and then meet up with Jamie Price at the office in the morning.

She could then get the rest of her things ready before catching the 2 p.m. flight up north. She hoped Rushton's sources would have the ID ready in time.

She decided to avoid the subway due to the late hour and keep to the streets. She would have caught a taxi but the roads were gridlocked – *at this time?* she wondered – and she knew it would be quicker walking. And anyway, she lived less than a mile away.

It wasn't long before she was questioning her decision, however; even though it was way past the time people were normally out – except for the regular die-hard party fans, of course – the streets were still clustered with people. She realized that it was possible that some of the apartment blocks had still not been cleared after the earthquake.

But it soon became apparent that it was something more than that. People were actually taking to the streets in protest, visibly shaken by the week's events. The various religious sects and cults were still plying their trade on the street corners, and seemed to be attracting huge followings. She checked as she walked and, sure enough, soon came across a preacher dressed in a white robe and wearing a gold headband. A few dozen people had gathered round him, listening intently, and he was urging them, in the name of the Order of Planetary Renewal, to prepare for the cleansing of the world.

The next street she chose was obstructed by a group of angry people – all ages, men and women, some wearing suits, others in rougher clothing – demanding to know what the government was doing to 'save' their country. Armed police were already starting to arrive on the scene, and Alyssa turned off, following a side road down to an intersection.

Things were quieter here, but only because the craziness had already been and gone. Storefront windows were shattered down the length of the street, the shops looted, empty. Cars lining the streets had evidently been set on fire at some stage; many were still smouldering, although most were gutted wrecks. A group of six men wearing greatcoats and carrying three-foot lengths of wood started marching down the street from the far end but were soon intercepted by a group of policemen. Alyssa turned down another street before she became embroiled in the confrontation; the sound of shouting and then heavy impacts, followed by two gunshots, made her quicken her pace.

It was one thing to hear about riots on the television, another thing altogether to see them up close. Alyssa had seen worse during her career but she wasn't used to witnessing it so close to home. It scared her.

She arrived at the minimart ten minutes later, her route mercifully unopposed by any more rioters or protestors. But instead of the minimart's normal night-time trade of a few dozen people at any one time, there were now several hundred crammed into it. People were buying all they could, just in case. In case of what? Alyssa thought about trying somewhere else, but soon decided against it. Another store might be even busier than this, and who knew what she might have to walk past to get there.

Pushing through the door, she entered the melee.

* * *

The store was busy but calm, people nervous but controlled as they moved along the aisles filling their baskets and trolleys with things they would probably never need. Alyssa tried to get what she wanted as fast as she could, but the sheer numbers were against her; it took her twenty minutes before she joined the long check-out queue. By then the mood was starting to change. The close crush of people and the interminable waiting was wearing down whatever patience people still had.

The first shouts came from the aisle next to Alyssa. *That's mine!* It was a woman's voice, coarse, penetrating. *Get your hands off it! I mean it!* The man's voice was equally coarse, threatening. Then others joined in, and there was scuffling as the man and woman went for each other. Shopping carts were pushed to the side and crashed into shelves as people tried to split them up. More shouts erupted, and then it sounded as if a full-scale fight had broken out down the aisle, and not just the man and woman now but many more, taking sides against each other. Alyssa flinched as the shelves swayed towards her, pushed by the struggling bodies on the other side. It held, but only just.

And then other fights broke out, all around the store, and Alyssa watched in mute desperation: two men kicking a woman on the floor, their feet repeatedly stomping on her belly, her head; another man driven face first into a refrigeration unit, the thick glass shattering and cutting him, blood pooling down his neck and chest to the floor; four women fighting in the queue directly in front of her, pulling each other's hair, kicking at each other with sharp heels; and then the man with the gun.

At its appearance, the whole store seemed to go quiet for a fraction of a second; or at least that was the way Alyssa would later remember it. Maybe it only went quiet in her own mind as her senses focused on the terrifying sight in front of her: the dull black metal of the pistol being raised by the panicked man in the pinstriped suit and glasses, the slight pressure on the trigger, the slide ratcheting backwards and forwards, the empty shell casing ejected; the head of the woman next to her exploding, covering her own face with the unknown woman's sticky, thick, bright red brain matter.

Despite herself, Alyssa screamed. The man dropped the gun in terrified recognition of what he'd done and was tackled to the ground by the people surrounding him. Alyssa clamped down on her scream. As she watched the gunman being mercilessly kicked to death by the crowd, his glasses broken across his bloodied, smashed face, she knew she had to keep her head together or she wasn't going to make it out of there alive.

Wiping the blood and brain tissue off her face, she went into a low, protective crouch and looked around, assessing the situation. The gunshot had acted as a catalyst for true chaos to break out, and her options were limited.

All around her, scenes of violence erupted, as people started fighting everywhere, most using just their fists but others using bottles, shopping carts baskets and any other improvised weapon that came to hand. People trying to escape were trampled underfoot, their screams muffled by dozens of pairs of shoes and boots.

And then the sheer force of the crowd smashed through

the storefront windows, glass shattering on to the street outside, people spilling out after it. The violence gave way to looting then. People gathered up as many items off the shelves as they possibly could and raced for the huge opening that was once a window. People fled from the store carrying piles of goods in their arms or in overflowing baskets. Some even pushed their shopping carts over fallen shoppers on their way out, crushing them.

Alyssa edged her way forwards, sidestepping as a man fell to the floor, hit on the side of the head by another man wielding a heavy piece of wood. She looked outside to gauge her chances of escaping through the window, and decided that they weren't good. Shoppers were being jostled and shoved to the ground by people pushing their way out of the minimart with their stolen goods; and Alyssa now noticed that other people were actually *entering* the store through the hole where the window had been, opportunists seeking to loot the store, maybe perfectly normal people until recently, now possessed by the mentality of the rampaging mob.

She looked to the check-outs and saw some of the staff fighting running battles with the looters, trying desperately to stop them, but it was hopeless, there were simply too many of them.

Alyssa sensed movement behind her and reacted, dodging to one side as a greasy fat man in a suit threw a punch at the back of her head. Without even stopping to consider why he would do such a thing, Alyssa stamped down on his knee. As the leg buckled, the man's weight collapsing on top of it, Alyssa grabbed him by the hair and pulled his head straight on to her knee. The impact knocked him out cold and his heavy body hit the floor. Alyssa was no stranger to fighting – had discovered years earlier that she was actually good at it – but she knew when discretion was the better part of valour. She couldn't fight them all.

You're a climber, she told herself. *Climbing's what you do*. Her eyes tracked upwards, following one of the nearest aisle's huge central shelving units as it led up towards the plasterboard ceiling, and knew that she had a chance. *Climb!*

She started to push against the crowd, avoiding punches, to her disgust even treading on some of the other shoppers who had fallen to the floor, until she was at the shelves. And then she started climbing, fingers gripping each shelf in turn as she pushed off with her feet, propelling herself upwards.

Hands started to claw at her from below, and she kicked out – hitting an arm here, a face there – and then she was at the top, pulling herself up on to the shelving unit, which ran from one end of the store to the other.

Keeping down, she quickly crawled along the length of the unit, ignoring the cans thrown at her by the people below. She saw the staff exit at the rear, saw how it was unobstructed, everyone's attention on the broken glass of the storefront, and knew that was going to be her way out.

She felt the shelving unit begin to sway underneath her, and looked down to see a group of women pushing against it, trying to send it smashing down to the floor. Again, Alyssa didn't stop to ask herself why they would do such a thing; instead, she looked at the shelving unit across the aisle, doing a quick mental calculation. Could she make it? It would be a standing long jump, with no room for a run-up. But it seemed so *far*. Logic told her that it was only two metres – far enough, but not out of the question. But up there, balanced precariously three metres off the ground, the women below screaming for her blood, it seemed much further.

But what choice did she have?

And so Alyssa braced herself, did a half-squat, and jumped straight over the aisle. For a few brief, terrible moments she felt she wasn't going to make it, would miss the shelves entirely and fall to the floor where she would be kicked to death by the angry mob; but then she was there, landing with a shudder on the top of the shelves opposite.

Her balance was good but she still almost lost it, struggling to compensate for the movement of the shelves that came from her weight hitting the top of it. But she managed to stop herself from falling over the edge, and composed herself. The exit was three aisles over.

The women below her pointed and screamed, rushing forward to push at the new line of shelves. Other people in the store started to notice her too, the mob mentality taking over, and they joined the women below and started to push at the shelves, for no other reason than that they could. They could take this jumping female down and kick her to death, and nobody there in the shop would judge them for it, they were free from all constraint. Alyssa could feel the violent energy, and jumped, just moments before the shelving unit collapsed.

She teetered on the top of the next one, getting her balance again, blocking out the screams of the people trapped beneath the crushing weight of the shelves behind her, and then jumped again.

She was a prime target now, people from all over the store were heading towards her, but it was quieter at the back, most of the crowds were at the front, and those coming for her were hampered by the crush and the obstruction caused by the fallen shelves.

Looking forwards once more, she made her final jump to the last shelving unit, her legs tired now, collapsing under her as she landed, spinning her off the top. She gasped in momentary surprise and panic but managed to correct herself as she went over the edge, catching hold of the top shelf with her strong hands; but her own weight, combined with the momentum of her jump, started to pull the whole unit down, and she shouted at the people below her to get out of the way, riding the shelves down as the unit arced towards the floor and jumping clear as it crashed down into the aisle with a deafening noise.

She saw a group of people – an unruly, violent mob – moving across the broken shelves and bodies to get to her, and she turned for the door to the staff exit, just feet away now. Sprinting forwards, she barrelled a man out of the way who had decided to block her path, kicking through the door just as the first hands were starting to reach her.

Then she was through into a whitewashed concrete corridor, and she pivoted on her heel and slammed the door shut behind her, sliding the locking bolt home even as the door bulged inwards from the weight of the ferocious crowd behind it.

She turned and fled down the corridor to the fire exit at the far end. Pushing through it, she heard the inner door break behind her and the flood of people rushing down the corridor in pursuit of her – their mind operating as one now, their only desire to track down and kill the jumping woman. Why?

Why not?

As Alyssa gulped in the clean night air of the service alley, she knew she didn't have much time before they would be upon her. She turned back to the minimart and looked up. The building was four storeys high.

She pulled off her shoes and threw them into a garbage bin opposite, then hauled herself up into a boarded-up window frame, her fingers and toes reaching for the ridges and depressions that would give her the purchase she need to climb.

Within seconds she was on top of the window frame, and then started on the harder part, her fingers and toes feeling for the gaps between the brickwork, using the tiny ridges to give her leverage to haul herself up the exterior of the old building.

By the time the first rioters broke out into the service alley, she was already two storeys up, but she didn't stop, she just kept on climbing, her mind focused on nothing else. Adrenalin coursed through her body, sharpening every sense; she could see the brickwork in exquisite detail, her fingers and toes probing the tiny gaps and depressions as she hauled herself upwards.

She could hear the shouts far below – *Where's she gone?* *– Where is the bitch? – Come on, down here! – Let's get her!* – and realized that they had never looked up; and now she was so high, she would be almost invisible in the dark.

She kept on climbing, until finally she pulled herself over the parapet of the roof; drained, exhausted, the breath simply drained from her.

But she'd done it. She was alive.

Alyssa spent the next few hours on the rooftop, watching with increasing horror the scenes around her.

The fighting and looting continued, spreading out from the minimart to engulf other shops on the street. And then innocent bystanders were pulled in, beaten, robbed of their money and jewellery. Cars and vehicles were set on fire, and then the shops too. Mercifully not the minimart – Alyssa felt safe on the roof, and didn't want to come down – but several other shops and business units on the street were set alight, some with people still inside.

And then the riot police descended on the scene and moved in with shields and batons, while water cannon and rubber bullets were used as suppressing fire from the rear.

The violence was terrifying, and surprisingly lengthy; the rioters held out for quite some time, despite the advantage of the police unit's weapons and equipment.

But slowly and surely some semblance of order was restored; the street was cleared, and Alyssa counted fifty-four people being loaded into the back of the police vans. Hundreds more fled across the city.

Finally, she felt confident enough to climb back down the building. She collected her shoes from the dumpster and made her way just two blocks further to her own apartment building. She avoided the police; she knew they were doing their job for her protection but if she'd gone to them, she would have been taken downtown as a witness, and she had no idea how long it would have been before they took her statement. Hours? Days?

But she was home now, finally; although – as the magnitude of what had happened to her began to sink in – she had to admit, she no longer felt safe anywhere.

11

Oswald Umbebe grimaced as he took a sip of sweet tea. The pain in his chest was agonizing, yet he knew that it was a not a problem with which he would have to concern himself for much longer.

He had been diagnosed with the disease just six months ago, after refusing to visit a doctor about the pain for several years. And by the time he went, it was inoperable; it had already spread from his lungs, outwards through his body. He knew he was going to die – the doctor had told him as much on that first day – but this didn't trouble him in the least. Everyone was going to die one day. And Umbebe knew something most other people didn't – that day was coming sooner than they thought.

He was the High Priest of the Order of Planetary Renewal and it was his firm belief that the world was going to end very soon. At least, the world in its present form was going to end, to make way for another to rise from the ashes. That was the beauty of it.

This wasn't just a way to cash in on the current situation, to part fools from their money. The order didn't ask anyone for money, they never had, not once in their thousand-year history.

Their philosophy was simple. The world had to periodically renew itself in order to survive. It had to cleanse itself, to cure itself of the malaise it periodically experienced. Catastrophic incidents had occurred on several occasions in the earth's four and a half billion-year history, and the ancient scientists who had established Umbebe's order had charted these events, discerning a pattern amongst the seeming randomness.

According to the ancient scholars, this year was due to see another Apocalypse, another renewal of the world's finite energy. Umbebe was thrilled that he would be presiding over the order during the time of final upheaval. It was an honour of the highest magnitude, and he had worked hard to build up the order, until now membership stood at over eighty thousand across the world. Not that they would have any sort of reward; they would perish along with everyone else. But they would die knowing that their deaths had purpose, and that was the real difference.

The year, however, was fast running out, and there was nothing on the horizon – no planet-ending comet, no tectonic movement presaging a gigantic earthquake, no sign of any catastrophic tsunami. But he wasn't without back-up plans. Years before, one of his most loyal brothers had come to him with news of some secret government research, and Umbebe's true mission in life had become clear to him in a moment of exultant revelation.

It was too much for him to expect to just sit back and let the world destroy itself. Technology was so advanced now that the earth might need assistance to cleanse itself.

The world was testing him, he began to understand that. And so he had started planning.

The phone beside him rang, the electronic handset obtrusive in the otherwise natural, wood-panelled setting of his private office. *My update*, he thought, wincing with pain as he picked it up.

'Yes?' he answered expectantly. He listened as his agent informed him of the latest occurrences, grunting occasionally in acknowledgement. When the man had finished, Umbebe asked simply, 'But how long until it is ready? *Truly* ready?'

As the man answered, many thousands of miles away, Umbebe smiled, the pain in his chest all but forgotten. It was a matter of great fortune that he had a loyal man deep inside such a project. Although, he had to admit, it wasn't entirely luck – Umbebe had spent years recruiting people; they were spread throughout the world for just such a time as this.

Yes, he thought happily. *The time is almost here. And our order will usher in a new dawn . . . with the destruction of the earth, and everyone in it.*

PART THREE

PART THREE

1

ALYSSA GLADLY ACCEPTED the steaming hot drink from the stewardess, then turned back to stare out of the airplane's small window.

The ground below was a complete white-out, although apparently the weather had much improved over the past few days, when commercial flights hadn't even been running. It made her shiver just looking at it out there, and she took a comforting sip of her drink.

After the trauma of her escape, she had barely slept at all, constantly checking the streets below for rioters or any other violence. She had been a bag of nerves, wired on caffeine and adrenalin, but had eventually managed a couple of hours of fitful sleep.

She still had to rise early that morning to meet up with Jamie. She'd checked out of her windows first and seen that a police barricade had been set up, which was cutting off and protecting the residential blocks. Would she be free to leave?

In the event, the police had let her pass, and the presence of a National Guard cordon on the streets even meant that the taxi sent by Rushton was able to proceed to the office at more than a snail's pace. And when she'd got there, she'd been relieved to see that he had received her message about the hair dye that she'd lost during the riot, and brought her in three bottles.

Jamie had had little to offer in the way of hard information about the base; he had never managed to get close enough to investigate properly. But the HIRP base scared him, that much was obvious. She didn't tell him that she was going, but he warned her off anyway, saying that he'd heard enough stories about people trying to get into the place and then never being heard from again to be wary.

She listened to the warnings, and would heed them – to a certain extent, at least. Nothing would deter her from going, but she would be careful. Jamie had told her about a man called Colonel Anderson who was responsible for security at the base, and his unsavoury reputation. Alyssa wondered if he'd had anything to do with Karl's assassination, and the attempt to kill her. She feared what would happen if she was recognized, but the simple change of hair colour, different wardrobe and thick spectacles changed her appearance entirely, and Rushton had provided her with identity papers. There was little more that could be done.

When Anna had died, Alyssa had volunteered to become an embedded reporter with the military forces in the Middle East. It had been her way of running from what had happened, of trying to escape. When she thought back on it now, she wondered if she hadn't perhaps been slightly suicidal; the survival rate of embeds during the worst part of the war was often as low as fifty-fifty. But she had made it through the shelling, the suicide bombs, the riots, the death and the mayhem imbued with a new sense of purpose in life. Reporting, showing the world what was *really* going on, had become her salvation.

As she stared out at the frozen wastes below her and felt the plane start its descent, she wondered what was really going on at the HIRP base.

2

BACK AT THE base, Colonel Anderson surveyed one of the large antennas in front of him. The radar field, known locally as the Ionospheric Research Array, was the real heart of the HIRP operation. It consisted of fourteen rows of fourteen separate antennas, each nearly fifty feet in height, laid out in a grid spread over a huge area of land. It was an incredible sight. The array amounted to a vast radio transmitter, beaming concentrated rays of pure radio-wave energy into the upper atmosphere at regulated frequencies. Each antenna was separated in its own square fenced housing, a small portable control centre nestled underneath each one. Each unit could pump out thirty million watts, meaning that the entire transmitter array had an effective radiating power of nearly six billion watts. The ionospheric research that the base was officially scheduled to carry out typically required only a fraction of the field's potential, but Anderson knew that Spectrum Nine would need it all.

Dr Martin King was the man in charge of the radar array, and one of the base personnel briefed on every aspect of the programme. He stood next to Anderson, arms folded and stamping his feet to keep warm.

'Welcome back,' King said through chattering teeth. 'I hear your trip didn't go too well.'

Anderson's stare cut King dead, and the scientist instantly regretted baiting him. 'Nothing we can't handle,' Anderson said calmly, the cold not seeming to affect him at all. 'Just make sure you're concentrating on your own job. How are preparations coming for tonight? I understand the aurora will provide excellent conditions for our test.'

'Absolutely,' King replied. 'Superb conditions. Do we have the authority to go ahead?'

'Breisner is dealing with that as we speak,' Anderson replied. 'But if we get the go-ahead, I need the system to be immediately operational. Understood?'

'Yes, Colonel. It will be ready to go.'

'Good,' Anderson said and turned to walk back to his jeep.

He checked his watch. *Damn*. He would have to hurry if he was going to meet Elizabeth Gatsby at the airport.

'Do you wish us to proceed?' Dr Niall Breisner asked General Tomkin over the secure telephone in his private office.

'Yes,' said Tomkin at the other end of the line, three thousand miles away. 'Secretary of Defence Jeffries and I both authorize phase three testing of the device, as previously discussed.'

'The target?' Breisner asked reluctantly; the science excited him, but he preferred not to think about the real-life ramifications.

'Again, as previously discussed. You are authorized to go ahead with a full-power test, to the coordinates you have already received.'

'Yes, sir,' Breisner responded mechanically. 'But there is . . . a problem of sorts,' he ventured carefully.

'What sort of problem?' Tomkin's voice was cold.

'We have a civilian visiting tonight. Karl Janklow's sister, coming to collect his personal effects.'

'Yes, I've already spoken to Colonel Anderson about her. We'll just have to ensure that she doesn't see anything. You and Anderson will have to deal with her if she does. Are we clear?'

Breisner swallowed hard. 'Yes, sir. Understood,' he managed to say with more conviction than he felt.

'Good,' Tomkin said. 'Because nothing must get in the way of this. Nothing, and nobody.' There was a pause on the line, before Tomkin spoke again, his voice grave. 'Good luck, Dr Breisner. Don't let me down.'

And with that, the connection was broken, leaving Breisner to sit there and wonder, not for the first time, what he had agreed to.

3

ALYSSA OPENED THE door to the Bear Tavern at just after six in the evening, local time, the sun already long gone over the horizon.

Now she was here in Allenburg, she didn't know what the protocol was. She had half expected a military escort to meet her at the airport, but there had been nobody there. She supposed that she shouldn't have got her hopes up – her presence was probably just a nuisance, and they weren't going to go out of their way to be welcoming.

She had ordered a taxi from the airport, but when they passed the bar – an old, decrepit building in a decidedly ramshackle part of town, well off the tourist track – she asked the driver to stop. It was the same tavern listed in the HIRP newsletter as the meeting place for Karl's Adventure Club, and she thought she might learn something. If Karl's club had met there, maybe it was a hangout for HIRP staff generally.

When she went through the door clutching her travel bag, a dozen heads turned to her, cold eyes appraising the newcomer. Typical small-town reaction, she thought. Outsiders were seldom welcome. The men – there were no other women here, she noticed – turned back to their drinks, and Alyssa approached the bar.

Half an hour later, she was sitting in a booth surrounded by faded wood and worn velvet, having finally found someone to talk to. Lee Miller was a local man, and the town drunkard by the look of him. But to Alyssa, this only meant that he might be a good man for information.

A group of men lined the bar, chatting to the humour-less bartender; across the room, another half dozen men sat drinking round a card table; two more booths were occupied by loud drinkers, whilst another held a solitary man. Handsome and seemingly out of place in this rough tavern, he had come in just ten minutes after her, ordered a drink and sat down by himself. Someone with troubles, she'd thought instantly.

Miller leant towards her over the small, scarred table. 'Ma'am,' he said gravely, 'you don't wanna be asking questions about the base around here.' He held her gaze, and it was clear he meant what he said. 'You see those guys at the bar?'

'Yes,' she confirmed.

'Four of 'em are base security. The six at the table playing cards are staff. This place gets crawlin' with 'em. The guys at the bar come here to keep an eye on things, make sure nobody's talking out of school, know what I mean?' He gestured to the barman for another drink.

'And what if they find someone who is talking?' Alyssa asked.

Miller shrugged. 'Hell would I know?' he said grumpily, accepting the glass placed before him by the bartender.

'Only thing I know is that they don't come here any more after.'

The barman paused at the table. 'Is old Lee here bothering you, lady?' he asked gruffly.

'No, not at all,' Alyssa replied.

Leaning closer, the barman said, 'You just be careful. We keep ourselves to ourselves here.'

The threatening tone of voice was all too clear, and Alyssa meekly nodded her head. Satisfied, the barman walked away.

Alyssa waited until he was back behind the bar.

'Lee,' she said quietly, 'what sort of things would these people have been saying? You know, before they stopped coming here?'

'Oh, the usual.' Miller grinned. 'The base has got some sort of secret programme, nonsense like that.' His eyes went glassy and he stared off into space, making Alyssa wonder how much alcohol he'd consumed before she arrived. 'One couple came in here, spouting off about how the radar field zapped a laser beam right up into the Northern Lights, they said it ain't never looked like that before, you know? All sorts of different colours, damn crazy stuff. Course, I seen some pretty weird stuff myself,' he continued, finding his flow now, glad to talk to someone who would listen. 'The lights happening during the day sometimes, or else maybe just shutting off altogether, just halfway through. And then there are the birds,' he said cryptically.

'The birds?' Alyssa asked.

'Oh yeah.' He leant back in the seat and stretched his arms over his head. 'Just the past few months, things have been messed up for the birds. Come and go at different times, you know, fly off during the wrong season. Fight each other. Found a whole flock of 'em dead one day, just scattered over the school playground, dozens of 'em just broken in bits.'

'What's causing it?' Alyssa asked, seeing the link between other recent events clearly but still not sure if Miller was just making the whole thing up.

'Damned if I know,' Miller grunted and took another swig of his drink. 'Only thing I know is, I lived here all my life, and I ain't never seen anything like it. Whatever they're up to, it's confusing the hell out of nature, is all I'll say.'

'And I think you said just about enough,' growled a male voice beside them. Alyssa's head whirled round to see four of the men from the bar now right next to their booth. How did she miss their approach? But it seemed Miller had been right, about this at least. 'Why don't you move along?' the man suggested, and Miller didn't have to be told twice; he picked up his drink and got out of there as fast as he could.

The man who had spoken slid into the booth across from Alyssa, into the space just vacated by Miller. 'And I think you've been asking too many questions, li'l lady,' he said.

Alyssa noticed the tension in the other three men; they were like coiled springs. She was anxious, but she still didn't feel true fear yet. What were they going to do, right in the middle of a public bar?

The man opposite her leant forward, his coat falling open to reveal a handgun in a shoulder holster. 'What say we take a walk outside?' he asked.

'And what if I say no?' Alyssa asked, the fear starting to creep up now.

'Then I guess we'll have to leave it at that.' The man shrugged his large shoulders. 'Can't force a lady to do anything against her will now, can we?' But as he spoke he pulled the coat further open, his other hand reaching for the gun. His message was clear, and Alyssa nodded her head.

'OK,' she said, the fear strong now, her heartbeat accelerating, the pulse thumping in her chest. 'We can go.'

The man started to slide out of the bench seat but stopped when he saw that Alyssa was not moving. 'Are we gonna have a problem here?'

'No,' Alyssa said hurriedly, 'no, not at all. It's just that if you work for the base, you know, for HIRP, I'm supposed to be here, maybe you can check or something. I'm the sister of Karl Janklow, he was . . . killed here in an avalanche a few days ago.' She used the fear, letting tears start to fall down her cheeks. 'I'm here to pick up his things,' she whimpered.

The man regarded her coolly. 'That may be so,' he said eventually, 'but I think we're still gonna head on outside until we can clear this up. Now come on.' He placed a large hand on hers. 'Let's go.'

'Hey, hands off the lady,' she heard a voice say from off to the side. Surprised, both Alyssa and the man turned their heads, to see the handsome guy from the other booth standing there, staring at them.

'Why don't you mind your own damn business, Jack?' the man asked, as his three friends started to surround him. 'We ain't got no beef with you, but if you get involved, you know Anderson will back us and not you.'

Anderson. Alyssa recognized the name as the security chief Jamie had told her about.

'Just don't threaten her, OK?' Jack persisted, moving closer. At his approach, the man opposite Alyssa swung round in his seat and swung a booted foot right at Jack's crotch.

The kick connected hard, and Jack doubled over in pain before being brought upright by two of the other men, one wrenching his arm up his back whilst the other slammed a vice-like grip round his throat. They began to march him outside.

Noticing that the man opposite her was momentarily distracted, Alyssa grabbed Miller's empty glass and smashed it across his face. The man was dazed but not out, and Alyssa instantly followed through, upending the table and driving it forward, smashing it hard into him.

The remaining man by the table reacted, going for his gun, but Alyssa was on him, driving the heel of her palm into his face, raising her knee an instant later to connect with his groin.

She could see Jack struggling with the other two men but it was clear he was getting nowhere. She started heading towards him but the man she had hit grabbed her ankle from his position on the floor, dragging her down with ferocious strength.

Alyssa kicked out at him, her boots lashing into his face once, twice, but still he held on, pulling her closer to him, until he they were face to face. She leant forward to bite him, but he anticipated this and thrust her head back into the floor, using his other hand to draw his gun and shove the barrel into her eye socket.

BANG!

The gunshot reverberated around the room, and everything came to a shuddering halt.

The gun moved away from Alyssa's eye, and she realized she was still alive. She felt the weight shift off her, and pushed forwards off the floor to see three men in the doorway in military uniform, one – wearing a colonel's insignia – holding a pistol aimed at the ceiling, where he had just fired his warning shot.

'Stand down,' the colonel ordered, and instantly the four men did as they were told, backing away from Alyssa and Jack as if they were diseased.

'Now get out of here,' the officer ordered, and the four men high-tailed it out of the bar as quickly as they could.

The two soldiers who had accompanied the colonel left with the other four men, presumably to escort them back to base, and the senior officer holstered his weapon and approached Alyssa, his hand extended to help her to her feet.

'Please accept my sincere apologies,' he said. 'Elizabeth Gatsby, I presume. I'm sorry I missed you at the airport. I'm Colonel Anderson, head of security at HIRP. I'm so sorry for your loss, and I'm horrified at my men's behaviour. They'll be reprimanded, believe me,' he said. Alyssa wasn't sure whether he was being genuine or not. His words sounded sincere, but his eyes were cold behind the friendly veneer.

'Colonel,' Jack said, nodding his head in greeting as he approached. Alyssa noticed one eye was swelling, his nose was bleeding, and he was rubbing the back of his head. Not much of a fighter, but she appreciated the effort. 'Your men could do with a few lessons in manners,' he suggested, quite gallantly in Alyssa's opinion, still pressing the issue despite his injuries.

'Quite so,' Anderson agreed. 'I'll see to it, Jack, believe me.'

At that, the injured man turned to Alyssa, hand extended in greeting. 'Hi,' he said with a quite charming smile, 'my name's Jack Murray. Sorry I wasn't much help back there. Guess fighting isn't really my thing.'

Alyssa shook his hand warmly. 'I thought you were great,' she said, meaning it. 'My name's Elizabeth Gatsby.'

She could see Jack thinking about it, then his head snapped up. 'Karl's sister?' he asked.

Alyssa nodded. 'Yes,' she said.

'I'm so sorry,' he said, embracing her. 'Karl was my best friend. I'm so sorry, really.'

'I've got a car just outside,' Anderson interrupted, putting a hand on Alyssa's arm and gesturing to the door. 'Shall we?'

4

ANDERSON SPENT THE next hour listening to Elizabeth Gatsby and Jack Murray chatting in the back of the big SUV he was using to chauffeur them back to the base.

He'd raised hell with Breisner when he'd found out that the woman had been invited to the base to collect her brother's things. Why couldn't they have just packed everything up and shipped it off? But Breisner had said that might seem suspicious, and in the end Anderson had been forced to agree.

But why had she stopped off at the Bear Tavern? And why had she been talking to Miller, that damned rumour-spreading drunkard? According to her, she had heard her brother talk about the place and wanted to have a look at it, try and find some sort of lost connection with him, and although it seemed feasible, Anderson had a hard time buying it. Could Elizabeth Gatsby have been the woman at the amusement park? Her story checked out – his men had confirmed that she had been somewhere else at the time – but where would a schoolteacher have learnt to fight like that? He had already ordered his men to start looking into whether Gatsby was a high-ranking martial artist of some sort, or had grown up in a rough neighbourhood.

But now, as she sat in the back of the car chatting to Murray, she seemed perfectly harmless, quite the little school ma'am. And it was clear that she was genuinely upset about her brother. Upset enough to try and cause some sort of trouble at the base? Anderson wasn't sure, he would have to be on his guard. That was his job, after all. And with Spectrum Nine so close to completion, he could not afford to take chances.

Murray had invited himself along for the ride, saying he'd had too much to drink to drive himself back to the base. Anderson had agreed, thinking he might learn something from listening to the two of them talk. For his part, Murray also seemed to miss Janklow, and Anderson found himself worrying about whether Janklow had ever said anything to Murray about the base's secret project. But Janklow had been closely monitored after he had found out, and it was evident that Leanne Harnas had been the only person he had confided in. No, Anderson decided, Jack Murray was no kind of security risk; he was just an overqualified desk jockey, a nobody.

But he still had to make his mind up about Elizabeth Gatsby. As the gates opened and they pushed on through the deep snow into the complex itself, Anderson determined not to let the woman out of his sight for a second.

As Alyssa spoke to Jack in the back of the car, she was aware of Anderson listening closely, probing the conversation for any hint of untruth. She played the role she had assigned herself, and felt she had done a good job; she'd known Karl well enough to share anecdotes with Jack like only a sister or close friend could.

She was glad when Anderson suggested that they all retire for the evening, saying that because it was late, she could go to Karl's office to sort through his things the next morning. It would give her more time at the base. But she didn't want to go to her room right away, so she had said she was hungry, and Anderson agreed to escort her to the cafeteria. It was clear he wasn't about to leave her alone. Jack offered to join them, which pleased her. He made her feel at ease, and he was undeniably attractive.

They continued to chat, Alyssa working hard to ignore Anderson's presence, and she started to wonder if Jack knew anything about the covert research programme which was supposedly going on here. Was it possible that Karl had told him anything? Or was Jack in on it anyway? She felt she might be able to get somewhere with him if Anderson wasn't there, but still the man stayed, preventing her from asking any important questions.

A vibration caused Anderson to check the pager on his waistband, and he looked up at Alyssa and Jack, obviously unhappy. 'I'm afraid I'm being called away,' he said. 'May I escort you to your room?'

Alyssa gestured at her unfinished meal. 'I'm sorry,' she said, 'I'm still really hungry and I'd like to finish this.'

'I can escort her back when she's done,' Jack offered instantly, and Alyssa tried to suppress a smile, watching as Anderson's eyes narrowed, calculating his options.

Finally, he nodded. 'Very well. Thank you, Jack. She's

staying in Room E14, common dormitory block. Her bags are already there.'

'Just across the hall from me,' Jack said happily. 'No problem. See you in the morning, Colonel.'

Anderson pushed himself away from the table, nodded, and was gone.

As he made his way back to the base's military command post, Anderson wondered if he'd been right to leave them alone.

But he had no reason to suspect she wasn't exactly what she claimed to be, and Jack Murray was a known woman-izer; he'd probably decided to try and add another notch to his bedpost. That probably wouldn't be a bad thing, Anderson reflected; it would distract her from being too curious about the base whilst she was here. Besides, he'd had no choice; the message had requested his urgent pres-ence back at the command centre. He wondered what his men had found.

He burst through into the busy command post, scanning the faces around him. He caught the eye of his chief analyst. 'What do you have for me?' he asked.

The man smiled at him. 'We cracked the system,' he announced proudly. 'The search on HIRP originated from the research computers of the *New Times Post*.'

Anderson stopped dead in his tracks. So, the woman in the amusement park was a journalist; his worst fears were confirmed. 'Who is she?' he asked.

'We're still working on that,' the analyst replied. 'Each reporter has a personal access key but we don't have a list of whose key is whose. Sometimes these guys log on under other people's keys anyway.'

'OK,' Anderson said, 'get a list of everyone who works at the *Post*, and I mean everyone, from the owner right down to the janitor. Then cross-reference the names with everything we've got on file for Janklow, see if he knows, or used to know, anyone who works there.'

The analyst smiled again and pointed at the computer in front of him. Anderson looked, saw huge swathes of electronic information racing down the screen, and understood.

The search was already under way.

5

Jack escorted Alyssa back to her room just as he promised, but they were both reluctant to part so soon. The connection was there and they both felt it.

'Well, I'd better be getting back to my own room now, Liz.'

'Yes, and thanks again for helping me out at the bar earlier.' Alyssa smiled and turned to her door.

Jack turned away too, but then his head snapped back. 'Hey, have you ever seen the Northern Lights?' he asked.

Alyssa looked at him. 'No,' she said. 'Although I've always wanted to.'

Jack checked his watch. 'Well, they're supposed to be happening tonight,' he said. 'These things are never exact, but they'll probably be starting about an hour from now.'

'Really?' Alyssa asked, very interested now. Her desire to see the lights was one thing, but she also recalled what Miller had told her at the bar, how the lights were somehow linked to, or affected by, whatever secret programme the base was running. Did that mean that something would be happening tonight?

'Absolutely,' Jack said. 'You should even be able to see them from your room. They're pretty amazing.'

Alyssa knew Jack was probably trying to get her to let him in, so they could watch them together, which in itself wasn't a bad idea. But she sensed a further opportunity here, and hoped Jack would go along with it.

'I've wanted to see them all my life,' she said earnestly, 'but I don't want to see them from inside. Is there any way to get out of here, see them properly?'

Jack frowned. 'Not really. At these hours, base personnel are kind of confined to quarters, it's a long-standing rule.'

'Why?' Alyssa asked.

'Not sure really,' Jack had to admit. 'That's just the way it is. They say it's too dangerous to leave the buildings at night, you know, due to wolves and bears, but I'm not too sure about that.'

She looked Jack in the eye. 'I'm not scared of wolves, Jack,' she said.

Jack laughed. 'After seeing you in action in that bar, I believe you.'

'So how about it?' she tried again.

'How about what?'

'Getting out of here to see it properly. I'm sure a guy like you knows a way.'

'Just what kind of schoolteacher are you?' he asked with a smile.

They arranged to meet outside Jack's room in thirty minutes; he said he had to take care of some things before they could go.

Alyssa decided to use the time to have a shower, and reached into the cubicle to turn the water on. It came out cold, and she let it run. The last thing she wanted was to freeze to death; it was cold enough outside as it was.

She had discovered that Jack worked in the base's computer section and ran all of HIRP's operating systems, many of which he had devised himself. The image of computer genius didn't seem to gel with his appearance or manner at all, but Alyssa knew you couldn't judge a book by its cover. She had genuinely enjoyed her evening so far and she found herself actually wishing she didn't have a job to do.

Since Patrick's death – nearly six years ago now – there had never really been anyone else in her life. For the first few years she had concentrated on Anna; then after her tragic death, she had just wanted to be alone. In the last couple of years, she had tried dating a few times but nothing ever came of it, and she wasn't sure she wanted it to. But there was something different about Jack, she thought as she stepped into the shower, stretching the kinks out of her aching body.

She tried to dismiss such thoughts and focus on the reason she was here. After tonight, she would probably never see Jack again.

She sighed.

Anderson strode back into the control room. 'Do you have a name?'

The analyst looked up at him with a wide smile. 'Alyssa Durham,' he said. 'Senior investigative journalist at the *Post*, and ex-climbing partner of Karl Janklow. From what we can see, she hasn't seen him for years. But it's a clear link. She's the one.'

Despite himself, Anderson let a smile cross his lips. The woman at the amusement park had a name. 'Good work. Is that the file?' he asked, gesturing at a folder on the desk.

The analyst nodded. 'Yes, that's all the information we have on her.'

Anderson picked up the file and started to flip through it, his mind already establishing the next course of action. 'OK,' he said, his head coming up, 'get people round to her apartment, see if she's there. If she is, have her picked up. At the same time, I want agents over at the *Post*. Let's find out who her contacts are, what she's working on at the moment. Get this file circulated to everyone. Treat this as top priority.'

The analyst nodded, already turning back to his bank of computers and picking up the secure telephone on his desk. Satisfied, Anderson put the folder under his arm and turned on his heel, heading back out for the radar field.

Good, he thought as he left the room. *Alyssa Durham will soon be mine.*

6

'It's BEAUTIFUL,' ALYSSA whispered to Jack as they sat huddled together under a thick blanket on the roof of the main control centre.

Jack had led her out of the dormitory building and across the area leading to the command centre, careful not to be seen by the patrolling guards. Jack knew they wouldn't be picked up by electronic surveillance but there was still the human element, and they had to keep to the shadows to avoid detection.

They had managed to get to the large concrete structure completely unseen, and Jack had then taken her to a metal ladder on one side. He had explained that there was no security on top of the building, just a bunch of air-conditioning ducts and a single access hatch for routine maintenance. As long as they kept down, careful not to get silhouetted on top of the building, they would be safe from prying eyes.

In the distance, Alyssa could make out a huge forest of antennas. Jack told her that it was called the Ionospheric Research Array, and gave her a brief breakdown of its purpose and how it all worked. It was interesting, but no more detailed than the information she had digested from

Jamie's research notes. On the other hand, seeing was believing, and it was a tremendous sight to behold. Alyssa could detect no activity at the radar field, except for what Jack seemed to think was an unusually large number of vehicles in the car park.

But now the first lights of the aurora started to illuminate the dark winter sky, a sudden flash of brilliant green, like bioluminescent sheet lightning. And then it started in earnest, and the sky all around them lit up with irradiated brilliance. The eerie green glow seemed to contract, then expand, then contract once again, twisting into seemingly impossible shapes as it danced across the sky. It was perhaps the most beautiful thing she had ever seen; and there was also Jack, whose heartbeat she could feel as her head rested on his chest.

Alyssa pushed herself up, keeping her body in contact with Jack's all the way, until her head was level with his. She turned away from the pulsating green aurora and looked into Jack's eyes, which looked back at her with burning intensity. Did he feel it too? She leant forward slowly, wanting so much to find out; and as the aurora flared once more above them, he moved towards her, accepting her invitation. Their lips met, gently at first, and Alyssa's heart seemed to beat louder and louder in her chest as Jack wrapped his arms round her. Alyssa responded by pressing harder into him, deeper, her arms seeking his body.

A feeling almost like electricity surged through her as their kiss continued, their bodies almost becoming one, and she felt free once more, the reality of the world melting away with their passion.

But then Jack pulled away, breaking the embrace, shattering the magical unreality of the moment. She felt cold instantly, separated from his warmth.

'What is it?' she asked, putting her hand on his.

'Quiet,' he said in reply, turning his head like a dog straining to hear some faraway noise. 'Do you hear it?'

Alyssa turned her head and listened. Nothing. What was Jack doing?

But then she heard it too, just faint, a low rumbling like a big-capacity car engine ticking over at idle. 'What is it?' she asked again.

Jack held up a hand as he struggled to make it out, but then Alyssa tugged at his sleeve and pointed towards the closest radar.

Jack looked too, and she felt his body tense. A spark of light exploded from the surface of the huge radar crosshead, and then the outer perimeter of radars lit up in the same way, one by one round the huge square. They watched as the inner 'rings' lit up, electricity surging across the vanes, until all one hundred and ninety-six antennas were crackling with barely contained primal energy. Alyssa and Jack could both feel the force of the radar array pulsating across the clear night sky.

'What's going on?' Alyssa asked breathlessly, but Jack could only look on in wonder, speechless.

They continued to watch as the huge sparks of light left the confines of individual radars, travelling through the air until the entire grid was criss-crossed with bright, crackling light. Minutes seemed to go past as they watched, the ghostly green of the Northern Lights above them all but forgotten as the energy coming from the radar grid seemed to build steadily in power, the light becoming thicker, brighter, more intense. Alyssa felt the need to look away to protect her eyes, but couldn't.

And then the light was directed upwards from the top of each radar mast towards a point thirty feet above the central group of masts. The beams met there, joining together in a single point, forming a covering of energy almost like a brilliant, luminescent parasol, and then both Alyssa's and Jack's jaws dropped open as they saw a huge flash of blinding light shoot straight up into the sky from this central point, the power from every radar mast converging in one single, arrow-like surge of pure energy into the aurora above them.

The single blast was over in the blink of an eye, and when it was gone, so too were the powerful, crackling lights of the radar masts, and the entire grid was inert once more, silent, unmoving.

A few moments passed, and then Alyssa turned to Jack. 'Have you ever seen anything like that before?'

Jack shook his head slowly, seemingly bewildered. 'Never,' he admitted.

Alyssa glanced skyward, and her eyes narrowed as she watched the Northern Lights continue their dance across the sky above them. But they were different now somehow, the snaking movements faster, more complex, perhaps even brighter. Yes, they were getting brighter, and she grabbed Jack's arm to get him to watch too. The aurora began to change. Alongside the familiar green light, streaks of crimson appeared; the two colours danced apart and then melted together, again and again.

Alyssa knew the lights were sometimes red, but this seemed different somehow; and then they changed again, an opaque blue light entering the procession, darting in and out of the green and red. The sky then went completely dark for a fraction of a second, and then glowed pure green, a flash of light that almost blinded Alyssa after the darkness that had preceded it. And then there was darkness again, and then a flash of red; then dark, before a third flash, this time of brilliant blue. Alyssa knew that such a display was unprecedented.

For several minutes, the sky above the HIRP facility raged with light – red, green and blue, but also yellow, orange, violet and white, all battling each other in a stunningly choreographed rhythm that took Alyssa's breath away.

And then the incredible light show was over and the sky returned to inky blackness once more.

After a few moments, Jack turned to Alyssa, his face serious. 'I think it's time we got the hell out of here.'

7

Just over thirteen hundred miles away, Jaywood Nblisi trotted gently along a beautiful white sand beach after his three-year-old son.

It was a glorious day, the sun high in the sky and blessing them with its warmth. He glanced back to his wife and four other children, all gathered on the large rug they'd brought down with them from their small home, just an hour's walk away.

They lived pleasant enough lives, although Jaywood had to admit that the conditions at the factory in which he worked left a lot to be desired. No plumbing, no sewerage, and no breaks in fourteen-hour shifts were not exactly ideal, but Jaywood was a realist; his small island had no natural resources to speak of, no tourist infrastructure, and there was no way of making a living save for working at the factory which, hellhole or not, he knew the country was lucky to have. And he fully believed that by putting in the hours without complaint, he would one day work his way up to be a supervisor. At least that's what his boss had told him, and he had no reason to doubt it.

At least he had every weekend off, which meant he could spend a couple of days a week lazing around on the beach without having to worry about how he was going to afford to feed his family – unlike some of his islander friends, who refused to work at the factory, and therefore suffered the ravages of abject poverty.

He had caught up with his youngest son, who had stopped to examine a multicoloured conch shell, when he felt the beach move beneath his feet.

The sensation was gone as soon as it arrived, and he began to wonder if he had imagined it; but then it happened again, even stronger this time, and he felt himself flipping into the air, the sky turning over him.

He crashed back to the ground, the wind knocked out of him. He looked immediately to his son, who was sitting there with a look of surprise – but not yet fear – on his young face. Jaywood scrambled over the white sand to him and gathered him up in his arms. He raced back towards the rest of his family, who he could see waving frantically for him to return.

Jaywood started to wave back but was sent tumbling once again as the earth shook for a third time. He collapsed, but managed to keep his son aloft, unhurt. Jaywood groaned, wondering if he had broken something.

The other people on the beach were running for the far treeline behind them. Jaywood watched as another shudder rocked the ground beneath him, and he saw a huge section of the jungle disappear right before his eyes, falling into the ground, swallowing the first people with it.

The screams started then, and sounds reached Jaywood from far away – car horns blaring, the sirens of emergency vehicles, house alarms, all from his home town, just a few miles away, on the other side of the jungle. And then he heard the klaxon sounding at the factory, the call for an immediate evacuation.

Earthquake, everyone was shouting, and Jaywood knew it must be true. He'd experienced tremors before, but something that destroyed an entire jungle in the blink of an eye? He could barely move with the shock of it all.

But he needed to move, he *had* to move, had to get to the rest of his family and make sure they were safe. And so he dragged himself to his feet once more and set out for them, weaving in and out of the other people on the beach who were panicking now, unsure of where to go or what to do.

As he ran, the rest of the jungle disappeared, it just seemed to be sucked down with no resistance, and he could see the buildings of his town, unobscured by trees and foliage. He winced as he saw the tallest of the buildings start to collapse, then turned back to his family, ignoring everything else. They were fifty metres away now; if the world really was going to end, as all the news reports lately seemed to predict, at least they would be together. But then there was another shudder, and the beach itself was ripped in two, leaving a deep crevasse that ran from the ruined remnants of the jungle all the way to the ocean. Jaywood himself was thrown clear, and he landed with his son, who was crying now, in a pile of sand.

The beach on his side of the rift tilted upwards at an impossible angle, so he couldn't see his family any more. He began to climb towards the top of the disgorged land, the sound of rushing water filling his ears as he went. He climbed steadily, powerfully, ignoring the pain in his legs and back, scrambling up the broken, sandy slope until he reached the lip. He saw his family over on the other side, scattered on the ground, frightened and bruised. But they were alive. His wife, three daughters and another son, they were all alive.

He looked down into the rift in the beach, and saw how the ocean was surging into it, creating a fast-moving river that pushed through the ruined jungle towards the town beyond. How many people lived there? Jaywood knew it must be ten thousand or more. He said a prayer as he watched the water crash towards them, before redirecting his attention to his family.

He whispered reassurances to his infant son, cradled in his arms, then looked again at his wife and other children. They were standing now, looking out to sea, immobile, frozen.

Jaywood turned himself and his eyes went wide with shock, with fear, and with simple awe at the sight that confronted him.

A wall of water – it must have been a *mile* high – was thundering towards the little island; an implacable, deadly force of nature. Jaywood shook his head in disbelief. Such a thing seemed impossible. But there it was, coming towards them, closer and closer with each passing second.

The roar of the tsunami filled his head, drowning out all other sounds, all other thoughts, and Jaywood turned to his family on the other side of the rift and waved goodbye.

He cradled his son closer in his arms, letting him feel

warm and safe. He bent his head to kiss the little boy on the head, tears in his eyes.

And then the tidal wave hit, destroying everything in its path.

8

'Just what is going on here?' Alyssa asked.

She was sitting on a chair at the small card table in Jack's room, while he lay back on his bed, hands covering his face.

He sat up and looked at her. 'I'll be damned if I know,' he said eventually.

'You must have heard talk about this place,' she probed.

Jack sighed and shook his head, and then got up from the bed and started to pace the room. Alyssa was worried that he wouldn't say anything else, but then he turned to her. 'OK. But before I tell you what the rumours are, you have to understand that I don't believe them, and I've worked here for years. OK?'

Alyssa nodded her head, and then he began. 'Well, obviously anything with any military connection becomes the target for conspiracy theories of all kinds, especially when some of the research is secret, and kept out of the public eye. But what some people – *crazy* people, in my humble opinion – believe is that the radar array can be used to influence the weather; you know, heat up clouds *here* and make it rain *there*, that sort of thing. Other people think that by influencing the ionosphere, sonic properties can be sent around the globe to be directed towards certain targets, to achieve all sorts of crazy things – natural disasters; electro-magnetic pulse waves which are supposed to shut off all electronic devices, sabotaging an entire country's infrastructure with one simple move; direct-hit weapons that can shoot missiles out of the sky; even mind control.'

'Mind control?' Alyssa asked.

Jack nodded. 'I told you the whole thing is crazy. Some folk believe the "light rays" shot out by the radars can brainwash people; indeed, they believe that we already are brainwashing people all over the world, our own citizens included.'

'It does seem a bit far-fetched,' Alyssa agreed.

'You bet.' Jack sat down on the bed once more. 'I'll tell you why this place attracts this sort of attention – because the real work that goes on here, quite mundane and boring as it is, is just too hard for most people to understand. And if people can't understand something, they'll create a story around it that they can understand. And people understand weapons, and they understand war.'

Alyssa knew that Jack was probably right, but she was convinced something more was going on. 'Look, I'll be gone tomorrow,' she said, 'and I'm sorry for being so nosy. I guess I'm just trying to understand the kind of place Karl was working in, you know, what he was doing for the last few years. We didn't see each other much after he started work here.' The manner of Karl's death came back to her in vivid detail, and she hugged herself, trying not to tremble.

She didn't resist as Jack pulled her on to the bed and put

his arms round her. And then, as they sat looking at one another, their hands suddenly sought each other's, entwining so naturally that they hardly realized it had happened. Their lips came together gently, then more forcefully, and Alyssa soon found herself lying next to him and he was brushing his lips across the smooth, soft skin of her neck. She felt herself melting under his touch and at that moment she wanted him more than she could remember wanting anything in her life.

9

As ALYSSA CREPT from Jack's room later that night, she hated herself.

It wasn't for sleeping with him, she didn't regret that for a second. In fact, lying in bed with him, his arm round her, she'd felt happier than she had in years. But after he'd fallen asleep, she had gone to his jacket and detached the security card that she had seen him using all evening. It was a betrayal of his trust but time was short. She would have to pick up Karl's things in the morning, and then she'd be on her way, never allowed on to the base again. She'd seen with her own eyes what the radar array could do to the Northern Lights, and if it could do that then surely it could also affect other aspects of nature, perhaps even create natural disasters. If there was even the slightest chance of a connection, she knew she had to investigate it. At the very least, she felt she owed it to Karl to make the attempt.

As she slipped down the quiet corridors, she hoped she would make it back before Jack woke up. At least she had a chance of remaining unobserved, thanks unwittingly to him. He had told her that while she had been taking a shower, he had returned to his computer station in the main command centre under the pretence of correcting a systems failure. Once there, he had logged on to the security mainframe and set about redirecting some of the computer systems.

That was how he'd thought of it – 'redirection'. It was much better than the arguably more accurate term of 'sabotage'. But the result was the same: certain key security cameras had been turned to face in different directions, other sensors had been fed inaccurate data, and an 'escape corridor', unobserved by the base's hi-tech surveillance, had been left open for their trip to view the Northern Lights.

Jack was in charge of all of the base's computer operating systems. He wasn't attached to the security section of the command centre, but because he had designed the software that the section used, he could control the base's electronic surveillance capabilities. He could shut down the entire system and replace it with a useless 'mock' system, and the security section would be none the wiser. Not that this had been his plan tonight; his intention tonight had been much more modest. And the redirection had worked. The two of them had managed to get up on the roof and back to Jack's room completely unchallenged. Jack told her he would switch the system back to normal in the morning, which meant that it was still streaming incorrect information through to the security centre. Alyssa hoped that this meant she would get to the computer centre undiscovered.

She retraced her steps from earlier, using Jack's access card to pass through doors, always alert for other people, and finally entered the main command centre instead of climbing up the side of it.

Despite the lights which still shone brightly from the mobile command centres over on the radar field, this building was mercifully empty, as she'd hoped it would be at three in the morning. She quickly found the signs for the computer centre, and had to hide only once as a security guard made his rounds. She made a mental note of the time, hoping that he wouldn't be back for at least an hour.

Eventually, she reached the computer centre, a room of glass-enclosed cubicles separated from the rest of the building by a huge smoked-glass wall. She used Jack's access card again, and a glass door slid open to admit her.

She searched the cubicles until she found Jack's – helpfully, all the desks had nameplates – and sat down, hunching over in the seat to minimize her shape, should any more security guards come round and peer through the glass. The desk was cluttered with work but empty of personal effects. There were no family pictures, nothing of any noticeable sentimental nature. The only thing that indicated a real person worked there at all was a canvas print hanging to one side. It was of a train crashing though the foyer wall of a station. She recognized it instantly as the main railway station of her home town. She wondered briefly if Jack used to live there too, or if he just thought it was an interesting picture.

She used the key card to turn on the computer, praying that the light from the screen wouldn't alert anyone.

'Are you sure?' Anderson asked the chief analyst. The security command centre was hidden underground, along with many of the research elements surrounding Spectrum Nine.

The place was a hive of activity after the successful test earlier, but nobody else working on the base would ever realize.

'Yes, sir,' came the reply. 'She's not there. Alyssa Durham isn't at her apartment, and she hasn't been seen at work since yesterday morning. It was hard getting information, but from what we can gather, she's gone away somewhere for a work assignment, although we haven't yet found out exactly what she's working on. Her editor, James Rushton, wouldn't give us anything. Her bags were gone from her apartment but we can't find plane tickets or any other type of ticket booked in her name.'

Anderson considered the matter, and could feel his blood pressure rising. After such a glorious evening, with the full might of Spectrum Nine finally being utilized, here was the bad news. Alyssa Durham was still out there somewhere.

Perhaps she had just been spooked and run off some-where. Understandable, considering he'd been trying to kill her. And yet from her performance in the park, and the information on her file, she didn't seem the type of woman to run away from anything. On the contrary, she seemed the kind of person who would just as soon attack.

He spun round to address the analyst. 'Do we have a home number for Elizabeth Gatsby?' he asked.

The analyst called up some data on his screen, and read it off to Anderson, who typed it into his phone and connected the call.

He held the phone to his ear and waited, hearing it ring and ring. No answer. He hung up. 'What time is it there?' he asked next.

'Er . . . eight in the morning?' the analyst suggested.

'Maybe she's already on her way to school,' Anderson muttered to himself. He asked for the school's telephone number and was put through straight away.

'Hello, I was wondering if Mrs Elizabeth Gatsby is expected in at work this morning?' he asked politely.

He listened as the receptionist on the other end of the line went to check her records. 'Yes, she's due in today. In fact, I can just see her pulling up outside now. Do you want to hold for her? Who shall I say is calling?'

But Anderson had already hung up and was racing towards the elevator that would take him from the control room to the dormitory block and Room E14.

10

Alyssa didn't know exactly what she was looking for. How did you go about finding a 'black' research project, something that wasn't ever supposed to be found?

But Jack had said that he had access to the base's security mainframe, and she was therefore confident that she would find something. She trawled security logs, staff records, maintenance requests; anything and everything. And then she stumbled upon some transcripts.

These were written records of conversations between certain base personnel – telephone calls, emails, even chats in the rest room, it was all there. Obviously anyone suspected of leaking intelligence was closely watched.

There wasn't anything that shouted at her, but she noticed continual references to S-9, Spectrum Nine, and something known mysteriously as the ninth spectrum.

With these key words, she inserted a search program into the system and set it running. Further security clearance was needed, but when she flashed Jack's card across the infrared reader, access was instantly granted.

Vast swathes of information came up, and it wasn't long before she found what she was looking for – technical schematics for a project known as Spectrum Nine, presumably the secret project that many people believed lay behind the HIRP base.

She quickly inserted a flash drive that she was carrying and started the download. Clicking off the page as the system laboriously downloaded the schematics to her portable memory stick, she began to go through the rest of the pages. The technical info should tell her what Spectrum Nine was, and what it was capable of, but she wanted names too, to find the people who were behind the project. Was it legitimate? And if so, who was authorizing it? Who—

'Would you mind telling me just what the hell you think you're doing?'

With a start, Alyssa looked up from her computer, to see Jack standing in the doorway.

Anderson knocked loudly on the door and when it wasn't answered within five seconds he drew his handgun and kicked it down, bursting into the room with his weapon up and aimed.

Nothing. She wasn't there. *She*, the woman who was impersonating Elizabeth Gatsby; the same woman who had evaded assassination and then capture at the amusement park. *Alyssa Durham*.

He raced from the room, thinking he had one last chance before he had to sound the general alarm. Across the hallway he came to Jack's room. Again he knocked, waited five seconds, and then kicked it down, handgun scanning the space beyond.

Empty.

Damn it! How could he have been so stupid? It was no coincidence that Jack had met her at the bar; they were obviously in on it together, which meant only one thing.

They would both have to die.

It took no more than a minute for Alyssa to tell Jack everything; her real name, what she did for a living, how she had seen Karl Janklow assassinated right next to her, which had set in motion all her subsequent actions.

'I'm sorry, Jack,' she said, hoping with all her heart that he believed her.

'And me?' he asked.

'Jack,' she said, 'please believe me, I never wanted to involve anyone else. What we did . . . I really wanted to. But I also needed information. I saw your card there, I remembered what you said about having security access, I saw my chance and I took it. I'm sorry,' she said again.

Jack stared at her silently, his expression unreadable.

'If what you've told me is true,' he said finally, collapsing into a chair opposite her, 'then I guess I—'

He was cut off by the shrill, ear-shattering blare of a warning klaxon.

The alarm had been sounded.

The security guard doing the rounds of the main command centre received the message over his intercom just as the alarm started.

Colonel Anderson was ordering all available security personnel to make a hard search of the base for two targets. Jack Murray was HIRP's chief computer technician, and the guard knew him well enough; Alyssa Durham/ Elizabeth Gatsby was an unknown entity, but her description was sent over even as the guard pulled his pistol from its holster and made his way down the corridor.

Anderson's orders were clear: the targets were to be shot on sight.

'We've got to get out of here!' Alyssa shouted at Jack over the sound of the siren, clicking frantically with the computer mouse, downloading any page she came across.

'We?' Jack asked. 'Why have I got to go anywhere? I haven't done anything!'

That was true enough, Alyssa thought. 'Then *I've* got to get out of here. Is there another way out of this room?'

'After what you've done? Why should I—'

The glass wall shattered behind them, a high-powered handgun round blasting through Jack's computer monitor.

Alyssa instinctively dropped down behind the cubicle, noticing that Jack did the same.

'Why the hell are they shooting at me?' Jack shouted across to her.

'They think you're helping me!' Alyssa shouted back, grabbing the flash drive from the computer and stuffing it into an inside pocket. She risked a glance over the desk but whipped her head straight back down as she saw the guard level his pistol at her. The next bullet tore across the room, destroying the next cubicle, showering her and Jack with glass shards.

'Well, thanks,' Jack spat. 'I guess I'll have to help now!'

Alyssa managed a grateful smile as Jack pointed back

towards the rear wall, ushering her towards it. Another way out? She really hoped so, knowing the guard would be upon them at any moment.

On her hands and knees, she started to crawl across the broken glass.

The guard snaked his way through the cubicles, angry that he'd missed that first shot. But when he'd seen the two of them sitting across from one another, he'd just raised his pistol and fired.

It was the smoked glass wall which had thrown his aim off, deflecting the path of his bullet just enough for it to miss Jack. And now they knew he was there, which would only make things harder.

Still, he figured, they would be panicked, scared and, most importantly, unarmed. What was more, they had nowhere to run. Reinforcements were already on their way, but if he played this right, all that would be left for Anderson and his men would be bodies.

Broken glass crunched under his feet as he turned past one more cubicle, his gun aimed down at the ground. But there was nothing there, just bloodstained shards of glass.

They must have crawled off, he realized, cutting their hands and knees as they went. Well, it didn't matter; they were only prolonging the inevitable.

'Son of a bitch!' Jack whispered, pain shooting through his hands and knees as they continued crawling.

They had made it undetected to the storage cupboard on the far side of the room. Jack had ushered Alyssa inside and then pulled out a rear panel to reveal a duct for electric cabling. It was small, but there was enough room to crawl in. Once inside, Jack had reattached the panel and gestured for Alyssa to keep moving forward.

Jack's curse drew Alyssa's attention to her own cuts. The pain made pulling herself through the cramped service space decidedly unpleasant. But it was infinitely preferable to being shot at, and so she just gritted her teeth and ploughed on. She hoped the security guard wouldn't be able to follow the trail of blood.

The cabling duct angled off in two directions, and behind her she felt Jack tap her right ankle. She veered off right, wondering why Jack knew so much about the ducts. Maybe she would ask him sometime, if they managed to survive the night.

'So where are they?' Anderson's voice boomed across the computer room.

'I . . . I don't know, sir,' the security guard stammered, unable to understand how the pair could have got away.

Anderson spent just seconds scanning the scene before he saw the spots of blood. There was quite a bit to start with, but then it petered out. He could see why the guard had failed to spot it, but Anderson was a whole different animal; to him, it was as plain as day.

He followed the trail to the cupboard and wrenched open the door. He was disappointed but not overly surprised to find it empty.

He saw the panel at the back instants later, observing how it hung at a very slight angle, as if someone had unsuccessfully tried pulling it back into place from the other side.

He reached forward and pulled it away, leaning through with his gun into the small, dark space. 'Where does this go?' he demanded.

When nobody answered him, he keyed his radio, contacting the chief analyst back in the underground chamber. 'The cabling ducts from the computer room,' he said without preamble. 'Where do they lead?'

There was a pause, the man obviously calling up the building blueprints on his computer. 'They terminate in an external access point, halfway down the building's north side, about five metres from the rear access doors.'

Anderson keyed the radio once more and directed his men to converge on the access hatch.

Alyssa and Jack were already in the shadows of a copse of trees fifty yards away from the command centre when a whole squad of soldiers descended on the access hatch they had left only minutes earlier.

'Well, we're out,' Jack breathed. 'But now what? The whole base is surrounded by a twelve-foot perimeter fence. If we get past that, we're still in the middle of nowhere.'

Alyssa tried hard to still her hammering heartbeat. Jack was right; they'd escaped the building and the immediate danger, but now what? They had to get out of the base somehow. She sank to her knees, thinking. There had to be a way; there always was.

Suddenly, kneeling there bleeding on to the crisp, fresh snow, she had a memory flash. HIRP Community

Newsletter number 324, second page. Karl's notice about the Adventure Club.

'Jack,' she said, 'where's the glider hangar?'

'So do you know how to fly one of these things?' Jack asked her as they stared at the sleek silver glider inside the large metal hangar they'd just broken into.

The hangar was not far beyond the trees; luckily, the search hadn't extended this far yet. They'd seen two soldiers pass by, but used the cover of the trees to avoid them. The hangar was barely protected at all; theft probably wasn't a big problem around here.

'No,' she answered simply.

'Well, what a superb idea!' Jack shot back. 'So what do we do with it now?'

Alyssa stared at it for some time, and the specially rigged tractor next to it. 'It's not a fighter plane, Jack,' she said, approaching it, figuring out how it might work. 'I mean, how hard can it be?'

'They're what?' Anderson exploded, already running towards the hangar.

The reply came back exactly the same as before: nearby security personnel had seen a tractor burst out of the hangar, dragging the glider behind it. What the hell were they thinking?

'Open fire!' Anderson commanded, and was gratified to hear the sound of automatic rifle shots just moments later.

* * *

This probably wasn't the best idea she'd ever had, Alyssa admitted to herself as she drove the high-speed tractor towards the northern perimeter, pulling the lightweight glider behind her, a terrified Jack at the controls. But all he had to do was hold it straight; she was going to have to do the real work.

Jack had told her that just a few hundred metres ahead, the northern edge of the base fell away down a sheer cliff face to the forest below; it was unclimbable, by all accounts, so much so that Anderson didn't even post security patrols there. But it offered everything she needed, and she accelerated towards it with every horsepower the tractor could muster.

She heard the sound of gunshots then, and felt the impact of rounds hitting the vehicle. She hoped the thin skin of the glider wouldn't be damaged, but there was nothing she could do about that now. And then suddenly they were there, at the edge of the cliff.

As the tractor started to tilt over the edge, she was seized by a feeling of absolute horror, a sensation of deep-seated, all-encompassing dread that chilled her to the bone. The view out across the moonlit, rocky terrain, the snow-covered landscape, the feel of the chill wind on her face – for several terrifying, panic-inducing seconds, she was back on the chair lift cable watching her eight-year-old daughter plunge helplessly to her death.

'Jump!' she heard Jack yell. 'Alyssa, jump!'

She snapped back to reality and started scrambling back through the tractor even as it fell from the top of the cliff, its weight pulling it inexorably downwards. With a last surge, she came out from the rear of the tractor, unhooked the towline from its attachment in one smooth movement and grabbed hold of the cable with both hands, gripping on for dear life as the tractor plummeted to the valley floor below. Momentum pulled the glider forward off the cliff until it soared out across the open sky, with Alyssa dangling beneath, swaying in the wind.

Anderson watched the glider as it pitched and yawed across the sky and emptied his magazine after it, ignoring the futility of such an action.

His men did the same, firing their weapons in a continuous barrage until there was no ammunition left. He watched in disbelief as the woman pulled herself up the towline and into the glider, marvelling at how strong she must be. How fearless.

He hung his head on his chest as the glider moved further and further away. He would just have to hope they would crash.

'We're going to crash!' Jack announced as soon as Alyssa pulled herself, agonized and breathless, into the cabin and settled into the second seat in the tiny aircraft. 'I've got no idea what I'm doing!'

'It's OK,' she said between ragged breaths. 'You're doing fine.' The most important thing, of course, was that they were leaving the base far behind them. Other than that, she didn't really have any more idea than Jack.

'How do we land one of these things?' Jack asked, handing over control of the stick to Alyssa.

'I've got no idea,' Alyssa admitted.

It was dark outside and despite the moonlight, she struggled to make out what was in front of them. Or, she realized, where the ground was. It was white below her, but they could be at any height at all.

'Are those branches?' Jack asked as he looked out of the side window. Before Alyssa could turn her head, the first impact made the glider lurch hard in the air.

'Yes!' Alyssa coughed as they were hit again, harder this time. 'We're landing already. In the trees.'

She just had time to assume the crash position before another impact jolted the glider up and over itself, the tail now the highest point, the nose aimed straight down at the forest floor below. The light aircraft bounced down between the tree trunks to the snow-covered ground, and the world went black as Alyssa passed out.

One hour later, General Tomkin put the telephone down and poured himself a drink from the cabinet behind his desk.

He tried not to get angry, but it was a struggle. He drank the amber liquid down in one and poured himself another, feeling a little better already.

The day had started off well, with news of the successful first full test of Spectrum Nine, but the phone call he'd just had from Colonel Anderson had soured his mood considerably.

To his utter disbelief, it seemed that the woman who had avoided being killed at the amusement park was a journalist. And not only that, she had also managed to infiltrate the base – *while the test was being carried out* – and access information from the computer files. She had then escaped from the base with a senior staff member, in a *glider*, of all things! Apparently the glider had crash-landed out in the forest, but when Anderson and his men had arrived, the pair were long gone.

Anderson still had search parties out after them but Tomkin wasn't holding out much hope. He would have to assume they would escape, and that they would use the information they had. What he therefore had to do was damage control.

What could the woman have found out? Jack Murray was a senior computer technician and had access to most of the information kept at HIRP, including full technical details of the weapon. He didn't have direct access but those details were on file, and if the pair knew what they were looking for, it was conceivable they would have found something dangerously revealing.

Tomkin sighed as he wondered what to do. Should he alert all the agencies, label them terrorists and have them picked up? The trouble there, of course, was that they would have the chance to talk to too many people before Tomkin's own trusted aides could get to them, and whatever information they had would be out in the open.

Tomkin studied Alyssa Durham's file, trying to assess what she would do. Assuming she had physical evidence with her of Spectrum Nine, would she just run to the nearest internet café and put it all on the web?

His instinct told him that she wouldn't; people published things on the internet all the time, and most of it was all but ignored. People only trusted information if it came from a reputable source, and that meant the mainstream media. Alyssa Durham would almost certainly contact James Rushton and convince him to publish a full report in the newspaper. She was a professional, after all, Tomkin reasoned. He would still order an instant block on all her email accounts, as well as her website and blog, just in case she did decide to post anything, and he would do the same for Murray too. But Rushton was the key.

Tomkin picked up the phone again to order round-the-clock surveillance on the newspaper editor and his assistants, including twenty-four-hour monitoring of all communications into and out of the *Post* building.

Satisfied that he had done what he could, he relaxed back in his chair and stared at his own computer, thinking about the additional information it contained.

At least, he thought, *they didn't break in here.*

11

ALYSSA LOOKED AT the man over the small desk, hoping he wouldn't notice the state she was in.

She had replaced her old clothes, which had been soaked through and muddy, but she hadn't been able to completely rid her face of the dirt which covered it, nor disguise the two-inch gash on her forehead from the crash landing, not to mention the numerous small scabs which now crossed her hands and knees from the broken glass.

Oh, who am I trying to kid? she thought. *Of course he'll notice.*

But strangely, the man paid almost no attention to her as he signed her in to the motel, concentrating instead on his computer. He was obviously watching the news, and seemed to be emailing and texting at the same time. Whatever he was watching, it had certainly got his attention; she just hoped it didn't have anything to do with her or Jack.

The phone rang and he picked it up instantly, all but ignoring his motel's new guest. 'Hey, man, so what do you think?' he asked, before his eyes went wide in disbelief. 'You mean you haven't heard? An entire island was destroyed,' he said. 'What? I don't know, one of the little ones out in the middle of the ocean. An earthquake ripped it in half, and then a tidal wave wiped it off the face of the planet. It's gone, man. Completely gone. It was little, but it still had thousands of people living there, and they're dead, man, dead and gone, every last one of them. It's on every channel. I can't believe it.' The man seemed so wired Alyssa wondered if he was on drugs of some kind.

He held out the cabin key for Alyssa, who took it and turned to leave, still listening to the conversation behind her.

'So what do you think, man? I mean, do you think we've had it? Is it gonna be the end of the world?'

And then Alyssa was gone, terrified by the thoughts which were flying through her mind.

Jack was waiting for her outside – they'd both thought it best that they weren't seen together, as Anderson was probably searching for a couple rather than a single individual. Besides which, Alyssa was the only one with money, as Jack hadn't been carrying anything on him when he'd left his room to find her back at the base.

After the glider had crash-landed, they had both been unconscious. For how long, they didn't know; but mercifully they woke up before Anderson and his men had made it to the scene.

The glider had gone further than they'd thought; the forest they'd crashed into was not the one surrounding the base but was actually a smaller bit of woodland past Allenburg and over towards the next town. They had managed to make it on foot into town and then buy bus tickets south. They were both busted up pretty bad, but bought some supplies and a first aid kit from a store, and also used the opportunity to buy new clothes. Alyssa had to use her credit card, which she knew would prove where they'd been; but she also knew that when Anderson found the glider it would be pretty obvious anyway.

The bus had taken them on a route south for several hours, Alyssa and Jack fearful at every stop that they would finally be found. Eventually, Alyssa suggested getting off before their final destination. It was possible that Anderson's men would find the office where they'd bought their tickets and discover the route, maybe even fly someone to the final destination to intercept them.

When they got off in a small town, they quickly managed to hitch a lift, going east to better mask their trail. They knew they had to turn south again eventually, and so when they saw the roadside motel, they'd asked to stop. They would rest the night and continue on in the morning; they were so exhausted that they just couldn't function any longer without some sleep.

Alyssa waved the key at Jack and gestured over to one of the linked cabins to one side of the horseshoe-shaped arrangement. He nodded and started to walk over.

As they met, Alyssa looked at him, worry and fear clear across her features. 'We need to watch the TV,' she said.

'Oh no,' Jack groaned as Alyssa unlocked the door to let them in, 'don't tell me we're on there already?'

'No,' she said uneasily. 'I think it might be much worse than that.'

* * *

As they watched in horror, everything Alyssa had heard the man say on the telephone was confirmed. The island nation had been destroyed in its entirety last night, every last man, woman and child swept to their deaths by the largest tsunami the world had seen in recent history.

Luckily, because the island was out in the middle of the ocean, and due to the direction of travel, the tsunami had over six thousand miles to go before it hit anything else, and the latest reports were that it had completely dissipated before hitting any major landmass. But the effect on the rest of the world seemed to be electrifying – citizens of every country were up in arms, demanding to know what their governments were doing to save them from similar catastrophes. The doomsday scenarios being preached on the streets of every major city in the world were now being taken seriously even by the conservative media.

But there was one piece of information which Alyssa found even more alarming. 'Jack,' she breathed, 'the earthquake that destroyed the island and created that tsunami started at about two o'clock in the afternoon, for that time zone. Which means it was about eight o'clock at night up here.'

Jack nodded his head. She didn't have to spell it out for him; it was barely minutes after the radar array had sent that unified blast of pure energy up into the heart of the aurora. He touched her hand and she knew he was as horrified as she was.

What was the purpose of such a device? Who was going to be using it? The obvious answer was the military forces of her own country. But did they have authorization, or was it hidden from Congress, the Senate, even the President himself? And more importantly, just what were they going to do with it? Alyssa still had no idea what the information was that she'd managed to get out of HIRP, or what use she could put it to. She felt her pocket, checking that the flash drive was still safe.

She knew she had to try and get in touch with James Rushton but she was concerned about how to do that. Anderson would surely be watching him now. And probably everyone else at the *Post* too, she thought uncomfortably.

She needed to relax if she was going to get any constructive thinking done. She stood up and moved towards the bathroom. 'I'm taking a bath,' she told Jack, who just nodded, still transfixed by the television screen.

Alyssa leant her head back on to the edge of the bath and luxuriated in the hot, foamy water.

She was thinking now about Jack Murray. It had been years since Patrick had died, and she knew it was silly, but she couldn't help feeling as if she had betrayed him in some way. Anna, too. What would Anna think? And she started to realize, perhaps for the first time since it happened, why she felt so much guilt in her personal relationships, why there hadn't been anyone else. It wasn't because of Patrick; it was because of Anna. Deep down, she hated herself for letting her little girl die. She despised herself, and the years hadn't lessened the feelings one bit. She blamed herself for Anna's death, it was her fault, no matter how much counselling said otherwise, and so she'd sabotaged any chance she'd had for her own happiness. This was why she had shut herself off from other people, why even when she went on dates, she was already pushing men away. It wasn't because she didn't like them; it was because she didn't like herself. She couldn't forgive herself, and wanted to punish herself.

But didn't she deserve some sort of happiness? Wasn't it time to let go? She thought again of Jack, and was again hit by feelings of guilt, this time for involving him. What had she done? Basically, she'd ruined his life. He'd really had nothing to do with any of it, and just because he'd been caught with her, he would now be marked for death. Patrick, Anna, and now Jack. It was too much.

But what could she do? The die had been cast. Even if they split up, Jack would still be a target. No, she decided, the best thing would be for them to work together until they cracked this thing. Jack was a computer genius, after all, and might even find some way of contacting Rushton covertly. It was worth discussing with him, anyway.

They hadn't talked much on the way here, not wanting people to hear what they had to say, but Alyssa could tell that Jack had accepted his lot; it was clear he understood he was a target and he had never even mentioned going alone. She knew it was selfish but she was glad; the truth was, she felt good being with him. Perhaps she liked Jack so much because he had made her forget to hate herself.

She sighed, and slipped her head under the water, the warmth cascading over her face, through her hair.

'Alyssa?' she heard him call from the main room. 'I think you should come and watch this.'

12

Oswald Umbebe was sitting in the newsroom, on a couch across from the anchor, a popular host called Jonny Watts. The title on the screen read, 'Are the Days of Planet Earth Numbered?'

Alyssa recognized the man being interviewed, it was the same charismatic preacher she'd seen that first day near the city square. He was even wearing the same eye-catching white robe and golden head- and armbands.

She turned to Jack, who seemed to be watching her for a reaction.

'I saw him once,' Alyssa told him. 'Back home, he was preaching after the bats came.'

Jack nodded. 'Yeah, they seem to be getting something of a following. I've been seeing news reports that membership is increasing by the thousands.' He stopped talking as the interview began on the small screen in front of them.

'So, Oswald,' Watts began. 'May I call you Oswald?'

Umbebe smiled graciously. 'You may call me whatever you wish,' he said, and Alyssa was again struck by his deep, melodic voice. 'As you know, I believe that we are all destined to die – very soon – and so names and titles have ceased to be important.'

'And yet you are still the "high priest" of your order,' Watts pointed out.

Umbebe raised his hands. 'What can I do? I have responsibilities that I cannot avoid. I want to live my life in a positive manner until the end.'

'But you are recruiting,' Watts persisted, 'are you not?'

'We are,' Umbebe confirmed, 'and I think I understand where you are going with this.' He smiled at the presenter. 'You are trying to suggest that our order is attempting to capitalize on recent events, yes? That we are in some way trying to profit from this calamity.'

Watts held Umbebe's gaze. 'Are you?' he asked.

'What do your reporters tell you? If they have done their research, you will know that we receive no financial contributions from our followers. What then would our purpose be?'

'To be honest, that's what I want to get to the bottom of. What *do* you want?'

Umbebe sat back on the couch, relaxed. His mode of dress, in stark contrast to that of Watts and utterly ridiculous in most circumstances, seemed to be the perfect choice for the man; he radiated confidence and charisma.

'I want everyone to accept the inevitable. I want everyone to accept the fact that they – *we* – are all going to die. All of us. It is a cycle, you see.' Alyssa was hypnotized by him, just as Watts seemed to be. 'The world's eternal cycle. The earth was created, and it is designed to go through cycles of destruction and regeneration, until it is finally sucked into the sun and obliterated in its entirety. But until this final ending – possibly billions of years away – it must still be periodically purged.

'We have seen this happen many times over the millennia. There is a great cataclysm, resulting in mass extinctions, the end of life as it is known at that time, and this is then followed by a period of renewal, of regeneration.

'Just consider everything we experience directly in life. We are born, we live – through various ups and downs – and then we die. Day turns into night, turns back into day. The sun rises, the sun sets. The tide comes in and it goes back out. Blood circulates around our bodies. If it stays still, it stagnates and dies. Every single cell in our bodies is destroyed and regenerated on a six-year cycle. Do you disagree with any of this?'

Watts just shook his head, entranced by Umbebe.

'Well, why is it so hard to accept that the earth itself follows just such a pattern? My order has charted each mass extinction event over the course of millennia, and we have predicted that the next will occur this year. We are certain of it. But I do not say these things to frighten, only to educate. Do we try and hold on to the cells in our bodies? No, we do not. We let the body get on with it, and regenerate itself. We, too, should not get in the way of the earth as it purges itself. It is necessary.

'And so you ask me *why*. Why do I recruit for the order if not for financial gain? I will tell you why. I recruit so that the people of earth can understand what is to happen, so that they can *welcome* it, rejoice in it, be a part of it. And I want to tell people, do not be afraid. We are to be sacrificed for a greater good. If we do not die, if life as we now know it is not purged, then the earth will suffer, and this will ultimately bring about its own early death. So, I implore everyone, accept your fate. There is no other choice.'

Alyssa watched as Watts, normally so quick off the mark, just stared at his guest, contemplating his words.

'This man seems so sure of himself,' she said in wonder. 'But why?'

'I don't know,' Jack said. 'Maybe he's crazy. Do you think there's anything in it?'

'What do you mean?'

'Well, you know,' Jack said, shrugging his shoulders, 'do you think he might be right? Do you think the world follows cycles, and needs purging?'

Alyssa frowned. Did Jack believe it? She hoped not. 'Listen, Jack, whether the earth needs purging or not, the premise of his beliefs is wrong. I mean, all these cults and sects, they're saying these things because they think the earth itself is rebelling. Well, we've now got strong evidence to show that this just isn't so. A lot of these recent strange events can be explained by the covert Spectrum Nine programme, whatever the hell it is, which was developed at HIRP. All of this "end of the world" nonsense will be killed off once we publish what HIRP is up to.'

Jack nodded his head, thinking it through. 'I guess you're right,' he said eventually. 'But you've got to admit, he makes a great case, doesn't he?'

Alyssa had to agree. 'He's very persuasive, I'll give him that. But at the end of the day, he's wrong. And we're going to prove it.'

'We?' he asked, and Alyssa was relieved when his serious expression broke into a smile.

Alyssa returned the smile, grateful hands finding his, holding them tightly. 'Thank you, Jack,' she said. 'And I'm so sorry for getting you into this.'

He shrugged. 'Hey, what's done is done. And now I've got to help you if I don't want to end up dead. But that means we've got some work to do. First we've got to find out what's on that flash drive you've got.'

Alyssa nodded, just as the windows exploded around them in a hail of concentrated gunfire.

13

ANDERSON WATCHED WITH grim satisfaction as the front of the motel room was obliterated by the small-arms fire of his men. His assault team had nothing larger than a single tripod-mounted machine gun, but the assault rifles the rest of his soldiers carried were all set to fully automatic and were capable of terrifying levels of destruction on their own.

If the frontal attack didn't kill them outright, if – by some small chance – they managed to survive and tried to escape through the rear windows, then a secondary team was there lying in wait for them.

After finding the empty glider, Anderson had almost lost hope; but he was not accustomed to failure, and would keep going until his mission was complete.

It hadn't been hard to figure out where they'd go from the crash site; the next town was less than a mile away. Anderson had already tagged Alyssa Durham's credit cards and he knew as soon as she used one. They'd missed her in town by bare minutes.

Interviews at the local transport hubs had revealed where they were headed soon after, and Anderson had immediately scrambled a helicopter from the base to follow the bus.

Conscious that the chopper could be overheard by his prey, Anderson ordered the pilot to fly high and use infrared and optical recording equipment to monitor the vehicle below. The footage was relayed directly back to Anderson, who followed from a distance, loaded up with his men in a convoy of jeeps and SUVs.

He watched a live feed as Durham and Murray got out of the bus and hitched a lift east, saw them eventually get out of the car at the motel, and Durham go into reception while Murray waited outside. He even saw which room they both went into.

He was on the scene not long after, and had spent the next hour setting up the operation. He spoke to the guy at the front desk, who then went door to door to the rest of the rooms, asking everyone to vacate the property, while Anderson's men positioned themselves for the assault.

The owner wasn't there, but Anderson called to explain the situation, and although he could tell the man wasn't happy, Anderson had given him no choice; besides which, the federal government would cover the cost of repairing the man's business.

The young guy working there had shut himself in reception ever since the shooting started, wanting to dissociate himself from the whole affair. Anderson couldn't blame him really; he knew it was going to be messy.

Alyssa pulled Jack to the floor as soon as the first rounds started flying, huddling close to him, trying to flatten herself on the ground as much as physically possible. It brought back instant, fear-inducing memories of full-scale attacks back in the Middle East. But she remembered the advice of the troops she had been shadowing, how she should try and push herself so low it seemed as if she was going *through* the floor.

As they waited there, heads down and breathless, her mind was racing. The fire all seemed concentrated to the front of the room. Which left—

'The rear?' Jack asked, panic all over his face. 'Maybe we could try and get out of the rear windows?'

Alyssa shook her head. 'No. That must be what they want us to do, they'll have soldiers out there waiting for us.'

'What then?'

Alyssa could see that Jack was on the verge of losing it, and she couldn't really blame him; she had felt much the same the first time she had experienced heavy gunfire. Although back then at least she'd had armed soldiers protecting her. Here, they were on their own. She didn't even have clothes, having left the bathroom in a towel and a robe.

Think, Alyssa, she ordered herself. *Think!*

'What's that?' Jack asked, pointing across the floor. Alyssa followed his gaze, and saw what he'd noticed. From this perspective, so low down, she could see that the room's rug was pulled back at the corner, and underneath it . . . Yes!

'Trapdoor,' she said.

She knew that in climates where the winters were very cold and the summers quite hot, buildings could sink into the ground when the frost thawed. Many structures were therefore supported on stilts to give some ground

184

clearance, and a space for the building to 'settle' in such conditions. She hadn't realized that the motel had this, as the raised portion was disguised from the front by a wrap-around veranda. She could only hope that Anderson and his men didn't know about it either, and that the motel owner hadn't told them.

'Stay here,' she whispered to Jack, crawling low across the floor to the foot of the bed. She took a deep breath, summoning her courage to raise a part of her body into the firing line, and quickly shot an arm up towards the bed, pulling down her jeans and blouse in one swift movement. The clothes weren't entirely necessary, but the flash drive was in her trouser pocket, and that really was essential.

Clothes in hand, she gestured towards the trapdoor. Jack nodded, and started moving towards it, wood and glass showering him as he went. Alyssa was right behind him, saw as he pulled the rug up and tugged at the trap-door. At first it resisted, but then it swung wide open. By the time she got there Jack was already through, and he helped guide her down after him.

She tried to position the rug over the door in such a way that it would fall naturally when it was closed, and slammed it shut over them.

Beneath the room, they had enough space to stand hunched over, and Alyssa quickly discarded her robe and put her clothes on. Once dressed she patted her pocket to confirm the flash drive was still there, and then motioned to Jack to move.

The ground was freezing cold under Alyssa's bare feet, and she could see that Jack was suffering too, although at least he had socks on. The crawl space was dark, only faint light from the roadside neon sign filtering through cracks in the wood.

They were out of the room, but they still had to get away, and they would have to do so with no jackets or boots, in a sub-Arctic winter, with a team of cold-blooded killers on their tail. The trapdoor wouldn't stay hidden forever. Sooner or later, when they hadn't appeared out of the rear window, Anderson would order a ceasefire and send his troops in to find their bodies. The hidden crawl space would be discovered soon after.

She thought back to the layout of the motel. The reception was on the far west end of the complex, round the horsehoe, past all the other rooms. She wondered if the cold, dark crawl space would take them all the way there.

'Come on, Jack,' she whispered urgently, moving past him and pulling him along, 'we need to move quickly. I think I've got a plan.'

'Cease fire!' Anderson ordered after five minutes of fully concentrated fire. The team at the rear hadn't reported any activity, which meant that Durham and Murray must still be inside. And if they were still inside, they were dead. 'Section one, move in.'

The motel room was almost entirely destroyed, and the interior lights could be seen clearly through ragged holes in the thick wooden walls. All the windows were completely gone, and Anderson wouldn't have been surprised if the structure was so weakened that it would collapse altogether in the not too distant future.

He watched from the shadows as his first eight-man section approached the front door cautiously. They expected the fugitives inside to be dead but their training made them inherently careful when it came to approaching the unknown.

They reached the door and Anderson watched as one soldier kicked it open and a pair of men swept into the room from one side, followed by another pair from the other.

There was silence for several long, uncomfortable moments as the section searched the room. *Come on*, Anderson said to himself. *Come on!*

His earpiece buzzed, and his hand went straight up to cut out the extraneous noise. 'Sir,' the report came through, and the nervousness in the man's voice told Anderson everything before he said another word. 'They're not here.'

The trapdoor to reception was situated in the back office, which was empty. Alyssa and Jack levered themselves out of the crawl space, shivering with cold.

Jack pointed to some coats hanging on the wall, and they slipped them on. There was one pair of boots, far too big for Alyssa but which fitted Jack just fine.

Alyssa pushed the office door slightly ajar and saw the reception desk right in front of her. The man she'd spoken to earlier in the evening was vainly trying to use the computer and make calls, frantically checking the connections. Obviously the lines had been cut.

Jack waited behind her as she crept forward, her bare feet silent on the wooden floor. She noticed that there was a revolver strapped to the inside of the desk – there in case of an attempted robbery – but the man was completely wrapped up in figuring out what was wrong with his electronics.

Within seconds she was right behind him, her first two fingers pushing gently into his back like the barrel of a gun, hand round his mouth. 'Make a sound and I'll shoot,' she whispered in his ear, and she watched as his hands comically went straight up into the classic position of surrender.

Jack raced past her, grabbed the real gun from the desk and aimed it at the young man's head. Alyssa moved past him, blowing imaginary smoke from her fingertips.

The man rolled his eyes to the ceiling, his arms coming down with sagging shoulders. 'OK,' he said quietly. 'What do you want?'

Anderson watched as the car approached from the rear lot, and he flagged it down, seeing the receptionist at the wheel.

The man rolled down the window. 'The boss is coming in,' he said to Anderson. 'He says he doesn't want me round here any more, wants me to go home. And . . . I'd really like to go, please.'

Anderson could see the man was scared. He was just a civilian, not used to anything like this. He didn't blame him in the least.

'OK,' Anderson said. 'But if you say anything about this, I know where you live, and we will come and see you. Do you understand?'

The man nodded his head frantically, and Anderson smiled. 'Good. So we understand each other.'

He watched the man nod his head again, and wondered

if he was about to soil himself. It wouldn't be the first time he'd seen someone do it, just from a threat.

'Thanks,' the man said weakly, and drove away from the shattered motel on to the deserted road beyond.

'Good job,' Alyssa said from the passenger footwell of the vehicle, where she'd lain hidden, the revolver pressed up into the receptionist's crotch.

She removed the gun, hearing a genuine sigh of relief as she did so, and slid up into the passenger seat just as Jack emerged from the rear footwell on to the back seat.

Alyssa felt sorry for the guy but it had been their only way out. He was never in any real danger though; she would never have used the weapon on an innocent man.

As she watched the empty road open out before her, she wondered how long it would be before Anderson realized that the boss wasn't coming into work and that the receptionist had just escaped with two high-value fugitives in his car.

She hoped it would be long enough.

'What do you mean the chopper can't fly?' Anderson demanded.

'Weather's taking a turn for the worse,' the pilot replied. 'Going to be coming down hard. I need to get back to base before I'm stranded here.'

Anderson put down the radio, his anger threatening to erupt. But he kept it inside, holding it tight, controlling himself. He needed eyes in the sky but it looked like this just wasn't going to be an option.

He'd finally put it all together, and was furious with himself for allowing them to pass out of the area right in front of him. Durham and Murray had at least twenty minutes' head start on them, which would be hard to get back, especially if the weather was going to get worse like the pilot thought.

There was another option, though, Anderson thought as he reached reluctantly for the radio and asked to be put through to the local highway patrol.

'That's a roadblock up ahead,' the motel receptionist said fearfully, already letting up on the accelerator.

'Ram it,' Alyssa instructed, having already seen it. It was just two cars, and driving right through it was undoubtedly their best option.

'I'll put my belt on,' Jack said, sitting back quickly into his seat.

But the fear was too much for the car's already nervous driver, and in a fit of panic he wrenched the wheel sideways, pulling the car across both lanes of the highway.

In the back, Jack had still not managed to put his belt on and sailed into the door, which sagged open. The car hit the kerb hard and the man pulled the wheel again, and then the door flew open completely. Jack spiralled out across the roadside, finally rolling to a stop in the snow.

One of the police cars was already heading towards them with four armed officers inside it. Alyssa whipped the revolver across the receptionist's head, knocking him out cold. With his feet still on the pedals, she turned the steering wheel across the other way, pulling the damaged vehicle back on to the highway.

She looked out of the window, saw that Jack had regained his feet and was heading away into the treeline, trying to lead the police away from her. He turned to her, the police car now between them. 'Get going!' he called. 'I'll see you back home, at the café in the picture in my office!'

And then he was gone, legs pumping through the snow, away into the trees, the cops moving in towards him from the other side.

With Jack gone, Alyssa dragged the unconscious man from the driving seat and took his place, gunning the engine and accelerating hard towards the roadblock's remaining police car.

Seconds later she was through, leaving the other vehicle spinning in her wake, her own car severely damaged but still going, and as the cops opened fire behind her, she pressed the pedal even further, accelerating away from the scene.

She could only pray that she would see Jack again.

Oswald Umbebe's pain was back, sharper than ever. And yet it seemed a blessing in its way, keeping his mind sharp, his appreciation for life vital. He pushed his medicine to one side, untouched.

He was a busy man, dealing with every aspect of his operations. He had followers in every nation, and their preaching – on the streets, in the few churches they owned, even on television and the internet – had to be guided, moulded, in the way he wanted. They were priests of the order but they still required guidance, especially now as the flock grew and grew with every passing day. Since the statue had moved, millions of believers had been recruited into the Order of Planetary Renewal. Umbebe knew it would do them no good physically – everyone was still destined to die – but at least they would understand why, and this would give them comfort in their last moments. They would see themselves as self-sacrificial martyrs, not helpless victims, and this would make all the difference to them. Instead of fear, they would feel joy.

And there were still many other aspects of his work he needed to keep on top of – intelligence briefings, reports from his agents around the world, which required him to modify and adapt his various plans.

He coughed up a little blood as the phone rang, and wiped it away with a handkerchief as he answered.

He remained silent as he listened to the report from the other end of the line. He had seen the news stories, of course, but this was further confirmation, what he had been waiting for: the weapon was ready, and the next phase of his plan could finally be put into operation.

But then came the bad news, and Umbebe listened as the caller explained what else had happened. He was silent for several long, painful moments as he digested what he heard. It was damaging, yes, that much was true. But the situation was perhaps still salvageable. His keen mind worked things out in instants, and he described the new plan to the caller. As always, improvisation was everything.

He replaced the receiver and smiled.

It was the smile of a man who knew that victory was just around the corner.

14

BY THE TIME Alyssa got back to the city, she was exhausted both mentally and physically.

She'd had to abandon the car eventually, and had then hitch-hiked her way southwards, a laborious and painful journey made worse by her justifiable paranoia that Anderson and his men could be waiting for her at any stage.

She was also unable to use her ID or credit cards, and after buying a cheap pair of shoes had to rely on the meagre cash she had left to feed herself snacks on the way. Until the last driver, at least. The woman had been so understanding towards Alyssa's invented story of fleeing from an abusive husband that she'd gone straight to a teller machine and withdrawn a large sum of cash, pushing it into Alyssa's hands, demanding that she take it.

But now she was back, where was she going to go? Anderson would have people at her apartment and at the office. She daren't risk contacting James Rushton, as they would no doubt expect her to do this and have his phone lines bugged.

Everywhere she went in the city she saw soldiers in full body armour, assault rifles at the ready. She'd never seen anything like it, and asked a man working at a news stall what was going on.

The old man looked surprised, peering up at her from his mug of hot coffee. 'You've not heard?' he asked. 'Oh, well, it's really only kicked in during the past couple of hours.'

'What's kicked in?' Alyssa persisted.

'Full martial law is in operation,' he told her, 'at least in this state. A few others too, although it's not national yet. But the city's pretty much under siege from rioters, protesters, you name it. The National Guard were called in, then the regular army. It's happening all over the country.'

Alyssa had seen signs of increased military activity during her long drive south, but nothing like this. She thanked the man and left.

She wondered whether there was the manpower to launch martial law everywhere. Surely there was a limit. And what if the soldiers started to ask questions? What if some of the commanders began to believe in this end-of-the-world talk? She shuddered to think of it. As it was, her home had been turned into something of an urban dystopian police state. It terrified her even more when she thought that many of these same people might be actively searching for *her*.

And yet she had to be here; Jack had told her to meet her 'back home', at the picture in his office – the train crashing through the wall of one of the city's most famous landmarks. The nearest café to that was the Grand Café, a beautiful coffee house situated in the main foyer.

If there was any chance that Jack had escaped capture,

she had to try and meet him. She'd got him into this, and she wanted to help him get out of it if she could.

Avoiding the concentrated CCTV surveillance of the subway system, she walked across the frighteningly un-familiar, militarized city to her destination, hoping against all hope that Jack would be there to meet her.

Four hours and eight coffees later, Alyssa realized that Jack wouldn't be coming today.

What did that mean? Did it mean that he wouldn't be coming at all? Had he been captured? Was he dead? Or was it just taking him longer to get down here?

Pushing away her last coffee cup, she rose to leave, vowing to come back first thing in the morning.

But the hours until then wouldn't be wasted, she thought. It was time to find out just what the hell was on the flash drive in her pocket.

'So when is the big day?' asked John Jeffries over the secure satellite link. The Secretary of Defence had been receiving regular updates, but due to the political nature of his job he was always one stage removed from the day-to-day practicalities of the project.

'I'll let Niall answer that, John,' said General Tomkin, who sat behind his desk staring at the live images of the men he was talking to on the dual-screen videophone in front of him.

Dr Niall Breisner cleared his throat. 'After the successful stage three testing of the device, there just remains some basic system debugging to complete, as well as the final analysis of the test data. But we're talking a matter of days.'

'I want the project signed off by the fourth,' Jeffries said immediately.

'That's just six days away,' Breisner said with concern. 'Why the sudden push?'

'We need to deal with matters on a political and tactical level, as well as just technological,' Jeffries answered. 'And with our own citizens rioting across the country, it's been decided that we need to strike soon, get this thing wrapped up immediately. My colleagues feel that if we do not use the device as planned within the next two weeks, we may have a civil war on our hands.'

'And that,' Tomkin added, 'is unacceptable. We've started this, and we need to end it. At the moment, we have the political will to go ahead with the plan. How long that will last, we don't know. John is a strong-minded sonofabitch but we all know people on the team who might not have the belly for what we need to do, especially if it takes much longer. We need to strike while the iron is hot.'

'The fourth,' Jeffries stated again. 'Six days' time. Can you do it?'

There was silence as Breisner seemed to weigh things up. 'Yes,' he answered finally. 'The device will be ready by the fourth. The plan can proceed as proposed.'

'Excellent,' Jeffries said. 'Thank you, Niall. Our country will soon be a safer place.'

15

ALYSSA WALKED THROUGH the main concourse of the central train station the next morning, her head a swirl of conflicting emotions.

She hoped she would see Jack today of course, but she was also horrified by what she would have to tell him if he was there. The information on the flash drive was just beyond belief.

The night before she had secreted herself in an internet café and opened up the disk, poring over the downloaded documents for hour after hour as she pieced together the mystery behind Spectrum Nine and what it might be capable of. What she found was simply terrifying.

She was now disguised yet again but she was more than ever aware of the personal danger she faced. This was actually quite a good location to meet Jack. The central station was as public as any venue in the city, and it was unlikely they would be executed in such a place. It was also secure, guarded by members of the city's municipal police, National Guard, and the regular army. Alyssa knew that Colonel Anderson was part of that same army, and the station could therefore very well be the lion's den, but she had decided to work on the premise that the project was not fully authorized, and Anderson's forces were limited in number. If the project was fully approved and everyone was in on it, she would be arrested or killed soon enough anyway.

She saw a large group of people on one side of the foyer, listening to white-robed preachers of the Order of Planetary Renewal. There were several of them, and they were preaching their message to as many as two hundred people. The armed patrols watched them with curious eyes. Would some of the soldiers pay attention to the message? Alyssa hoped not; the result could well be chaos and anarchy.

She sat down at a free table in the Grand Café and ordered herself an espresso. She'd not slept well; she'd used some of the cash from the friendly woman driver to rent a room in a cheap hotel, but her mind would not relax.

She checked her watch. It was 8.28 a.m. She sipped her drink, wondering if today would be the day. How much longer would she give him?

She had information, but what was she going to do with it? If she approached Rushton or anyone associated with the media, she would be found and killed. Her email accounts had been deactivated, as well as her blog and website.

Could she go to the police? Maybe the feds? But HIRP was an authorized government project. Maybe Spectrum Nine was too. Which meant she would also have to stay clear of federal law enforcement.

She hoped Jack would show up; he might be able to circumvent computer security protocols, get her accounts reactivated, allow her to post some of this information in plain sight, see if anything came of it. But it wasn't a course of action guaranteed to get results. She knew what they really needed was to find out who was behind the project, something that the documents she'd downloaded did not reveal.

Again, she knew that Jack would be able to help her access the information.

But these weren't the only reasons she wanted Jack to be there, she finally admitted to herself. She wanted him close to her, simply because of the way she felt about him.

'Where the hell are they?' Anderson exploded at Bill Jenkins, his chief intelligence analyst.

'I'm afraid we just don't know at this stage,' Jenkins said apologetically. 'After they got away from the road-block, they might have done anything – hitch-hiked, caught a bus, a train; hell, they might still be hiding out in the woods, for all we know.'

'You've got a description out?'

Jenkins nodded. 'Yes, to those people we can trust. As discussed, we're not going to widen the loop until we know what they've managed to find out, until we know just how compromised we are.'

'How's it going with that side of things?' Anderson asked, calmer now; he knew that Jenkins was doing all he could.

'We're just reconstructing the computer records now,' he answered. 'We'll know soon enough what they managed to get.'

'Good,' Anderson said. 'As soon as you find out, let me know.'

'I will.'

'Best guess as to their location?'

'You know how these things go. People on the run typically go back to their home base. Not every time, but nine out of ten. No reason to suspect they'll be any different.'

Anderson nodded, having come to the same conclusion. He turned his back on Jenkins, picked up his phone, and started to make some calls.

It was just before nine o'clock when Alyssa saw the familiar figure emerge from the subway stairs into the grand marble foyer, striding purposefully towards her.

'Jack!' Alyssa exclaimed as he got to the café, unable to help herself. They hugged, and Jack kissed her on the cheek. Alyssa could see that he was exhausted, with a look in his eye that reminded her of a cornered animal – fearful, but in its own way still dangerous.

'How did you get away?' Alyssa asked. 'I thought I might never see you again.'

Jack shrugged his shoulders, taking a seat opposite her. 'After I got into the treeline, I lost the cops pretty easily. Spent the night in the woods, almost froze to death.' He grinned. 'Then I headed back to that first town, thought it would be just about the last place they'd look, and caught a bus again, same as the first time. Had to pawn my watch to buy a ticket, but what the hell. Changed buses a few times, and here I am. How about you?'

'Hitch-hiked,' she said, smiling at him.

Jack ordered a coffee, and then Alyssa leant forward and gripped his hands across the table, looking into his eyes with an intensity that he could literally feel. 'It's real,' she said.

'It's real?' he asked. 'The weapon?'

Alyssa nodded her head. 'It's codenamed Spectrum Nine,' she whispered. 'They've discovered something they refer to as the "ninth spectrum", a group of soundwaves that can be used to produce controllable fluctuations in the weather. They've programmed the radar array to reproduce this soundwave pattern, and when they transmit it up into the sky, they can transfer it across the ionosphere to any point on the globe they want. Nobody else even knows about the existence of this ninth spectrum, which is why nobody can see any link between the strange events that have been occurring. Nobody can detect it,' she breathed. 'It's perfect.'

'That explains how the statue moved,' Jack said. 'One of the only possible explanations was soundwaves, but of a type unknown to current science. This ninth spectrum must be powerful enough to cause the atomic structure of solid state objects to alter.'

'But who's behind it?' she asked. 'That's the question we really need to answer. Obviously Niall Breisner is in on it, as he's the one that's been signing off on all the testing. And Anderson almost certainly knows about it. But who's really behind it?' Alyssa held up her hands. 'I've got no idea. But if we're going to stop it, we need to find out.'

'Stop it?' Jack asked, surprised. 'I thought you were writing a story on it. Once it gets out, they'll have to pull the plug. You're talking as if we have to stop it ourselves.'

She looked at him, her eyes serious. 'We do,' she said gravely. 'They're going to use it again. We have five days.'

*   *   *

Anderson was with Dr Breisner on the radar field when the call came through from Jenkins back at the command centre.

He tried to control his expression, trained never to reveal anything to anyone who might be observing him, but a muscle beneath his eye started to twitch involuntarily. He tensed his face to get rid of it, but this only made it worse. Damn them. Damn them to hell!

Jenkins' news was the worst it could have been. He had managed to decipher Murray's computer files, find out what he and Alyssa Durham had been looking at. And, as Anderson had feared, they had hacked into the secure HIRP database and accessed the classified information about Spectrum Nine. So now they knew everything. Well, everything technical anyway; there was next to no information on the base's files about how the device was going to be used operationally or tactically.

He would have to inform Tomkin, who may or may not then decide to inform Jeffries. Doubtless Tomkin would throw more men at the task of finding Durham and Murray, before the pair revealed anything.

Anderson just hoped – for his personal satisfaction if nothing else – that his own men would find them first.

16

'I NEED TO get a look at the data on that disk,' Jack said over a plateful of food, his suppressed appetite suddenly returning with a vengeance. 'Maybe I'll see something that you missed.'

'That's a good idea,' Alyssa agreed. 'We can't use any of my resources at the paper but we can hire a computer at an internet café. We don't need to connect to the web, so they won't be able to trace us.'

Jack nodded, bowing his head back to his food, and Alyssa watched him as he ate; then he raised his head once more to speak, but something behind her left shoulder caught his attention.

Alyssa tensed as she saw his eyes widen in shock.

Major Rafael Santana was an ex-Special Forces operative, semi-retired and now a unit commander with the local battalion of the National Guard.

He had served under Easton Anderson back when the man was a major, both in central Asia and the Middle East, and they had remained close ever since. Santana had received the call from his old commander just an hour earlier, along with a picture of a man called Jackson Edgar

Murray and a woman named Alyssa Durham. These characters were supposed to be agitators, people who wanted to cause some sort of disturbance; home-grown terrorists, apparently.

Anderson had contacted many of his old colleagues, asking them to keep their eyes out for this man and woman, and to 'terminate' the subjects on sight if possible. Santana was told that General Tomkin was willing to issue a nationwide arrest order for the man if necessary, but due to 'sensitive' issues, everyone would prefer the problem to be wrapped up with a minimum of fuss. Santana hadn't asked questions; he knew the score. It wouldn't be hard to kill the pair if it came to it. He could always say that he thought the subjects were armed, and were reaching for a weapon. It happened all the time, and in a nervous, keyed-up environment like the city was at the minute, nobody would bat an eyelid.

And so it was that he had spent the morning scouring the train station for Durham and Murray. He had provided the pictures to his section of soldiers, and they were also out there looking for them. They didn't know that Santana was going to kill them, but they would alert their chief as soon as they found the pair, and Santana would do the rest.

And there, across the foyer, as arrogant as you could get, the little terrorist scumbag was sitting having coffee with a woman. Who was she? She looked different from the picture, but it had to be Durham.

'Targets located,' he said into his two-way radio. 'Grand Café, central concourse. I'm approaching now.'

He edged forward, past the crowd of worshippers who

were taking up one side of the hall, tuning out the white-robed preachers' messages of death and destruction. He would soon be doing enough of that himself.

As he moved forward he took the safety off his automatic assault rifle, but then he stopped dead in his tracks. Murray had looked up from the table, looked over the shoulder of the Durham woman.

He had been spotted.

Jack saw the soldier headed towards them, watching in disbelief as the man started to raise his rifle to his shoulder, aiming it towards them.

'Get down!' he screamed, grabbing Alyssa and pushing her to the floor as the air above them erupted in gunfire.

Jack quickly upended the table, using it as a temporary shield between them and the soldier. Alyssa peered round the edge of the table, pulling her head back quickly as another barrage of high-velocity rounds impacted the steel that protected them.

Jack and Alyssa exchanged looks of terror, but then Alyssa heard a *click*. 'He's empty,' she shouted at Jack, over the screams of the other patrons of the café, who were running away in all directions, or else cowering behind tables and chairs.

Alyssa grabbed Jack by the arm and pulled him further into the café, through the double glass doors that led to the interior. They heard the glass shattering behind them – the solider must have reloaded – as they raced past the counter towards the rear.

She didn't know exactly where she was going, but there

had to be some sort of rear service access for the café. Jack was looking for the same thing. 'Here!' he shouted, pushing through a swing door into the kitchen.

As Alyssa and Jack raced into the busy, hot kitchen, they had to jump over the people who were cowering on the floor, keeping their heads down at the sound of gunshots. They crashed through another door at the end of the kitchen, and found themselves in a long concrete corridor that accessed all of the retail and restaurant units along this side of the terminal.

'Come on,' Jack said. 'Let's get out of here.'

Santana cursed out loud. He'd missed them. Luckily he'd not shot any civilians, but the café was a mess.

He got on his radio instantly. 'All team members to converge on the main concourse,' he ordered. 'Louis,' he said to his communications specialist, 'get on to the security chief here, inform him we're in pursuit of suspected armed terrorists.'

He broke off to shout at the staff and customers of the café to stay down. He looked around, searching for the pair, and saw one of the waitresses pointing towards the kitchen. He peered through the access hatch, saw the door swinging at the other end.

'Where does it go?' he barked at the waitress.

'S-service corridor,' the waitress stammered.

Santana cursed again, getting back on his radio. 'Team members to enter eastern service corridor,' he shouted as he ran through the kitchen, kicking the door open at the other end.

He turned into the passage and saw the man and woman racing away, footsteps echoing off the concrete. Immediately he opened fire again, spraying the corridor with bullets.

Alyssa heard the door opening behind them and instinctively grabbed Jack and dived for the floor. Keeping low, they started to crawl. She heard boots pounding behind them. Then another sound echoed from in front, and she looked up to see three more men enter the corridor ahead of them, rifles up and aimed.

She tried to resist as Jack pulled her up off the floor, flinching as the soldier behind and the three in front opened fire, concrete erupting around her as the high-powered rounds chewed up the passageway.

Santana watched as Murray managed to pull the woman up, narrowly avoiding the gunfire as they slammed through another access door. *Dammit!* Where the hell did that door lead?

'Louis,' he spoke over his radio, 'do we have CCTV feeds through here?'

'Negative,' Louis reported. 'No surveillance in the service areas.'

'Schematics?' he asked as he ran down the corridor, meeting his colleagues at the access door. 'Blueprints?' He signalled his men to get after the targets.

'I'll see what I can do,' came the reply.

His men kicked through the door into the room beyond, guns at the ready. There was a yell as the first man to enter the dark chamber tumbled down a flight of stairs.

The second man flicked on a torch and shone it down the narrow staircase.

When the soldier came to rest at the bottom, Santana had no sympathy. 'Joe,' he called down after him. 'Can you see anything down there?'

Joe got unsteadily to his feet, turned on his torch and scanned the area. 'Nothing,' he called back up. 'There's nothing down here.'

Damn. Santana took out his cell phone and called Colonel Anderson.

Idiot. What was Santana doing? Anderson cursed to himself. He wasn't even airborne yet, still on his way to commandeer the fast jet stationed at the airport which would get him to the city in a little over three hours, and he had to rely on men like this? Santana had been a proven combat vet, once upon a time. Obviously, his time in the reserves had made him soft. The man had lost his edge. Tomkin had wanted to keep things low-key if they could – the less people involved the better, it was felt, which was why Anderson had contacted some of his own people in the city to deal with Durham and Murray. But now he got on to the terminal's chief of security, a civilian but nominally in charge of all of the units currently on patrol in his building – over a hundred armed men and women. It was time to activate them.

In the dark, Jack and Alyssa had also fallen head over heels down the concrete staircase.

Alyssa had fallen right on top of Jack and bounced off

the other side, bursting through another door they may never otherwise have seen. Jack groaned in pain but managed to pull himself to his feet and haul himself through the narrow opening. Once through, he wedged the door shut tight.

This corridor was narrow, and Alyssa could feel both walls with her hands. There was still no light, and she felt her way by touch, ignoring the sounds coming from the room behind them. Ahead she could see a very faint, hazy light. Was it another door? She edged forward cautiously, but no more light came through; it just remained a vague fuzz. Then she bumped into something hard. Her hands went up, feeling ahead of her. Metal. It was another door.

Her fingers quickly scoured the surface for a handle, her hands sweaty now as she heard the door behind her being forced. They'd be trapped like rats if they didn't get out quickly.

And then she found it, a metal lever. She yanked it up and spilled out through the door, instantly blinded by lights and deafened by the sound of a blasting horn.

Jack grabbed her as the subway train shot past, just inches from her face. Her whole body shook, rippling in Jack's hands as the high-speed vehicle blasted through the tunnel.

And then it was gone, leaving her reeling. Jack pulled her round, slapping her face lightly. 'Come on,' he said. 'We need to go. Now!'

Alyssa nodded her head, forcing herself to regain control. Jack pulled the metal door shut behind them and they raced over the tracks, careful not to touch the electrified rails, heading for the door on the other side of the illuminated tunnel. As they reached it, they saw the lights of another train barrelling towards them, the scream of its engines filling the enclosed space.

Alyssa tugged at the door lever but it wouldn't move. She felt Jack's body pressing against her, squashing her against the door, and then the train was going past them. Jack's body was buffeted by the train's slipstream, threatening to rip him from the door frame, but he hung on for dear life, protecting her, until the train was gone.

She tugged the lever one more time with every ounce of strength she had left, and at last it opened, on to another narrow access corridor.

They pushed through, running for their lives.

'We've lost them.'

Santana's words came through to Anderson over the satellite phone, and he clenched his fists in rage. 'You've lost them?' He struggled to control himself. 'Could you please explain to me how one hundred armed, trained professionals can lose two untrained civilians?'

'They got into the subway system,' Santana explained. 'There's no surveillance down there, no way to track them.'

Anderson was disgusted. But he also felt something else – *fear*. The consequences of the pair escaping were too much to handle. If they got word out about Spectrum Nine, he, Jeffries, Tomkin, Breisner – they'd all be sent to jail. And Anderson was *not* going to allow himself to be put in jail.

'Do I have to do your job for you?' he asked through

gritted teeth. 'If you can't find them in the tunnels, you monitor the CCTV coverage at the stations and you post your people on the exits for when the pair finally emerge, which they will have to do at some stage. Can you do that?'

Santana replied in the affirmative, and Anderson grunted as he cut the connection. *Amateurs*. He was counting down the minutes until he could land in the city and take over the manhunt himself.

17

JACK AND ALYSSA emerged back on to the city streets less than an hour after they'd entered the tunnel system.

For almost thirty minutes they had wandered the concrete service corridors – some lit, others pitch black; some wide, others barely big enough to push through side on. There was no way to navigate and soon they had become hopelessly lost. So when they had stumbled out of a door on to another track, they decided to trace their way down it until it met a platform. Luckily the timing had been good, and they hadn't had to dive out of the way of any oncoming trains.

As they neared the platform, they heard human voices, dozens of them, raised in anger. A small-scale riot seemed to have broken out. As they emerged from the tunnel they saw people armed with knives and bottles trying to attack a cordon of riot police, who pushed back against them with their shields and batons.

Jack and Alyssa both saw the cameras mounted on the platform walls and instinctively lowered their heads. A train came along then and stopped at the platform. Those who were going to get off here thought better of it and backed away inside as scared commuters pushed and shoved their way on to the train, Jack and Alyssa among them. The doors closed and the train pulled away, leaving the violence and chaos behind.

Feeling safe at last within the crush of other passengers, Alyssa took Jack's hand and squeezed it.

The next station was much quieter, and there were no armed guards on the platform; perhaps all personnel near the scene of the riot had been called on to help quell it.

Jack and Alyssa stepped off the train and made straight for the ticket barriers. They were stopped by a ticket officer, but Alyssa told him they'd come from the riot on the next platform and had lost their tickets in the confusion. The officer, obviously used to such stories over the past few days, simply sighed and buzzed them through. There were more important things to worry about, it seemed.

'Where are we?' asked Jack as they emerged into the bright light of day. Alyssa just turned and pointed across the main road. There, opposite them, was the central park, famous around the world. 'Well, how'd I miss that?' he asked brightly, trying to dispel the fear and desperation that had been filling him.

'So what now?' Alyssa asked, looking around for cops or soldiers.

'Right now, we stop a taxi and get the hell out of the city,' Jack said.

Alyssa nodded. A taxi wouldn't be monitored in the same way as buses or trains – you didn't need to buy tickets, for one thing – and the only person who would see you was the taxi driver.

'A taxi's fine for now,' Alyssa said, raising her arm to flag one down, 'but we might need to ditch it before we leave the city. There are roadblocks and security checks everywhere, and taxis are bound to get stopped.' She lowered her arm as a yellow cab stopped in front of them. 'We'll take it as far as the city limits, then we may have to get past the security checks on foot.'

Jack nodded as he opened the door for her. Alyssa got in the back, and Jack slid in next to her.

The driver turned round in his seat. 'Where to?' he asked in a strong local accent. 'Just so long as wherever it is, you ain't gotta be there anytime soon, know what I mean?'

Alyssa and Jack smiled. 'No problem,' Alyssa said. 'We can see how crazy things are. Just to the bridge will be fine, thanks.' She would have liked to go further, but she realized that all choke points such as bridges would be monitored. *Damn*. How were they going to get out of the city?

The driver turned back to face the road ahead. 'Damn shame what's happening to this city if you ask me,' he said as he indicated to turn into the heavy traffic. 'But it's not the first time. I remember when—'

But Jack and Alyssa would never hear what the man was going to say, as the back of his head exploded towards them, his brain spraying through the chicken wire grill and covering their faces with greasy, bright-red blood.

It was a shame he'd had to kill the cab driver, Santana thought as he raced with four of his men towards the car; but he couldn't afford for the man to pull out and his prey to escape. Not after it had taken him so long to find them.

But now, trapped in an immobile vehicle, it would be like shooting fish in a barrel; he'd simply run over and empty his magazine into the two fugitives through the window.

The pair had been picked up by CCTV footage as they emerged from the tunnel on to the station platform – Anderson had arranged for facial recognition software to be connected to the city's system in order to quickly identify them. They had tried to hide their faces after they'd spotted the cameras, but by then it was too late.

They were tracked getting on to the train, and then cameras were monitored at the next platform along the route, where they were seen exiting. The station personnel had been sent over to help control the riot, but Santana was there with some of his men on foot in a matter of minutes.

He ignored the screams from fearful bystanders, who threw themselves for cover behind parked cars, and just kept his attention on the taxi, its windscreen now shattered and smeared with blood. His men were close behind him, their own weapons raised.

But then he heard the sound of the vehicle's engine gunning, and the taxi was moving, not waiting for a gap in the traffic but smashing its way out, knocking another car sideways as it accelerated towards him.

Santana couldn't help the cry of panic that escaped his lips as he dived to the side, the taxi's fender missing him by an inch.

Jack cried out he was thrown back into his seat, Alyssa wrenching up on the handbrake as she violently twisted the wheel all the way round.

The taxi slid across the road, oncoming vehicles having to jam on their brakes, as the cab made a one hundred and eighty degree turn. Now pointing in the opposite direction, Alyssa gunned the engine again and accelerated off down the busy city street, towards the oncoming traffic. She kept her hand on the horn, gratified that the cars, vans and bikes were all moving out of her way. She wasn't going fast, but it was fast enough to get them away from the armed soldiers behind them.

'Where are you going?' Jack asked. He pulled the dead cab driver back through the broken grille to the rear seats and climbed over into the front passenger seat.

It was a good question. Where the hell *was* she going? She could already hear sirens behind her. How far could they hope to get in a stolen taxi without a windshield and with a corpse in the back, in a city that was on full military lockdown?

'I've no idea,' she said through gritted teeth as she forced the cab onwards, weaving in and out of the oncoming traffic, one hand glued to the horn. 'But anywhere's better than here.'

There was a break in the traffic, a slight easing in the number of vehicles coming towards them, and for a time Alyssa managed to surge forwards, travelling parallel to the park. But then the reason for the break became all too clear, and Jack and Alyssa watched in horror as a sixty-ton main battle tank turned a corner on to the wide boulevard in front of them.

'Are you sure about that?' Jack asked quietly.

18

THE TANKS HAD recently been brought into the city because of the growing unrest, more as a visual deterrent than anything else. It was never anticipated that they would be used but the sight of a sixty-ton hunk of armoured metal with a gun on top that looked as if could take out a small army on its own did wonders for crowd control.

Santana and his men were running down the street after the out-of-control taxi when the regular army M-251 main battle tank trundled on to the parkway ahead of them, its huge 120mm smoothbore cannon aimed down the street at the yellow cab.

Well, Santana had to admit, Colonel Anderson had certainly come through in spectacular style. Anderson was monitoring the situation and acting as the main point of liaison between the different security forces. Santana understood that General Tomkin had given the colonel temporary field command, and he was now authorized to do anything in his power to bring the two terrorists to justice.

Santana had seen what these tanks could do when he'd served in the Gulf. An armour-piercing flechette round had been fired at an enemy personnel carrier, and when Santana had arrived on the scene to arrest any survivors, he had been sickened by what he'd seen. The round had pierced the hull and created a vacuum inside the personnel compartment which instantly vaporized everything organic within it, air pressure sucking it back out of the vehicle. The image of the charred, burnt and bloody remains of the enemy soldiers that were scattered around the carrier had been forever imprinted on his memory. But – despite the devastation he knew such a weapon could create – he now *wanted* such a result. His eyes opened wide in anticipation.

Alyssa, too, had seen the devastation caused by such weapons during her own time in the Gulf; and she had also seen how the front end of the tanks gave a telltale lift a fraction of a second before they fired.

She kept on driving straight for the tank, even as its barrel swivelled towards them, locking on to its target. Closer, ever closer she drove, waiting for the front end to lift. If she missed it, she'd never know – they would both be dead instantly.

The cab was just four hundred feet away now, then three hundred, then—

The front end lifted and she yanked the wheel hard left. The gun fired, the ground shook with the sonic boom, and the cab mounted the kerb and smashed through a thick row of bushes into the park beyond.

Santana watched in disbelief and horror as the taxi swerved left and disappeared into the park, and the tank's 120mm high-velocity projectile streaked up the road towards him.

With a yell, he and his men dived for cover, heads down. Santana heard the explosion – could feel the heat from the blast – and when he looked up, all he could see were the smoking, devastated remains of a haulage truck.

He keyed his cellphone to speak to Anderson, unsure what to say, but the colonel spoke first.

'Don't bother,' he said. 'I already know. I want you and your men to locate transportation and be mobile in case the cab leaves the park. I've notified other units as well.'

'Yes, sir. And the tank?' Santana asked.

'The crew has its orders,' Anderson replied.

'It's following us!' Jack yelled at Alyssa, twisting in his seat to look through the rear windscreen.

'I know, I can hear it!' Alyssa yelled back, swerving to avoid a family, then swerving again to avoid a teenager riding a bike.

The sound of the tank trampling bushes, trees and benches was tremendous. Day-trippers, alarmed by the sight of the yellow cab careening through the park, now scattered in every direction as the tank bore down on them.

Alyssa pushed the car hard, jumping hills and tearing through underbrush, all the while struggling to avoid people who still hadn't fled the park. She gunned it between a gap in a row of high trees, gasping as she emerged on to a softball pitch. There were screams from all over as the players scrambled to safety, spectators dropping down behind their seats.

'What the hell are people doing out playing softball?' Jack yelled. 'Don't they know the city's on lockdown?' He grunted as the car hit a hillock on the far side of the pitch and he was tossed painfully in his seat.

There was an explosion directly behind them, and their car was hurled twenty feet further forwards before it landed, regained traction, and accelerated off.

Jack turned in his seat again and gasped. The tank had driven straight through the line of trees, destroying them, and had loosed off another shell, obliterating the small hillock they had just driven over.

'I think you're going to have to drive faster,' Jack said.

Alyssa just nodded and floored the pedal. There was another row of trees on the left and she yanked the wheel that way, breaking out on to a wide path with the trees providing a barrier between them and the tank.

Alyssa and Jack both let out involuntary screams as another explosion rocked the air. The rear passenger window smashed and they both turned, and saw a tree branch jammed across the back seat. The row of trees was now just a jumble of smouldering vegetation.

They had now almost reached the far side of the park. But what would they find on the other side? Probably more police officers and army soldiers, Alyssa thought bitterly, before she cut the thought off. There was no use in thinking like that. They would keep going until they were stopped.

Santana had put local resources of armed riot police and state troopers at every exit to the park. He was receiving real-time surveillance drone footage and had positioned himself at the most likely exit. He now waited – with his

own men, three cars, two vans and twelve state troopers
– as the taxi drew near.

He wondered if the tank would be able to get another
shot off before the cab left the park. If it did, that would
be great – Santana would see the cab and its occupants
destroyed before his very eyes – and if not, then Santana
would just have to do it himself.

'We're not going to make it,' Jack breathed. He could see
the exit block ahead, and behind them the tank was
tracking its barrel to aim at them again.

'Just keep watching that tank,' Alyssa said, 'and let me
worry about the roadblock. Watch the front end, and shout
loud when it lifts.'

'What?' Jack asked in confusion.

'Just do it!' Alyssa yelled, struggling to keep the car
straight on the gravel path.

The park exit was just a quarter of a mile away, a ten-
foot-wide open gate in the middle of an eight-foot-high
steel fence.

'It's on the path!' Jack cried out next to her. He knew
that once its position was stabilized, the tank would fire
on them again.

Alyssa ignored him.

'Are you going to ram them?' Jack asked. 'There's no
way this little thing can break past all of them. What are
you doing?'

'Shut up, Jack,' Alyssa snapped. 'Just tell me when that
front end lifts!'

They were so close now, just a hundred yards away.

'Now!' Jack yelled.

Instantly, she jerked the wheel to the right, careening off the path on to the trimmed entrance lawns. The tank's 120mm shell streaked past them and through the open gateway, obliterating the waiting police vehicles. The air around them was filled with flame and heat but Alyssa kept her mind focused and her hands gripped tight to the wheel.

Jack turned from the scene of devastation outside the park exit to look where the cab was headed. He barely had time to close his eyes before the taxi hit the steel fence at sixty miles per hour.

As soon as Santana had seen the taxi swerve right, he had leapt to one side himself; he had seen this happen before.

And then all hell was let loose as the tank's high-explosive shell hit the lead van head-on, destroying it totally, bits of metal shearing across space into the other vehicles, flames bursting across the open space and igniting the fuel that spilled out from damaged engines until the whole damn area was on fire.

He watched helplessly as state troopers rushed to carry the injured to safety, straining his eyes through the twenty-foot high flames to see what had happened to the taxi.

The impact knocked Alyssa's breath right out of her, but the robust cab managed to smash through the steel fence with an almighty crash, the speed of the vehicle dropping from sixty to thirty miles per hour as she bumped on to the northern parkway.

The front end of the cab was crushed, a steel railing embedded in the engine, but it was still moving. Alyssa pulled the wheel to the right to straighten the car but it didn't respond. She tried to turn again, harder, but the cab wouldn't turn with her. The wheels were locked in place from the impact.

Ahead, the concrete bulk of a skyscraper loomed. She tried to let up on the accelerator, switched her foot to the brake, but it was no good; the yellow cab was still travelling at twenty miles per hour when it hit the building head on.

Santana watched as the taxi hit the one-hundred storey skyscraper. *Yes*. Then he saw the tank appear at the edge of the park, its turret-mounted gun aimed at the stricken taxi.

He counted the seconds until the gun sounded its ferocious sonic boom once more, almost giving a little hop as it did so. The taxi disintegrated; the roof popped off and the doors exploded outwards while the rest of the chassis collapsed inwards in a fiery, smoking ruin.

Santana let out a sigh of satisfaction.

It was over.

19

Secretary of State John Jeffries strode out of another emergency cabinet meeting, keen to get back to his office to check up on the current situation.

The meetings had been coming thick and fast over the past few days. Decisions had to be made about the involvement of the armed forces in city security, disaster prevention and recovery, emergency protocols activated to ensure uninterrupted chain of command, protection of the national infrastructure prioritized; the list was endless. Endless, and endlessly tiresome.

Jeffries was not overly concerned, for he knew the truth – there were not going to be any more disasters. Not in their home territory, at least. Jeffries knew that the cabinet was worrying without need – it was their own country that now controlled the ability to create disaster. They had nothing to fear.

There was the civil unrest, of course. But the military would easily be able to control that problem if local police could not.

The only fly in the ointment now was this pair of characters on the run from Colonel Anderson. Jack Murray, a computer technician at HIRP, and Alyssa Durham, an investigative journalist, which was a much more terrifying prospect.

General Tomkin, through Anderson, had already ordered the targets to be executed on sight, and Jeffries had spent the meeting biting his fingernails in anticipation. He didn't want to risk communicating with Tomkin or Anderson via his cellphone, and knew he would have to wait until he could use the secure landline back in his office. As the meeting dragged on, he could feel his ulcer starting to burn his stomach.

But now he was out. He walked purposefully down the stately corridors of the Senate building, and two minutes later he passed his secretary in the outer office and pushed through into his inner sanctum without a word.

He sat down at his desk and dialled Tomkins' secure line. It was picked up after just two rings.

'John,' the voice on the other end of the line said. 'I thought I'd be hearing from you earlier.'

'I've been stuck in a damn meeting all morning,' Jeffries fumed. 'Status report?'

'The news is both good and bad,' Tomkin said cagily.

'Meaning?'

'Meaning that Murray and Durham are still alive, but we have them contained.'

'Contained how?'

Tomkin gave a brief breakdown of how the pair had escaped, without revealing too much about how one of the army's tanks had all but destroyed part of the city. 'It seems they were able to make it out of the cab before the shell hit and entered the foyer of the Landers Building through one of the shattered windows.'

'And where are they now?' Jeffries demanded.

There was a pause, almost as if Tomkin was checking real-time surveillance – which Jeffries presumed he was – and then he spoke. 'They're on the fifteenth floor, running up the stairwell.'

'What assets do we have there?'

'We have thirty armed police officers in the lifts and on the stairs getting after them right now, and we also have a full SWAT team en route. We have snipers placed in the park and buildings opposite to take them out if they appear in the windows, and we have a special ops team coming in via chopper to land on the roof and enter the building from above. They're not going to escape,' Tomkin said confidently.

'This Durham,' Jeffries said, 'this *journalist*. Can we be sure she can't get her story out before she's caught?'

'We're monitoring all communications into and out of her offices, and also the private cell of James Rushton, her editor. We've also cut all communications links to the Landers Building, and to that entire city block. Even when she's finally cornered and tries to get the message out, she won't be able to do anything.'

'And Rushton?' Jeffries asked next. 'What does he know?'

'We're unsure,' Tomkin answered. 'We assume that she infiltrated the HIRP base with Rushton's knowledge and consent, and obviously he might be suspicious that he hasn't heard from her since, but we think it's better to leave him hanging, see what we can learn from him.'

'Are you evacuating the Landers Building?'

'No. At the moment we have the pair confined to the stairwells. We've locked the access doors through the building's security mainframe, so they're trapped. If we evacuate, we'll have those same stairwells clogged with about two thousand people, and our targets could well escape in the confusion.'

'OK. As you say, it's good and bad. I can live with that. Just don't let it get any worse.'

Jeffries ended the call and sank back into his leather chair, holding his stomach. He reached for his medication, wondering when the stress would ever end.

20

ALYSSA WAS BREATHING hard now, Jack still behind her as they sprinted up the stairwell.

In her prime, running up the stairs all the way to the top would have been just a good morning's workout to her. Now, however, she felt as if her heart was about to leap out of her chest, and her legs were on fire, lactic acid building up in her thighs to excruciating levels.

Still, she was doing better than Jack, who really seemed to be struggling. He was naturally fit and athletic, without the excess fat people often accumulated from too much time spent behind a desk, but he obviously didn't get out and exercise too often.

They were both somewhat the worse for wear from the impact with the building. Twenty miles per hour wasn't exactly a high-speed crash, but it had been enough to loosen a few fillings. Alyssa had smashed her head against the steering wheel, and it was bleeding profusely. She wondered if she was concussed, as she was starting to feel dizzy. Jack had damaged his legs, jamming them up against the dashboard as the cab hit the wall. The injury to his shins and knees would do nothing to help his chances of escape.

They reached the twenty-fourth floor. 'How about . . . that one?' Jack wheezed behind her.

She reached for the handles of the big double doors and pulled, but the result was the same as it had been on every other floor. 'Locked,' she called down to him. 'Let's keep going.'

She waited for him at the landing, then took his arm to help him onwards. She could tell he wanted to refuse her help, but the pain in his lungs and chest gave him no choice.

The twenty-fourth floor. Only seventy-six left. Not that it seemed likely they would ever get to the top floor; Alyssa could hear the heavy boots and shouts of the men below her – armed, and no doubt ordered to kill them on sight. And she was under no illusions about finding any of the remaining doors above them open; it was obvious that the building's security system had locked it down tight. The only way they would open now would be when more police officers or soldiers – who were undoubtedly racing ahead of them in the fast elevators – entered the stairwell from above, trapping them finally and fatally.

But it was not in Alyssa's nature to give up; she would not surrender, not while there was breath left in her. She'd tried to call James Rushton both at the office and on his cellphone, but her own phone was dead. She realized that all communications must have been cut off, and she would be unable to contact anyone. There were probably snipers observing the building, but at least there were few windows in this service stairwell; they crouched low every time they passed one, and Alyssa wasn't sure how much longer Jack would be able to keep it up.

On the twelfth floor of the Landers Building's eastern service stairwell, Santana led the troops ever upwards.

Murray and Durham had a head start on them due to the length of time it had taken his people to realize that they weren't in the vehicle, but the fugitives didn't have the training he had, he was racing up the stairs two at a time, and they would have been shaken and bruised at the very least from the crash.

According to the latest updates, the SWAT team was still fifteen minutes out, whilst the special ops team that was going to secure the roof was due in ten. Santana hoped he would need neither.

He was leading one section of men up behind the targets, whilst two other sections made their way up in the high-speed elevators. According to the heat sensors that were monitoring the movements of Murray and Durham, they were now on the thirty-second floor. The other two sections were in the elevators on the far side of the building. Having quickly calculated the size of the building, how long it would take for the teams to cross it, how fast the targets were running, and how fast the elevators were travelling, Santana got on to his radio and spoke directly to the section leaders.

'Exit the elevators on the sixtieth floor,' he told them, 'then start sweeping your way down the stairwell. Execute on sight.'

He listened to the dual affirmation, then concentrated

on upping his speed. He hoped he would get to them before the others.

Jack paused halfway up one of the flights of concrete stairs, out of breath and panting raggedly. He collapsed in Alyssa's arms, and she took his weight as he sagged, propping him up against a wall.

'I'm . . . I'm sorry,' he panted. 'I don't know if I can . . . go on.' Alyssa studied him. He could go on, she was sure. Was he just giving up?

Then she realized. Jack was giving up for her, he felt he was holding her back. He thought she would have a better chance without him.

'You can make it,' she told him. 'And I don't want to make it without you.' She didn't tell him that she didn't know what she meant by 'making it'. Her plan, if it could be called that, was essentially to keep heading upwards, but nothing more than that.

Jack looked completely done in, but then something sparked in his eyes. 'What if . . .' He was suddenly focused, his mind switched back on. 'Let's get up to the next door,' he said urgently, pulling forwards.

They came to the next landing, with another set of locked double doors. Alyssa checked the number. The forty-eighth floor. Nearly halfway up.

Jack started to feel around the edge of the door frame.

'What are you doing?' Alyssa asked.

'Trying to find a control panel,' Jack said. 'It just occurred to me, the doors must have them, for manual override in case of an emergency.'

His fingers found the panel, which was hard to see in the reflected white paint on the surrounding wall. He pulled with his fingers, but the panel wouldn't move. He drew back his fist and punched through the wooden cover. He clawed away the broken wood to reveal a computerized control panel underneath. He tried inputting some codes but they were rejected instantly. 'Damn,' he breathed. 'They've really got it locked down.'

'What's the plan if you manage to get through?' Alyssa asked.

Jack continued to play with the controls as he spoke. 'Our only purpose now is to get this information out, right?'

'Yeah, I guess that's right,' Alyssa agreed. The sound of boots on the stairs below was getting louder.

'Well, we're going to get out of this death trap and try and access some computer systems. They may have shut everything down, but I might be able to override their programs.'

Watching Jack's hands work steadily, Alyssa's attention was suddenly caught by a noise from above – more boots on the stairs, heading downwards.

'Whatever you're doing,' she urged, 'do it faster.'

21

'THEY'VE WHAT?' SANTANA asked, not yet out of breath but starting to feel the first faint signs of fatigue.

'They've exited the stairwell,' Anderson's voice came back over the radio. 'Murray must have overridden the system somehow.'

'Which floor?'

'Forty-eighth.'

Santana looked ahead to the next landing, checked the number. 'We're there,' he said, holding up a gloved fist to slow the men behind him. Shouldering his rifle, he approached the door cautiously.

His head snapped up at the sound of boots above him, and he saw the other team hurrying down the stairwell, their own weapons up and aimed.

Santana signalled them to stop.

'Do we have their location?' he asked next.

'Negative,' Anderson replied. 'This is an office level, approximately thirty separate rooms and over a hundred people.'

Santana said no more and reached for the door handle, the index finger of the other straightened next to his trigger guard, ready to move at any second.

He pulled the handle.

'It's locked!' he said through the radio to Anderson. 'The damned thing's locked!'

Anderson cursed. How had Murray done it? They had been pinned, trapped, with no possibility of escape; and now Murray and Durham were free to roam the building, and the state troops were locked in the stairwell!

Anderson immediately got through to the building's security control room. 'Get those doors open!' he bellowed. 'Right now!'

'We . . . we can't!' stammered the man on the other end of the line. 'I don't know what they've done, but the system's not responding!'

'You've got to be kidding me,' Anderson moaned. 'You're telling me I've got to send all my men down fifty floors to get back into the building?'

'I'm sure I can do it,' the man said nervously, 'I just need some time.'

'You've got two minutes,' Anderson barked. 'If it's not open by then I'm going to shoot you in the head the minute I walk through your door, do you understand me?'

'Yes, sir,' the man said, and Anderson could hear the fear in the voice. If it was possible, it would be done.

'Santana,' Anderson said next, back in touch with the leader on the ground, 'can you break through?'

There was a pause before Santana replied. 'No, sir. The doors are thick steel units, and we don't have explosives. The SWAT team would be able to, but they're not here yet. Besides which, we don't know if there are civilians on the other side.'

'OK,' Anderson decided, 'split into three groups. Group one is to go downstairs and find an alternative route into the building, group two is to go up and do the same from the roof, and group three is to stay put and wait in case security manages to get those damned doors open.'

Anderson waited for the acknowledgement, then put the radio down, fingers pinching the bridge of his nose as his head began to throb with a dull, heavy pain.

'Where are we going?' Alyssa asked as Jack pulled her by the hand through a huge open-plan office, work cubicles on either side of them.

The office workers had obviously been warned that Alyssa and Jack were dangerous and cowered behind their desks, keeping their heads down and avoiding eye contact.

'An enclosed office somewhere,' Jack answered. 'Somewhere with a computer and a bit of peace and quiet.'

Alyssa suppressed a laugh. Peace and quiet? Not likely. Jack had somehow managed to relock the door behind them, but she knew it wouldn't take long for their pursuers to get through and come after them again.

They turned and weaved through a maze of cubicle corridors, Jack seeking out an office almost like an animal smelling its next meal, using his instincts to guide him.

They came to a wooden door in a long wall on the northern side of the building. Jack pulled the handle and barged through, Alyssa right behind him.

The office was big, with a stately desk holding a

flat-screen monitor dominating the space. A large man in a suit sat behind the desk, his back to a huge picture window. Six other people were in the office with him, three sitting on a couch against the opposite wall, two on chairs on the other side of the desk, and one sitting cross-legged on the floor; all obviously hiding out in their boss's office.

'Out!' Alyssa shouted. 'Now!'

The seven people widened their eyes, and Alyssa could almost smell their fear. She wondered what they had been told. Something to do with terrorism, she assumed; they probably thought she and Jack had explosives strapped to their bodies.

A thought occurred to her, and she stopped the big man in the suit. 'Not you,' she said, ushering him back inside the office. Terrorists took hostages, didn't they? She felt bad about it, but a hostage might make a SWAT team think twice before they blew the doors off and ran in, guns blazing. She hoped.

She saw Jack heading towards the other side of the desk, keen to get behind the computer.

'No!' Alyssa shouted to him, gesturing to the window behind him. Jack stopped, understanding instantly. *Snipers*.

He came back round to the other side, and he and Alyssa dragged the desk further into the office. Once it was at a safe distance from the window, Jack turned the monitor and keyboard round to face the other way and sat down on one of the other chairs.

'Pass me the disk,' Jack said, and Alyssa fished it out of her trouser pocket and handed it to him.

As Jack got to work, Alyssa grabbed the sofa by one of its arms and started to drag it across the thick wool carpet, ignoring her hostage who stood off to one side, watching her. She pulled the heavy couch across the doorway. It wouldn't stop their pursuers altogether but it would certainly slow them down. Especially if she added a little something extra. She looked at the suited executive.

'Sit down on the couch,' she told him. He stared at her with disdain. There was no fear in his eyes, and Alyssa knew he must be a man of some power and, hopefully, some importance. Eventually, he grunted and reluctantly lowered his hefty frame onto the couch, which creaked under his weight.

Alyssa sat down in a chair opposite him, keeping herself away from the windows. 'Look,' she said to him, 'I'm sorry about this. If there was any other way, believe me we'd be doing that instead. But there isn't, and that's the bottom line. Despite what you've been told, we're not terrorists. I mean, do we look like terrorists? I'm a journalist, my name is Alyssa Durham. I work for the *New Times Post*.'

There was a flicker of recognition in the man's eyes. 'I've read your work,' he said eventually, 'if you are who you say you are.' He gestured with his head to where Jack worked feverishly at the computer. 'What's he doing?'

'That's Jack Murray, and he's trying to get a line out of the building, open up communications somehow. He's a lead technician at the High-frequency Ionospheric Research Project.'

'What?' he asked.

'It's a government research centre which we've discovered

is a front for a covert weapons programme. That's why we're here now, being chased by government agents.'

The man shook his head. 'Whatever,' he scoffed.

'It's the truth,' Alyssa said. 'What's your name?'

The man seemed to consider not answering, but then thought better of it. 'Stevens, Ray Stevens. I'm the vice president of York Investments, the multi-billion dollar financial giant whose offices you've just barged into. And whatever your reasons are, you're both in big trouble.'

'From you?' Alyssa mocked. 'We've just had to drag your desk away from the window so we don't get shot by snipers. A stolen taxi we've just driven across the park got blown across the street by a damned *battle tank*. The weapon we've discovered is capable of destroying entire countries. And you think we should worry about a fat banker? Mr Stevens, you really need to get over yourself.'

Stevens spluttered, outraged, but then caught himself. 'A weapon that can destroy entire *countries*?' he asked, his interest aroused despite himself.

He watched Alyssa nod her head gravely, then leant forward on the couch. 'Tell me about it.'

'They're in the northern office,' Anderson informed Santana.

Santana was still in the stairwell, having decided to lead this section. If Murray could unlock and relock them, he was sure the building's security experts would also be able to do so. And he didn't want to waste twenty minutes running up and down the stairs again.

Anderson went on to tell him that the pair had taken

a hostage, and even more unfortunate was the fact that it was Ray Stevens, one of the richest bankers in the city and a personal friend of the mayor's.

Good news came next, though, when Anderson reported that security had finally managed to override the door locks; they would be open any moment.

22

THERE WAS BANGING on the office door and Stevens jumped. He quickly recovered himself. 'They're not going to shoot their way through with me sitting here,' he said confidently. He turned to the door and shouted, 'Hey! This is Ray Stevens! I'm right on the other side!'

The banging stopped, and Stevens turned back to Alyssa with a look of satisfaction.

As Jack continued to clack away at the keyboard, Alyssa scanned the walls of the room. 'Is there another way out of here?' she asked.

Stevens hesitated. Eventually, he nodded his head. He gestured over to the side of the office, where some large mahogany bookcases stood in an alcove. 'Over past the bookcases,' he said. 'There's a private elevator, goes from here up to the executive lounge on the hundredth floor.'

'Does it go down?' Alyssa asked.

Stevens shook his head. 'No, it's only for the chosen few of us on the executive board. Bit of a luxury gentlemen's club. Not many people even know about it.'

'Is there another way down from there?'

Stevens nodded. 'I guess so. There are four offices like this one, and each has its own private elevator. So there are at least three other ways down, although none of them come down further than this level.'

Alyssa looked at Jack. 'How are you getting on?'

He carried on typing as he talked. 'Nothing so far,' he said in exasperation. 'I'm not sure if I'm going to be able to get through. I think they've shut down the building's actual external communications hardware on a physical level, not just performed a software command protocol. They've pulled the plug, so to speak.' He looked up at Alyssa. 'We're going to have to get our message out in person.'

Alyssa nodded. She could hear activity on the other side of the door. It was time to move, although she had no clear idea how they were going to get out of the building. She motioned Stevens over to the private elevator. 'Lead the way,' she said.

Minutes later the three of them stepped out of the elevator into the executive suite on the one hundredth floor of the Landers Building.

Alyssa could scarcely believe her eyes as she gazed at oak flooring covered with rich wool rugs, mahogany-panelled walls hung with works of fine art, breathtakingly turned antique furniture – and this was just the foyer. There were private dining rooms, Stevens explained, a bar area with an entire wall of glass that looked out over the city, a library of rare first editions and antiquarian delights, kitchens and service rooms, and even bedrooms in case the valued executives needed to stay the night.

Alyssa's eyes strayed to one of the large windows in the

foyer, but there was no view today; the hundredth floor was enveloped in low cloud, At least that meant there would be no threat of snipers.

'That's strange,' Stevens said as he walked through the foyer, starting to check through the rooms. He had listened without interruption when Alyssa had explained what she knew about Spectrum Nine. She wasn't sure if he believed all of it, but his manner had certainly become less antagonistic. And they had all heard the assault team blasting through his office door just seconds after the elevator started its ascent. It seemed clear that while Stevens might not be a primary target, his life was considered dispensable.

'What's strange?' Jack asked, trailing after him.

'There's nobody here,' Stevens answered.

'Well, they probably went down in the other elevators when this whole thing started,' Alyssa said, catching up with them in one of the private dining rooms.

'Perhaps,' Stevens said. 'But where are the service staff? This area has over twenty people working here and they don't have access to the private elevators.' He grunted. 'So there must be some other way out. Stands to reason really, though I've never considered it before.'

Alyssa and Jack exchanged looks. 'Maybe directly to the ground floor,' Jack said hopefully.

Stevens just shrugged his shoulders. 'Maybe.'

'Then what are we waiting for?' Alyssa said. 'Let's go and find it.'

'A private lounge?' Santana exclaimed with barely concealed rage. 'Why the hell didn't we know about that before?'

The cop before him just stared back, unfazed. 'Who knows? SWAT just got here, remember? You've been on the scene for an hour already. Why didn't *you* know about it before?'

Santana wanted to punch the puke in the face, but thought better of it. Besides, the cop was probably right. He *should* have known about it. And yet the executive suite didn't show up on any of the blueprints to the building, and nor did the private elevators which accessed it. There was just a big open space for the hundredth floor, labelled as still 'under construction'.

The SWAT team had placed explosive charges round the office door frame and smashed their way in with a battering ram, with little regard to the well-being of the bank's vice president. Anderson had told Santana to get the job done, whatever it took. When they found the elevator at the back of the office, Santana had instructed one of his men to ask if any of the employees knew anything about it. One man had explained about the private lounge, and how there were three more elevators that accessed it.

Now Santana snapped out orders to his men and the SWAT team, creating four assault sections, one to each of the elevators. They would time their arrivals to coincide, burst out into the lounge foyer and clear the floor one room at a time.

Locking and loading their weapons, Santana and his section of eight men squeezed into the elevator and checked their watches.

One minute and ten seconds left before they would set off into the kill zone.

23

'Well, here it is,' Stevens called to the others, standing at a large concealed panel in the main kitchen, much like the panels that were used to disguise servants' access corridors in the large houses of the past.

'At least I think it is,' he added. 'There's a control pad right next to it, the same as next to our own elevators.' He sighed. 'The trouble is, I have no idea what the code is.'

Alyssa looked at Jack.

He answered her unspoken question with a nod. 'It's going to take about ten minutes.'

They heard a pinging sound from the foyer and raced back to check it out. The light had come on above all four private elevators.

Alyssa turned to Stevens. 'OK, *think*. Is there any other way out of here?'

Stevens thought. 'Well, there is one way,' he said finally, 'although I don't know if it will do us any good.'

Jack gripped him. 'What is it?' he demanded.

'There.' Stevens pointed towards another elevator door, positioned in a corner of the room behind a huge potted plant.

'Why didn't you mention it before?' Alyssa asked as they raced towards it.

'Because it doesn't go down,' Stevens said evenly. 'It goes up. To the roof.'

Santana re-checked his assault rifle, making certain the magazine was properly inserted and he had one round chambered, ready to go.

They would be in the foyer in seconds, and he flicked the safety catch of his weapon to the 'off' position, watching as his men did the same. Drilled into keeping the weapon safe until a target was identified, the SWAT officers sharing the elevator with them decided to follow normal protocol with their own; but Santana was too far gone now to worry about protocol. The three people upstairs had to die, and they had to die the second those elevator doors opened.

There would be no more mistakes, Santana promised himself as the elevator began to decelerate, weapon coming up to his shoulder as they came to a stop on the hundredth floor.

The foyer's fifth elevator, Stevens explained, was to access the building's rooftop helipad. Stevens had to admit that there was no helicopter there at the moment, and he wouldn't be able to fly it even if there was, but it was mutually decided that it was better to avoid the destruction that was about to be brought down upon the executive private lounge. They would keep heading up, until there was nowhere else to go.

Stevens keyed in the code and the steel doors slid open. Stevens and Jack hurried inside. Alyssa, however, paused, her eyes drawn to the far side of the room.

'What are you doing?' yelled Jack, reaching out to yank her inside.

She snatched her arm away, pointing to the bar in the far corner. 'Is that a radio?' she asked Stevens.

'I don't know,' the big man snapped. 'I suppose it could be, the staff use them. What does it matter? Get in the damned elevator!'

Alyssa sprinted across the room. If she got that radio, they would be able to get a message out from the roof. Radio communications were always possible; Anderson and his men wouldn't have thought of this possibility, she was sure.

'Come back!' called Jack, but Alyssa ignored him. She grabbed the radio off the bar top and held it triumphantly aloft.

And then the lights above the private elevators clicked off, the doors opened, and all hell broke loose.

Santana saw Murray and a large, heavy man in a suit – presumably Ray Stevens – in another elevator across the foyer.

As the flash-bang grenades went off, Santana opened fire at them, watching as they hunkered down and hit the elevator button. He cursed as the doors began to close, his bullets ricocheting off the metal surface, noticing Murray's pained expression as he looked across the room towards . . .

Alyssa Durham. She was running through the smoke as rounds from the rest of the assault team tore up the oak floor and wool carpet behind her, grabbing a bar stool as she went.

Santana turned his own weapon towards her, watching in disbelief as she hurled the stool at the huge window on the eastern side of the building. The glass shattered and she followed the bar stool, throwing herself straight out of the window, one hundred storeys above the earth.

Alyssa had placed the radio in her belt as she ran, and with both hands free, she swivelled in mid-air and grasped hold of the bottom window ledge. It was wide, made of rough concrete which gave her fingers purchase, but the wind at fourteen hundred feet was strong, threatening to rip her hands off the ledge and send her into the abyss below her.

But the building *did* have a surprising amount of places where an experienced climber could place fingers and toes. Calming herself, she swung one leg up and levered her body up on to the ledge. She moved to the side of the window and pulled herself upright, fingers sunk deep into the half-inch gaps between the concrete blocks. She shut her mind to the fearsome wind and the freezing low-level cloud, and started to climb.

Santana looked out of the window straight down, but he could see nothing. Then his peripheral vision caught movement to the left, and his rifle came out of the window at the same time as he saw Alyssa Durham's leg pull round a concrete abutment to the side of the window ledge.

He squeezed the trigger but the rounds ricocheted off

alongside splinters of the concrete wall, Durham already safe behind the abutment.

What was she going to do? Hide there forever? Climb to the roof and join Murray and Stevens? The special ops team should have arrived by now but they had hit a delay due to air restrictions over the city and were circling two miles out whist paperwork was sorted.

Santana thought for a moment, then pulled his head back in and ordered men to guard the window while he went further down the wall to another window, to check if the target could be seen from the other side of the abutment.

As he moved down the wall, he called over to the men working at the door to the rooftop elevator. 'How you doing over there?'

One of the men shook his head. 'It's not responding,' he called back. 'They must have jammed the doors open up on the roof.'

Cursing, Santana got on the radio and verified the estimated arrival time of the special ops team. The clearance to fly over the city had still not been granted but Anderson was working hard to get it approved.

Santana stuck his head out of the next window but all he could see on this side was another abutment, which meant that she had managed to find a channel between two abutments and was now covered on both sides.

He wouldn't normally have considered it, but he'd seen the Durham woman putting a radio in her belt as she ran for the window. With that, she might be able to contact the outside world, which Anderson had explained was completely unacceptable.

He called the SWAT officers and his own men into the centre of the room and explained the situation to them; they were going to have to follow Alyssa Durham out onto the building's exterior.

A plan was quickly agreed upon, and the well-equipped SWAT team began to unravel their rappelling ropes, ready to finish their mission once and for all.

24

WHEN THE BULLETS had come, Alyssa had almost lost her precarious grip on the concrete blocks, at one stage only holding on with two fingers of one hand as she dangled perilously above the cloud-shrouded abyss below. But she had managed to hold on and haul herself back onto the building's façade.

Her cheek and arm had been cut and torn by concrete chips which had been shot loose from the high-powered rounds, but that only served to increase her focus as she started once again to climb.

Slowly, painfully, Alyssa climbed up the channel between the wide concrete abutments. It should protect her from rifle fire all the way to the top. But what would she find up there? The assault team waiting for her? She had no way of knowing. She hoped Jack and Stevens had kept the presence of mind to block off the elevator doors once they'd hit the roof; if not, then there would surely be a less than friendly welcoming party once she made it up there herself.

When she got to the roof, she figured she'd use the radio to make an emergency distress call. She knew that news agencies routinely scanned the radio waves for such things, and she hoped that hers would be picked up. At the very least, the presence of the media would make it less likely that they would all be shot out of hand.

As her fingers continued to work against the wide edges of the building's huge block-work, pulling herself as close in as possible to avoid the worst of the buffeting winds, a new sound drifted up to her. The sound of men shouting.

She paused momentarily, trying to identify the words, but she could not. She recognized the tone though; they weren't shouts of shock or anger, but the shouts of orders being transmitted across open space. She knew instinctively what it meant; they were coming out after her.

'This is an emergency distress call; I repeat, this is an emergency distress call.'

Anderson looked up as he heard the words coming over the radio network. Who the hell was that? He paused. Alyssa Durham? He shook his head. It couldn't be. But the message continued, and he knew it was her.

'Anyone who is on this channel, please listen!' She sounded scared, desperate, and Anderson knew this would also make her dangerous. *Damn it!*

'My name is Alyssa Durham, and I am heading towards the roof of the Landers Building. Police officers and soldiers are trying to kill me, and they are also trying to kill Jack Murray of the High-frequency Ionospheric Research Project, and Ray Stevens of York Investments.'

Anderson started to pace the enclosed confines of the aircraft, his pulse rate rising. He turned to his communications operator. 'Is there anything we can do to block this?' he asked in exasperation.

The operator shook his head. 'These channels are always open, it would take hours to get them blocked.'

Still with one ear to the message, he dialled the number for General Tomkin.

'We have uncovered a government plot to use HIRP research as a weapon to—' the message continued, even as Tomkin answered his secure phone.

'Colonel Anderson, what's the situation there?' came the gruff voice.

But Anderson didn't answer, all his attention focused now on the radio message. He heard Alyssa Durham's breath catch in her throat, in shock, no words coming now; and then there was a piercing shriek coming through the equipment, and he realized that Alyssa Durham was screaming.

Aboard the special ops chopper, Major Dan Edwards smiled. *Finally*.

The word had just come through from the state aviation office that they had at last been cleared to fly over the city.

The pilot eased the helicopter out of its circular holding pattern, aiming the nose across the city to the Landers Building just five miles ahead of them.

Edwards nodded to his team. 'OK, men, let's lock and load. We have three high-level targets, and it's up to us to take them out.' He racked the slide on his personal weapon, putting a round into the chamber. 'You know the score. No prisoners.'

* * *

The radio fell out of Alyssa's hand as she screamed, grasping onto the ledge above her with both hands and pulling her legs up just instants before the concrete façade below was ripped to pieces by high-velocity rounds.

Without looking back, she pulled herself all the way up onto the next block, instinctively pushing her body further into the left-hand abutment to shield her from the bullets. There was a pause then, and she assumed the men were edging further out onto the building. Without a moment's hesitation, she used the opportunity to climb even further upwards, hoping the thick cloud might obscure their aim; although she knew deep-down that if they reached the channel, they couldn't possibly miss.

Santana edged along the window ledge, cursing himself for shooting prematurely, before he definitely had a target.

He looked back at the seven armed men behind him, all joined by the rappelling rope, which in turn was anchored to a table and six other men back in the executive lounge, and nodded at them.

Cautiously, careful not to look down, Santana edged his toes and fingers along the ledge, a slow and painful process that nevertheless brought him closer and closer to his quarry. She wasn't going to escape this time, he was damned certain of that.

But his mind rebelled at what he was asking his body to do. His conscious mind told him that he was well secured, and even if he fell, he wouldn't die; but the instinctive side, the part of his inner nature that could never be fully controlled, was horrified by the height of the building, the sheer surface, the fact that they were in the *clouds!* What had he been thinking?

But, despite the reservations of his subconscious, he drove himself onwards step by step, easing across the surface of the huge skyscraper one hundred storeys above the city streets.

He was close now; so close. Just three more painful, tortuous sideways steps and then he would be there in the channel, and then it would be all over.

Two feet now, and he eased his assault rifle forwards on its sling, ready to aim it upwards the instant he leaned around the corner. He looked back to his men, lined up along the ledge, ready to back him up. He edged the final foot to the corner and nodded to them.

Turning back to the edge of the left-hand abutment, he slowly breathed out, trying to calm and centre himself. He wasn't going to waste any shots this time; each one would count.

And then he was stepping out off the ledge, easing himself around the large concrete post that was providing his target with her protection. One step, two steps, and then he was there, in the channel.

He looked up, raising his weapon skyward as he did so.

And then his eyes went wide with shock; he never had the chance to scream.

Alyssa had looked down, saw the man's hands reaching around the concrete abutment twenty feet below. She knew that as soon as he was in the channel, her chances were zero.

At least she'd managed to send something out over the radio; maybe it would be picked up by someone. There really wasn't anything left to do, and so she decided to take her life in her own hands and not wait to die at the gun of some faceless government thug.

She waited until she saw the man's head and shoulders swing around the concrete pillar, and then let go her grip of the building. Hands, feet, body; she simply let go of everything and plummeted towards the earth.

Santana took the full impact of Alyssa's fast-moving weight after her twenty-foot fall, her boots planting themselves firmly into his face on her way down.

The savage impact knocked Santana clear off the wall, his own momentum stripping his team-mates from the wall's concrete surface after him.

As the men fell into the abyss one by one, already the commands for full brace were being given back in the office, the knots attaching the rope to the table checked quickly as the six officers prepared to take the strain.

Even with preparation, the weight of eight armed men falling to the earth was enough to pull both the desk and the other officers inexorably towards the open window. But then the men got their grip right, the desk hit the window and stayed tight on the frame, and the eight falling men came to sudden, back-breaking halt in a wild, swinging line down the face of the building, fourteen hundred feet above the earth.

Alyssa filled with satisfaction as she felt her boots hit the man on her way down, glad as his grip was ripped from the wall.

The impact with the man's head served to slow her own fall sufficiently, enabling her to grasp the nearest concrete block with the strong, vice-like fingers of one hand.

Although the soldier had broken her fall, the shock of saving herself with one arm threatened to dislocate her shoulder, and she winced in pain as she swung out over the clouds, trying to numb the pain.

She tried to calm her breath as she watched the momentum of the first man pull all the others away from the wall, and although she was pleased they were no longer a threat, she was also happy that they hadn't fallen to their deaths but were still secured by the rope; she wouldn't want all their deaths on her conscience, despite the fact that they were trying to kill her.

She reached up and gripped with her other hand too, then pulled herself higher to get purchase with her feet, her toes straining for grip through the thin leather of her shoes.

She looked down the façade of the building at the soldiers all spread out like ants on a spider's web, then gasped in horror as the man at the bottom pulled out a pistol from a belt holster and started firing.

Santana had blacked out momentarily when the woman had hit him during her suicidal plunge, although now he had regained consciousness he realized it hadn't been suicidal at all, but was instead a carefully calculated risk. And one that had paid off too, he noticed in rising anger as he saw the woman clinging to the concrete blocks above him.

His adrenalin making his heart feel as if it was on fire, Santana didn't even have time to consider himself lucky that the rappelling rope had held, didn't allow himself to wait until the rope and seven other men had stopped their pendulum-like swing from one side of the building to the other.

Instead, filled now with a murderous anger the likes of which he had never before felt in his life, he processed the fact that he had lost his rifle in the fall and immediately reached for the hand-gun at his waist. Still swinging upside down, battered and dazed, he pulled it free and started firing wildly.

The first two shots hit one of the men above him, the next three threatening the crew on the rope behind the window; but Santana paid this scant regard as he aimed again, fuelled by bitter rage.

As he loosed off round after round, he heard orders being shouted from the window to the men above him on the rope, but he paid them no attention, focused purely on shooting Alyssa Durham to death.

But then he felt the rope pull, jerking his body to the side, and he finally looked up to see the man above him sawing through the rope with his combat knife.

He understood instantly what was happening; he was being cut loose, his actions endangering all the men on the rope. He was being sacrificed to save everyone else.

He gestured with his hands, eyes wide and pleading, offering to put the gun away; but it was too late, the rope was already cut, and Major Rafael Santana's last words consisted of a single, piercing scream that could be heard all over the city as he plunged fourteen hundred feet to his death.

Dan Edwards ordered his men to check and re-check their equipment, despite the fact that he knew he didn't have to. The men in his crew were professional through and through, and didn't have to be told anything.

The chopper was sailing through the clouds on a direct line with the roof of the Landers Building, which was only two miles away now although they still couldn't see it in these conditions.

The latest news was that two of the targets – the two men, Jack Murray and Ray Stevens – were on the roof, whilst Alyssa Durham, the lone female target, was climbing up the exterior of the building, approximately one more storey from the top.

An attempt to kill her outside the building had evidently gone completely haywire, resulting in the death of the field commander, and Edwards thought again that the men should have just been patient and waited until the real professionals were on the scene to handle things. Special operations forces weren't given the label 'special' for nothing.

When all other options failed, Edwards and his men could be relied upon to get the job done.

'What the hell's going on down there?' Jack asked Stevens, heading towards the roof edge.

'Hey, I'd get back from there if I were you,' Stevens yelled over to him. He'd heard the gunfire too, but there was no way he was going to the edge of a one hundred and two storey building to see what it was. So long as nobody was shooting at *him*, he was happy.

The gunfire stopped then, and another sound started to emerge through the thick, dense cloud. 'Hey Jack, wait!' Stevens called again with renewed urgency. 'Stop!' he called, even louder, and Jack paused and looked round at the banker.

'What?' he asked irritably, keen to see what was happening, aware that any sound was a possible indication that Alyssa might still be alive.

'Do you hear it?' Stevens asked.

'Do I hear what?' Jack responded, but then grew silent as he began to perceive the noise Stevens had heard. What was it? A slow, steady, mechanical beat. Rotor blades. 'A helicopter!' Jack said in panic. 'They're sending a damned gunship after us!'

Just fifteen feet below the roof parapet, Alyssa continued to climb steadily, trying her best to ignore the searing pain in her shoulder. Once, she reminded herself, she'd had to make a four hundred-foot vertical descent with a badly broken collarbone. It had been hard, but she'd made it. She always made it. She cut the pain from her mind completely, as she concentrated on making the next foot of height up the building. She would make this too.

The men on the rope below had ceased to bother her, far more interested now in saving themselves, and Alyssa was able to concentrate more fully on her climbing. But then another noise intruded on her, and it was only seconds before she realized what it was. *A helicopter.*

She looked up at the roof edge above her, just scant feet away, and cursed her bad luck. So near. But she understood that the chopper would be on them within minutes, and they wouldn't stand a chance.

But, she told herself, if she made it to the roof, at least she could spend her final moments in Jack's arms. And, with renewed vigour and purpose, she continued to climb.

Jack and Stevens were crouched behind an air-conditioning duct. It wasn't much of a hiding place but at least it gave them some shelter from the wind. They had wedged the elevator doors open with a long piece of broken metal antenna which they had worked into the sliders on either side. The doors showed no signs of moving.

Jack was staring morosely across the expanse of the rooftop when he thought he saw a hand clawing at the edge. He stared, disbelieving, but it was definitely a hand. He'd raced towards the edge and saw another hand appear, and then Alyssa's exhausted, beautiful face as she pulled herself up and over the parapet.

And suddenly he was there with her, pulling her up the rest of the way, arms tight around her, kissing her cold cheeks, her lips.

'Alyssa,' he breathed. 'I thought you were gone.' He embraced her tightly, and she hugged him back, her body still strong despite what she had been through.

And then they both turned towards the sound of a helicopter, hovering just ten feet over the roof on the far side of the building.

* * *

'What the hell are they doing here?' Edwards exclaimed in fury. WBN News? Who had given *them* permission to fly?

But dammit, there they were, hovering right over his targets, their cameras on live, broadcasting the scene to the whole damned world.

Edwards' own chopper was still one mile out, and he got on the radio immediately to Colonel Anderson. He was going to need new orders.

Anderson couldn't believe what was going on.

Getting permission for the special ops team to fly over the city had stretched his patience to the limit, and it was now clear that it was the mayor's office that had been the real cause of the hold-up. It seemed that Stevens really was a good friend of the mayor and he was unhappy about how the situation was developing.

That damned newspaper editor James Rushton, too. Anderson wished he had pulled the man in when he'd had the chance. When Alyssa Durham's distress message had come over the radio, Rushton had seized on it instantly, appealing directly to the mayor for his help and convincing him to keep the news helicopters flying.

The mayor could not withdraw permission for the special ops chopper to approach the Landers Building – Secretary of Defence Jeffries had stepped in and declared the situation to be an issue of national security – but he was still in a position to authorize flyovers by media news crews.

Anderson sighed, and put another call through to General Tomkin.

* * *

Alyssa, Jack and Stevens waved their arms at the TV news helicopter, showing the world at large that they were helpless, unarmed. The cameras picked up everything.

And then another helicopter arrived, and Alyssa noted with dismay that it was military. It pushed its way past the civilian chopper – which moved round, cameras still on the scene – and then it hovered over the roof's expansive flat middle section, dust kicking up high into the air.

None of the three fugitives attempted to flee as the doors of the helicopter opened and a team of eight special operations personnel fast-roped down to the rooftop, weapons up and aimed as soon as they landed; they just raised their arms in surrender.

The media chopper kept on filming, and Alyssa knew that WBN would be sending live footage out over the satellite network. Would they all be gunned down live on TV?

She swallowed hard as the men approached, wondering what orders the soldiers had been given.

Seconds later, the lead man was upon them, hand up to halt the men behind him. He looked at the three people over the top of his assault rifle. 'Alyssa Durham, Jack Murray, Ray Stevens,' he announced coldly over the continued thrum of the helicopter rotors, 'you are under arrest.'

Relief flooded Alyssa's body so powerfully that she collapsed on to the rooftop.

PART FOUR

PART FOUR

1

ONE HOUR LATER, Colonel Anderson's airplane touched down. He had to show his military credentials to be allowed the continued use of his cellphone, although he still experienced a dead spot as he was ushered through the airport.

When he reached the arrivals lounge, there were several military officers waiting for him. 'Where are they?' he demanded before anyone had the chance to introduce themselves.

'Due to the helicopter being forced to circle for so long, fuel was a problem,' the nearest officer said. A tall, athletic man in his mid-thirties, he led the group through the glass doors and outside to a waiting army limousine. Other men moved ahead to open the doors for them.

'They had to land at DuPont Airfield, just outside the city,' the tall man continued when they were inside the car. 'The airfield's only about ten miles from the city's internment camp where the rioters and protesters are being held. It's the most secure place in the area at the moment, so the prisoners are on their way there now.'

Anderson considered the situation. He would have liked Durham, Murray and Stevens to be isolated, but it could have been worse. At least they were in custody, and on the way to a secure location. He could deal with Durham and Murray, but Stevens posed another set of problems entirely. How much did he know? And what could be done about him? It was clear that the mayor was taking a keen interest in this, and Anderson didn't want the situation getting blown out of all proportion. Would a 'tragic accident' be too obvious?

The majority of the government wasn't involved in the Spectrum Nine programme. Almost nobody had any idea it even existed, and that was the way Tomkin wanted it kept. So yes, Anderson decided, an unfortunate accident for Ray Stevens seemed best. Anderson was pretty sure that Tomkin would authorize the same fate for the mayor himself if he continued to pry too deeply.

There was James Rushton too of course, the editor of the *Post*. What should be done about him? Urgent action was required. It just wasn't worth taking the chance that Rushton would say or, even worse, print something about what he thought he knew. Any hint of what was really going on would cause untold damage to the plans.

From the car, Anderson called Tomkin. There was going to have to be a media curfew put in place, connected to today's 'terrorist' incident; and then he would need authorization for James Rushton to be dealt with.

'My hands are tied, James,' said Harry Envers, the city's mayor, regretfully.

James Rushton was sitting on the other side of the desk in Envers' large, well-appointed office. 'I understand that,

Harry,' he said reasonably, 'and I appreciate what you've done so far, I really do. But is there really nothing we can do to get them out of there?'

Envers raised his palms. 'My remit is this city, James, you know that. Only this city. And hell, martial law is in action here anyway, it's amazing I've got any pull left at all. But outside the city limits I've got no authority at all. And that camp is way out of the city limits.' He shook his head. 'It's under full military jurisdiction too. You know I'd help if I could. Hell, I've known Ray Stevens for over thirty years; I've had his wife on the phone most of the morning wanting to know what I'm doing about it – that is, when I've not been trying to explain things to the board of York Investments.'

Rushton looked down at the desk. He knew Envers was right; there was nothing he could do. But there was something Rushton himself could do. He still had no evidence, no cold, hard facts, but he now believed in his heart of hearts that Alyssa was right. Elements of the government were using the HIRP base as a covert weapons programme. She'd gone up there to investigate – *with my blessing, damn me!* – and then days later had become a 'dangerous terrorist', at least to hear the authorities tell it. He'd known Alyssa Durham for years and knew she was nothing of the sort. It was obvious what had happened – she had found out too much and was being silenced.

Well, to hell with it. He was going to run the story anyway.

Still sitting across from the mayor, Rushton pulled out

his cellphone and called his office. His deputy editor, Hank Forshaw, answered.

'Hank,' he said, 'I want you to compile everything we've got on the story Alyssa's been working on and get it in this evening's edition.' He paused as Hank spoke excitedly on the other end of the line. 'What?' he asked in anger. 'When?' He listened for a few more moments, then hung up.

Envers looked at him. 'What's wrong?'

Rushton shook his head in disbelief. 'They've shut us down,' he replied.

'The *Post*?' Envers asked.

'All of us,' Rushton answered. 'Jeffries has declared a national emergency due to the terrorist threat and ordered a total media blackout.'

'I don't believe it!' Envers exploded. 'That's completely unconstitutional!'

Rushton opened his mouth to add his own vitriolic opinion when the large mahogany double doors behind him burst open and armed military police marched into the office.

Behind them, the mayor's secretary looked close to tears. 'I'm sorry,' she said, 'they just walked straight past me.'

They approached Rushton, who jumped up out of his chair and backed away as two of the men reached for him, ignoring Envers' shouts of outrage.

'James Rushton,' the lead officer pronounced, as his men managed to secure the newspaper editor and cuff his hands behind his back, 'you are under arrest for assisting in the planning and execution of terrorist attacks against your country.'

'What?' Rushton cried out as he was escorted from the office. 'Harry, do something!' he yelled.

The lead officer nodded to two more of his men, who went round the desk towards the mayor, handcuffs at the ready. 'Mayor Envers,' the man intoned, 'I hereby arrest you for the crime of treason.'

Harry Envers, the anger leaving his body to be replaced with the cold, helpless feeling of total despair, uttered not a further word of protest as the arresting officers led him away after his friend.

The prison bus bounced along the dirt road that led from the well-paved highway to the makeshift internment camp just a few more miles away.

'Don't worry,' Stevens said to Alyssa and Jack from his seat behind them. 'I know the mayor, known him thirty-four years. There's no way in hell he's gonna let anything happen to us. That's why we got arrested and not just shot. He—'

'No talking!' came a shout from the front, and Alyssa watched as a uniformed guard strode down the bus, brandishing a night stick at Stevens. 'You shut your mouth, you hear me?' He regarded the three prisoners with contempt; hatred, even. 'You traitors make me sick,' he said with true vehemence, following up with a gob of spit to their feet.

He walked away, shaking his head and muttering to himself. Alyssa wanted so badly to speak to Jack but she wasn't willing to risk the wrath of the guards. They'd obviously been told what she and the others were supposed to have done, and with things as heated as they were right now, it was possible that someone would just lose it and shoot or beat them to death. And so she remained quiet.

But what would happen next? The relief when the hand-cuffs had appeared and they had merely been arrested instead of executed was wearing off now. Stevens seemed confident of the mayor's intervention but Alyssa wasn't so sure. She thought it more likely that they hadn't been killed because they were being filmed at the time. When the cameras were off, and they were ferreted away in some government installation somewhere, what would happen then?

To make matters worse, in the frantic race for the rooftop, Jack had left the flash drive still connected to the computer in Stevens' office, leaving them once again with no evidence. She prayed that someone might pick it up and hand it on to the authorities but didn't hold out much hope.

But maybe the right people had been watching the broadcast from the news helicopter; maybe Rushton, or even the mayor himself. But then again, maybe—

The next thought never materialised in her head however, as an explosion burst from underneath them and sent the bus spinning on to its side, sliding across the wasteland next to the track. The impact knocked the breath from her, and she thought that she must have lost consciousness at least for a short while, because when she opened her eyes, there were masked gunmen on board the bus, coming towards her.

She looked to her left and saw that Jack, too, was only just regaining consciousness, blood leaking from a gash to the side of his head. They both hung down from their tipped-up seats, their hands still secured to the guard rail of the bench seat in front.

She looked beyond the gunmen and saw the driver and three prison guards lying in pools of blood on the side of the bus interior, executed by the men who were now approaching.

She again peered beyond the men with guns, tensing as she prepared to take the bullets she knew were meant for her, and saw a curious sight: other gunmen, instead of executing the prisoners, were freeing them with bolt cutters.

The masked man nearest to her and Jack now did the same thing, slinging his rifle and using a pair of bolt cutters to free them of their cuffs. He must have seen the quiz-zical look on Alyssa's face, and he winked at her over his mask. 'We're the Resistance,' he said conspiratorially.

'The Resistance?' Jack asked from beside her, rubbing life back into his wrists.

The man nodded as he moved past to free Stevens. 'You better believe it. You think we're just gonna take this federal government crap?' He shook his head. 'No way, pal. In that camp up there,' he continued, gesturing with the bolt cutters towards the windscreen and beyond, 'they've got over two thousand red-blooded patriots, imprisoned ille-gally. And we're not gonna take it any more. Soldiers on the streets? Dammit, we're gonna take the streets back.'

The man released the prisoners behind them and headed back to the front, where he turned to them. 'Well, what you waiting for, a signed invitation? You've been rescued, say thank you and get your asses off the bus!'

Alyssa took the lead, murmuring thank yous as they

followed the other prisoners down the sabotaged, half-destroyed bus, careful to avoid the flames that licked at the broken windows.

Out on the road, Alyssa could see the camp in the distance, a huge place for a temporary internment camp, covered with barbed-wire fences and gun posts. She watched as the gunmen made their way towards the camp; some on foot, some in vehicles, but all armed to the teeth.

Alyssa shook her head. 'What the hell is happening to this country?'

Jack put his arm round her and checked behind for Stevens just as the ground shook beneath them.

Alyssa recognized the impact as being from an artillery shell, and realized that the camp must have seen the 'Resistance' coming. She heard Jack gasp and then she turned to look for Stevens too.

But instead of the big, heavy, well-dressed banker, what she saw was a horrific mass of blood, internal organs and widely-strewn body parts. Stevens had been hit by shrapnel from the shell, and the result was devastating.

Alyssa noticed that Jack's eyes were wide, and knew that the sight of all that blood and gore might well cause panic to set in, and so she grabbed him by the arm and started to run, pulling him with her.

To all sides she saw masked members of the Resistance, along with many of the transport's escaped prisoners, fall like leaves from the trees under a hail of gunfire; cars, bikes, trucks and people were shredded by more artillery shelling, until the scene was exactly like the worst parts of her tour in the Middle East. It was a slaughterhouse out there, plain and simple.

She thought she saw some of the masked gunmen make it as far as the fences, their impressive numbers making up for their suicidal tactics, but had no time to watch any more; she was leading Jack over the broken wasteland, stumbling over rotten dirt tracks and unused paths until the sounds of battle started to grow fainter and fainter.

They were in a protected lee now, the low lip of the bank providing some much-needed protection. Alyssa had no idea for how long they had been running, but the other prisoners were all gone, either run off in their own direction or killed by the horrendous cross-fire, and Alyssa and Jack were alone, their breathing ragged and hoarse.

'What are we going to do?' Jack whispered to her.

Alyssa looked at him with steely determination. 'I think we should count our blessings,' she said calmly, 'and get the hell out of here.'

2

'This whole thing is getting out of hand, David,' John Jeffries said, looking his old friend in the eye. General Tomkin stared straight back, until Jeffries had to turn away.

The two men had decided to meet in private and were now ensconced in a duplex apartment which Jeffries kept for his mistress, who was out of town for a few days. The apartment was registered in a false name, and had no connection on paper to either of the two men. Tomkin had still insisted that his own bodyguards conduct a thorough check of the building for both physical and electronic surveillance, but the place was clean.

'It's too late for second thoughts now, John,' Tomkin warned. 'Way too late. We're past the point of no return, I hope you understand that.'

'I think you're wrong,' Jeffries replied. 'I don't think we've gone too far yet. The weapon's been tested, yes. But we still haven't gone ahead with the plan. We don't have to.' He shook his head. 'We don't.'

Tomkin sighed inwardly. He had been waiting for this moment; it was bound to come sooner or later, and he was surprised it hadn't been sooner. The week's events had been enough to test any man. First, the repercussions from the

274

testing of the device; not only the strange phenomena themselves but the chaotic, violent backlash that had been unleashed across the globe as a result. People were literally scared for their very lives, thinking the world was about to end. Tomkin sympathized with Jeffries on that score; there was a hell of a job on to control the rioters and protesters.

And then there were those two fugitives that Anderson was chasing, the only people who had so far made the connection. The newspaper editor and the mayor had been taken care of, and bits of Ray Stevens had been identified scattered about the wasteland near the prison camp, after an unsuccessful attempt to liberate it by a group calling itself the 'Resistance'. The existence of such a group was another major worry, of course, but of more concern was the fact that no remains had so far been found of Alyssa Durham or Jack Murray. He had to assume that they were still alive, and potentially dangerous.

Still, at least the media was now under control. Tomkin relaxed into one of the comfortable leather couches which dotted the apartment's oak-floored living area. With the mayor under arrest, Jeffries had been worried about the political implications, but the attack on the internment camp had played right into their hands. 'Evidence' was fabricated that linked both Envers and Rushton with the resistance movement, and they had since been transferred to a tactical base for further investigation, a decision backed by the President himself. Other figures, in media and politics, would be scared to move against the authorities now, even if they knew anything, which they probably didn't.

So, while Tomkin understood that the past few days

had been testing, he did not see the problems as insurmountable. In fact, a lot of it played into their hands; when the entire thing was over, his country would have not only a military grip on the rest of the world, it would be able to claim the moral and even spiritual high ground.

Tomkin knew what was really bothering his friend. He took a sip of his drink. The fact was, Jeffries was getting cold feet about the agreed utilization of Spectrum Nine. Tomkin knew that it was one thing to talk about things in the abstract, but to see the results – as they had with that little island recently – tested the mettle of even the strongest man.

'John,' Tomkin said reasonably, placing his drink down on the coffee table between them, 'I know you are a patriot of the first order. You want what's best for your country. You want what's best for your countrymen. Isn't that so?'

'Of course it's so!' Jeffries exclaimed. 'But—'

Tomkin cut him off with a wave of his hand. 'But nothing,' he said firmly. 'But *nothing*. This country is being attacked on all sides. Terrorists everywhere, regimes building their own long-range missiles to wipe us off the map.' He banged his hand down on the coffee table. 'And are we going to just sit here and take it? Are we going to let them?' He shook his head. 'We sure as hell are not. I can't even believe you're faltering at this stage. Don't you remember what happened to Adam?'

'Don't you dare speak to me about that boy!' Jeffries spat back, but his vehemence was short-lived. 'Don't remind me about him,' he added softly.

Adam Jeffries, John Jeffries' eldest son, had lost his wife

and child in a terrorist bomb attack. Adam had been a fireman and was first on the scene, horrified that it was his own dead family he had to pull from the burning wreckage. He had left the fire service and signed up with the army the very next day. Sent to the Gulf, the young man only lasted three weeks before an improvised explosive device blew both his legs off, leaving him to bleed slowly to death in a ditch by the side of the road, his fellow soldiers unable to retrieve the body because of enemy sniper fire.

Terrorists had taken John Jeffries' son, daughter-in-law and grandchild in as horrible a way as could be imagined. Tomkin knew all of this, and it was one of the reasons why he had approached his old friend with the plan. Tomkin had needed some real political muscle behind the scheme, and Jeffries was the perfect match.

The trouble was, he was not a military man himself. He was the Secretary of Defence for the world's largest superpower but he had never fired a shot in anger, nor been shot at himself. He saw things like a civilian, and had a civilian's weaknesses.

Tomkin understood compassion, but compassion would never win wars. And that was what they were fighting. A damn *war*.

'Look, John, I know it's a morally repugnant act, what we're doing,' Tomkin said. 'Maybe we'll even be sent to hell for it. But that's why we need to be strong. You and me. Willing to sacrifice ourselves, even our mortal souls, to protect our great nation.'

Jeffries picked up his glass from the table and took a long drink, then looked across at Tomkin. 'You said we were going to present Spectrum Nine to the President. It was going to be his decision to use it, not ours.'

'I'm sorry about that,' Tomkin said. 'But we both know that he would never give the go-ahead. The project would just end up being mothballed, never used. Or even worse, the technology would get into enemy hands and then be used against us. How would you feel then?'

Jeffries' hands tightened round his glass. 'It would just be . . .'

'Easier?' Tomkin finished for him. 'Of course it would be. Give the responsibility to the other guy. Pushing the button yourself is much harder. You need to be stronger, much stronger.' Tomkin paused, levelling his gaze at his friend. 'John,' he asked, 'are you strong enough to go through with it?'

Jeffries finished his drink in one action and lifted his eyes to the ceiling as he asked himself the same question. Eventually, he looked at Tomkin.

'Yes,' he said evenly. 'I am. We will proceed as planned.'

Tomkin nodded his head, pleased.

Now he just had to hope that Anderson could find Murray and Durham, and take care of the only two people who could still cause problems.

3

'So what do we do now?' Jack asked as they sat shivering under the trees.

The forest protected them from the wind, but it was unseasonably cold, chilling them to the bone. They still had on the clothes they had been wearing since the meeting at the train station – jeans, pullovers and thin jackets – which had been sufficient for daytime in the city but were proving to be grossly insufficient for night-time in the forest.

'Now,' Alyssa said with chattering teeth, 'we make a fire.'

She set about telling Jack what type of leaves, twigs and branches to look for, and then they set off to gather what they needed.

As Alyssa searched in the undergrowth which bordered the clearing they had found, she suppressed a smile, despite their situation. Jack was such a city boy, she didn't think he'd ever had a night outdoors before. Luckily for him, she'd had plenty. Yet another thing that she and Patrick had liked to do together; nights out camping went hand in hand with the adventure sports they had always enjoyed.

Alyssa could at last think of Patrick without guilt; she

was with Jack now. Through circumstance perhaps, but she was with him nevertheless, and she was finally able to accept it.

She and Jack had walked – or rather limped in exhaustion – for the entire day, careful to avoid roads and any other signs of civilization. She didn't know how far they'd gone, but estimated their pace as no more than two miles per hour; twelve painful hours would have put them about twenty-four miles from the internment camp. Not far enough, to her mind. An attack on a federal internment camp? A resistance movement in her own country? And the response from the camp! Returning gunfire was one thing, but the use of artillery shells on native citizens was just too much. She truly never thought she'd live to see such a thing.

She had no idea where they were now, but assumed they'd made it to one of the vast national parks that bordered the city. Wherever it was, they should be safe for the time being. Nobody would be out here now; there was a curfew in place, and it wasn't likely that people would be allowed out of the city.

They were lucky in a way, she considered as she brushed aside some surface leaves to gather the dryer leaves below. If they hadn't been arrested and transported to the internment camp, they might never have made it out of the city. She paused, thinking about Ray Stevens. It was a shame he'd not been so lucky.

'Alyssa!' Jack called. 'Alyssa! Get over here!' He clearly didn't seem to consider the fact that other people might hear him.

She found him kneeling by a tree, his hands hidden down some sort of large hole.

'You've got to see this,' he said, beckoning her over with a muddy finger.

The hole Jack was looking down seemed to be manmade and out of it he was lifting wallets, mobile phones, car keys, money.

Alyssa bent down to look at the cache. There were passports, driving licences, social security cards for a whole host of people, men, women and children, probably about two dozen in all.

Jack looked up at her. 'I was looking for dry wood, like you said, and I found a big pile right here. I started to pick it up,' he pointed to the stack of branches and twigs he'd placed to one side, 'and then found this hole, covered with a bit of earth on top of a tarpaulin.'

'What does it mean?' Alyssa wondered.

'I don't know,' he said, pocketing two of the wallets, along with car keys and some cash, 'and I don't care. But now we've got ID, transport, and money. That solves a lot of our problems. I've got IDs for a man and a woman, about our age and description. The photos are no good, but we can work on that later. I've no idea where the cars are, but we might get lucky.'

Alyssa knew it made sense, although she felt guilty about taking other people's things. And that was another thing, she thought. 'Never mind the cars,' she said to Jack, 'where are the people?'

'Who cares?' Jack said.

'Why would they bury their ID and money out in the

middle of a forest like this?' she wondered out loud. 'The only reason would be if they wanted to leave their old lives behind, start afresh.'

'Why not burn it then?' Jack asked.

'In case they need it again. Once the threat has passed.'

'What threat?' Jack asked.

'The end of the world. I would guess these people have escaped into the woods to get away from what they think might be coming. They must be survivalists, maybe even extremists of some kind. You know the sort,' she said. 'But they don't know for sure if it's really true, so they're hedging their bets.'

All of a sudden, Jack looked unsure. Scared. 'They probably . . . They probably wouldn't go too far from where they buried it, would they?' he asked nervously.

'I'm not sure,' Alyssa answered, looking around the small clearing anxiously. 'But—'

She never finished the sentence, interrupted by the supersonic blast of a large calibre handgun echoing from the trees behind them, and the spray of wood bark as the tree in front of them erupted from the bullet's heavy impact.

'Get the hell away from there!' an angry male voice shouted from the woods and then Alyssa could hear other voices too – *Did you get them? – Where are they? – Come on! – There!*

There was another loud crack, and Alyssa pushed Jack aside as the tree trunk exploded just where they had been crouched, more wood splinters hitting them even as they raced for their lives into the forest, angry screams and gunfire pursuing them all the way.

* * *

Five minutes later, Alyssa and Jack crouched low, motion-less behind a long row of ferns. After an all-out sprint through the forest, they were struggling to control their breathing, trying to keep as quiet as they could. They hadn't heard the sounds of feet crashing through under-growth for a while now, and hoped that the survivalists had either gone the wrong way, or given up altogether.

'Do you think it's safe to move?' Jack asked, his voice strained from the chase.

'I'm not sure,' Alyssa whispered back to him.

'It ain't safe to move, darlin',' came a cold, hard voice from directly behind them.

Alyssa and Jack turned to see a large bearded man in a camouflage bush jacket staring at them, a wicked-looking hunting knife in his hand, the serrated blade ten inches long.

'I've got 'em!' he called out loudly. 'Over by the stand of ferns!'

Alyssa felt her heart rate quicken even more as the sounds of people moving through the forest reached her once more. They were running out of time.

'Damned government pigs,' the man drawled through his thick beard. 'How the hell did you find out about us?' When his captives didn't answer, he inched towards them menacingly. 'Ain't no matter,' he said. 'Ya goin' tell us everything anyway.' He turned his knife to admire the blade. 'Ol' Carol-Ann's gonna see to that, ain't ya, darlin'?'

He was talking to the knife, Alyssa realized with a sick

feeling. She heard footsteps getting closer, and knew that she had to act.

The man was still admiring his knife and Alyssa surged forward, her fingers snaking out towards his face. She ignored the knife, knowing she wasn't strong enough to wrestle it from his grasp. Instead, she drove her thumbs into the inside corners of his eyes, gouging deeply, the way she had been shown by some of the special ops soldiers she'd worked with in the Gulf.

The man screamed and dropped the knife. Alyssa ignored her feelings of disgust as she continued to drive her thumbs in, before turning them outwards, scraping the eyeballs from their sockets.

Clear, warm liquid ran down her thumbs on to her hands and wrists; one thumb slipped out with the fluid, whilst the other one came out with the eyeball itself, still attached by the slick, greasy optical nerve.

The man continued to scream as he went into a seizure, jerking in Alyssa's hands. She let go, disgusted with herself, and felt no satisfaction as the man fell to the floor, writhing in agony.

Jack just stared in stunned amazement. Alyssa picked up the hunting knife, grabbed him by the arm and pulled him away from the ferns.

She pushed through bushes and leapt over small streams and scattered branches, her mind on nothing at all but getting out of there alive. She could hear gunshots now, from different weapons – a big handgun, what sounded like a small-calibre hunting rifle, even a shotgun – but the rounds never found their mark. They came close once or twice, but mainly Alyssa could hear the bullets impacting trees well wide of their mark.

The darkness of the forest, occasionally punctuated by the light from the stars and moon whenever they reached a clearing, was both an advantage and a disadvantage. On the one hand, they couldn't see very well where they were going, which meant that they tripped up over logs or found themselves wading through muddy bogs too many times for a fast getaway. On the other hand, their pursuers were equally disadvantaged and the likelihood of their hitting anything was remote. They were probably aiming towards the noise that she and Jack made as they crashed through the forest, but sounds could be deceptive in such an environment. Anyone aiming a weapon would also have to stop to listen and then take aim, which would slow them down. The shotgun, whose scatter-shot effect covered a large area, was a worry, though. These guys also would undoubtedly know the forest much better than she and Jack did; it was possible some of their group was circling round to some known point ahead of them to cut them off. But what options did they have? They had to keep on running, it was as simple as that.

She could hear Jack's ragged breath next to her. At least he was keeping up. She had worried about his condition before, when they were working their way up the skyscraper's stairwell. Sheer terror was probably doing the work for him now. Sure, there had been armed men chasing them back in the city, but out here, things were different; the alien environment and irrational, unseen pursuers ratcheted up the terror to a whole new level.

Yes, she thought as they continued to race along, terror would keep Jack right by her side.

After all, it was having the same effect on her.

Five minutes and two terrifyingly close shotgun blasts later, Alyssa and Jack came bursting out from the forest's undergrowth into bright moonlight.

They could hear rushing water, just feet away. 'A river!' whispered Jack. He tugged at her arm. 'Come on!' he said. 'Let's go!'

But Alyssa could hear that the river was strong; they would have no chance crossing it. Instead, the current would simply take them downstream – to where? There might be rapids, and she imagined their bodies being smashed to pieces on the rocks.

'Have you got a better idea?' Jack asked, taking her hands and looking into her eyes. 'Come on, we've got to do this. It's our only chance.'

Alyssa was still reluctant. Maybe they could make their way down the river bank instead? But then another shot-gun blast sounded, and Alyssa felt the passage of warm air over her shoulder as the wide-spread pellets barely missed her.

She knew he was right. She gripped his hands, nodded once, and then they turned and threw themselves into the crashing river.

The two bodies were carried downriver at a frightening pace, swept along by the violent current.

Alyssa kept trying to find Jack, grasping hold of him

before losing him, time and time again. She struggled to keep her head out of the freezing, surging waters, gasping for breath in the small moments she had before the water came crashing down on her again.

The channel narrowed, the pace quickened and swept them towards huge boulders that glinted in the moonlight. But they came through unscathed, the path of the water guiding them straight down the middle, between the rocks which would have meant instant death if they'd come too close.

Alyssa lost all sense of time as the river swept them along, and was starting to lose all sensation in her body too. Somewhere in her mind, she realized she was starting to become hypothermic. She looked across the dark river for Jack, and found him moments later. Was he still alive? Spun this way and that by the current, it was hard to tell.

They would have to leave the river soon, she knew that in her befuddled mind. If they didn't, they would die.

'Jack!' she called out, swallowing river water as she was taken under by the current. Her head pulled free and she called again. 'Jack!'

'Alyssa!' she heard him call back, a huge wave of relief flooding her. 'We need to get out of this river!' he shouted.

'Start to head for the left-hand bank!' she yelled back. It was the closest, and would also put them on the other side of the river to their pursuers.

'OK!' Jack shouted back, and she watched as he started to struggle sideways against the current. She did the same, pushing hard against the seemingly solid wall of water.

They weren't going to make it. It was just too fast, too

powerful, and she was too weak now, her body failing after all it had been through.

'I can't do it!' she heard Jack call through the dark night, hearing the struggle in his voice as he continued to try and push towards the riverbank.

'Me neither!' she answered. She closed her eyes. Was this the end? After coming so far, would they die in this cold, dark river?

But then the sensation of the river changed ever so slightly, seeming both to widen out and get even faster at the same time; and then she heard the roar ahead of her, a sound that began to fill her head completely.

She was carried forwards faster and faster, only able to get small breaths now and again when she forced her head up out of the water. She thought she could hear Jack screaming but couldn't make out his words.

And then the vista opened out ahead of her, the moonlight showing the river coming to an abrupt end just twenty feet away, and she understood.

'Waterfall!' she heard herself screaming, even as she was pulled under and her mouth filled with cold water. Her mind went blank as she was pulled inexorably over the edge, her body plummeting two hundred feet into the watery abyss below.

4

It was over three hours later when Alyssa finally awoke, coughing and spluttering as her eyes opened, still convinced she was drowning.

But then she saw Jack, his arms wrapped close around her, and her anxiety eased. But where were they? She felt warm, at least. Then she realized there was a fire. She looked around her and saw they were inside a small shelter made from branches lined with ferns. Maybe Jack had more of an idea of what he was doing than he let on, she thought idly.

She saw their clothes hanging on makeshift drying poles over the fire, and realized that they were both naked, entwined on a bed of ferns.

'What happened?' she asked at last, when the dryness in her mouth eased slightly.

'We came down over the waterfall,' Jack explained. 'The water was deep, and you must have passed out when you hit, but it was a lot slower at the bottom and I managed to drag you to the bank. The left-hand side, like you said.'

She clutched his arm. 'Thank you,' she breathed.

He squeezed her back. 'You would have done the same,' he said.

She licked the dryness from her lips again. 'What happened then?' she asked.

'I realized we were both going to go hypothermic if we didn't get warm, so I followed your advice about how to make a fire, and got one started. You didn't tell me how hard it was!' he said light-heartedly. 'Without matches or a lighter, it must have taken me about forty minutes to get the damned thing going.' He smiled. 'But finally it caught, and I used some other bits of wood to make this little shelter, then stripped us both off, and . . . well, here we are.'

Alyssa nodded. 'Here we are,' she murmured and kissed him, a gesture of relief in being alive more than anything.

Jack reached forward, checking their clothes. 'They're nearly dry,' he said.

'Good,' Alyssa replied. 'It's must be nearly dawn. We're going to have to move.'

Jack nodded. 'Bad news about our travel plans,' he told her.

'Oh?'

'The car keys have gone, all of them. Not that we'd have been likely to find the cars anyway. I mean, they could have been parked anywhere.'

'The IDs?' Alyssa asked anxiously.

Jack pointed to the fire. 'Drying out along with the clothes. About three hundred in notes too, and some bank cards we might be able to use.'

'OK, that's not so bad. At least with ID we can rent a room or a car.'

Jack shook his head. 'I've been thinking about that. I don't think we're going to be able to do that,' he said. 'At least not until we've had a chance to change our appearance somewhat. The likelihood is that our pictures have been flashed across the country on every news channel in existence. They've probably had time to sort through the bodies by now, and realized we weren't there.'

'Did you manage to think of a plan while I was out of it?' she asked hopefully.

Jack smiled at her. 'Kind of. We need to find out who's behind Spectrum Nine. We can't go to the authorities; we've already seen that they're willing to kill friends of the mayor himself. The media's out too, as they've probably already spread stories about us which will make us less than reliable sources. Essentially, if we present ourselves, we'll be arrested again, and they're unlikely to make the same mistake twice and let us escape. So we're on our own. But I noticed back in Stevens' office that a lot of the information you found on the base's files was authorized by the user of a computer based in the headquarters of the Department of Defence.'

'And you can trace the user?'

'Yes, I think so,' Jack said.

'So all we need to do is get to a computer, right?'

Jack shook his head. 'The DoD uses a closed system, probably one of the most sophisticated anti-hacking programs in existence. You can't pull the user ID from outside.'

'You mean . . .'

'Yes,' he confirmed. 'We're going to have to break in.'

'But that's impossible!' Alyssa exclaimed. 'We're wanted fugitives, and you think we can just walk into one of the most secure locations in the entire country and access their computer systems? And what do we do then, even if we can get in?'

'I told you,' Jack said with a wink. 'I have a plan.'

They decided to follow the river, which eventually led them to a tourist parking lot. There were a couple of cars parked up, but luckily no people. Neither of them knew how to hot-wire a car so they followed the access road through the trees on foot, and out on to a main highway that cut through the park. They debated about what to do, whether to keep on walking or try and hitch a lift. Desperation won; they had no idea where they were, or how long they would need to walk before they came to civilization.

Traffic was light, no doubt due to the curfew and military lockdown, but the road did still have a fair number of users, people who were probably designated as having jobs vital for the economy or industrial infrastructure.

Alyssa and Jack were aware they looked bad – their clothes torn and barely dry, their appearance dishevelled and covered in cuts and bruises – but at least it meant they looked quite different from any photographs of them which might have been shown on the news recently.

When they saw a likely car – an ancient SUV driven by a kindly looking elderly couple – they showed themselves, and were rewarded when the car stopped moments later. Alyssa gave them a hastily concocted story about going on a camping trip days before and getting lost in the wilderness, which evoked the couple's sympathy and got them an invitation into the car.

The man told them about the roadblocks in the area and Alyssa asked to be dropped off at the nearest shopping mall, hoping there would be one before the first roadblock came up.

They arrived at a medium-sized retail park just forty minutes later, without having had to pass through any roadside security checks. They also discovered that they were now over sixty miles south-west of the city. They thanked the couple and made their way inside, careful to keep their faces away from the mall's CCTV cameras.

Alyssa went shopping for clothes for the two of them – conservative, muted colours that wouldn't attract attention – and also for spectacles and hair dye. She picked up two new cellphones at the same time.

Jack, meanwhile, found an internet café. As well as checking out the latest news on their situation, he spent the next hour researching how to make fake IDs.

When they met up later, Jack told her that very little information had been reported in the press – there was next to nothing about the attack on the internment camp – but their pictures had indeed been flashed across the nation's media as dangerous terrorist suspects.

In the bathrooms, they changed clothes, put on the clear-glass spectacles, and dyed their hair. Then they went to a passport photo booth to have their pictures taken.

While Alyssa shopped for more supplies, Jack went to

a stationery store to pick up scissors, superglue and plastic laminate and then made his way back to the bathrooms.

When they met up another hour later, Alyssa showed Jack the fleece tops which she had bought, with embroidered logos on them that another store had done for her. Large lettering across the back, company logo on the breast.

'Perfect,' Jack said, before showing her their new IDs.

Deciding that they had stayed long enough at the mall, they went to a car rental desk and used their new identification to hire a small family car. Their fake IDs were accepted with no sign of suspicion. Sterner security faced them at the roadblocks but there, too, they got through without a hitch and continued their journey southwards to the capital. On the outskirts of the city they stopped at a small roadside diner, where they changed into their fleece tops and pinned their brand-new company ID cards to their lapels before sitting down to eat, and to wait.

Jack had just picked up the menu to select a dessert when Alyssa's cellphone rang.

Jack looked up at her, and their eyes met, searching for mutual reassurance.

Alyssa answered the call. 'Beltway Security Systems, how may I help you?'

Phase one of the plan was about to commence.

5

THE HEADQUARTERS OF the DoD was one of the world's largest buildings, at least in terms of floor space.

Built to house an amalgamation of several government departments, it had been decided to position the huge structure just over the river from the President's own famous residence and the rest of the congressional and senatorial machinery on the hill beyond.

It was a bulky, ugly structure made out of visually unsympathetic concrete built on three hundred acres of what had once been swampy marshland, but it was an architectural marvel nevertheless; its creators had managed to cram nearly twenty miles of corridors into its floor plan. With close to seven million square feet of internal space, the building housed over thirty thousand employees. Almost four thousand of these employees worked within the Cyber Warfare Division, trying to protect the DoD's fifteen thousand separate computer networks from the ever-increasing threat of cyber attack and cyber terrorism. The department was based right in the heart of the building, in a huge cluster of offices connected to the main server rooms where the building's supercomputers and internal mainframes were housed.

Lieutenant Colonel Evan Ward was the lead cyber

warfare technician currently assigned to the operations room, and he contemplated the department's problems as he stared at the three separate flat-screen monitors that sat in front of him.

The main trouble was the large number of networks that operated within the building. Most office complexes used one system, but here, mainly as a result of numerous departmental mergers over the decades, there were now fifteen thousand vaguely interconnected systems. This was simply too many for the staff to even monitor, never mind adequately protect against external threats, especially for those networks connected to the outside world via the internet.

The really sensitive stuff – black projects, lists of agents, details of ongoing sensitive operations – was held exclusively on so-called 'closed' systems, able to be used internally only. Someone would have to get access to the room Colonel Ward now stood in to have a chance of accessing the information on those computers.

But still, he thought, his task was an unenviable one. Although he was good at his job, he was a military man first and foremost, as DoD protocol dictated. An outside computer expert – although arguably better at the job – would never be allowed to run a DoD department. And the problem ran right through the Cyber Warfare Division's staff from top to bottom. The government simply didn't pay enough to attract the very top people, which meant that Ward often had to outsource to private companies, at great expense. It was a perverse irony that more money was spent on external contractors than on the four thousand men and women directly under Ward's command.

The system was archaic, the staff underpaid and under-valued, but they somehow managed to struggle on. Ward took a sip from his steaming mug and thanked his lucky stars that the intelligence resources of other countries were in an even worse state than his own. It would be a dark day indeed if any enemy nation were to launch a concerted, technically thorough attack on the country's computer infra-structure.

'Sir,' a voice said from behind, and Ward swivelled in his chair to face the man.

'Yes, Sergeant,' he replied.

'We've got something in one of the systems.'

'What sort of something?' Ward asked, not too concerned. There was always *something*.

'A virus,' the sergeant replied. 'We've been working on it a while now, I know you don't like to be bothered normally, but it's a tough one.'

'Which system?' Ward asked, still not unduly concerned.

'Alpha Two Bravo,' the man said, then stopped as his boss's phone rang.

Ward answered instantly, listened for ten seconds, then put the phone down. 'Four more systems have gone down,' he said, more urgently now.

And then he saw more people heading for his desk, messages began to appear on his computer, and the phone started to ring again; all of his fears appeared to be coming true.

The virus was spreading everywhere.

* * *

Half an hour later, Ward received his damage report.

An unknown but highly dangerous virus had infected two hundred and forty-five of the DoD's 'open' networks, and although its progress had seemed to slow, other networks were still being sporadically infected. No major systems had yet gone down, but it was just a matter of time unless Ward could get a grip on it.

Nothing his staff was doing seemed to be working. He had called in people from across the division, pulling them from all but the most vital projects, until he had seven hundred people trying to stop the virus. But another half an hour later, a hundred more networks had become infected, and Ward knew the time had come to bite the bullet. It went against the grain, but he had to do it nevertheless.

He picked up the phone and dialled a number he had memorized long ago.

'Beltway Security Systems, how may I help you?' a cheerful female voice answered.

Reluctantly, Ward explained the situation and asked for help.

Alyssa hung up, smiled at Jack, and zipped up her Beltway Security Systems fleece.

Back at the mall, Jack had not only spent time in the internet café learning how to make fake IDs; he had infected the live, internet-connected part of the DoD's internal mainframe with a virus. He had also found out which external companies were used to deal with hacking and virus problems, and discovered that one communications security contractor was used almost exclusively.

Beltway Security Systems was based just outside the capital and did a wide range of work for the government, and for top multinational firms in the area. Its own security systems were good, but Jack had nevertheless managed to get his and Alyssa's new identities registered on to the company's database as long-term employees.

Jack knew that when the virus was detected, procedure would dictate that the DoD's own internal people would try and deal with it, and when they failed – as Jack was confident they would – they would contact Beltway Security Systems and arrange for contractors to come in and deal with the problem. He had hacked Beltway's telephone system to redirect calls from the DoD's computer centre to one of the cellphones Alyssa had bought. Pretending to be the Beltway control centre operator, she had taken Colonel Ward's direct number and told him a senior technician would call him back immediately. Ward had demurred, demanding the technician's number instead, which Alyssa had provided.

As they reached the car, Jack's own phone began to ring.

'You're on,' Alyssa told him, and Jack answered as he opened the car door.

'Dave Jenkins, Beltway,' Jack said, sliding into the passenger seat.

He listened to the voice on the other end for some time before speaking himself. 'Yes, sir, I understand. You've been passed through to me because my colleague and I are only twenty minutes away. We'll take a look, report back to Beltway, and then decide what sort of resources need to be mobilized.'

There was another pause before Jack gave the details of their new identities, including their employment codes at Beltway. He knew Ward would check the names against Beltway's database, but was confident their new identities would be there; security passes would be duly issued.

'Yes, sir,' Jack said again, before hanging up and turning to Alyssa, who was manoeuvring the car on to the highway. 'He's sending a man to meet us at the east gate. He'll escort us straight to the offices of the Cyber Warfare Division.'

Alyssa smiled. 'We're in.'

6

Oswald Umbebe surveyed the young men and women in front of him with pride.

They came from all over the world, members of elite special operations forces from a huge variety of countries. Indeed, some of the men and women in this room would once upon a time have been sworn enemies of one another. They may even have faced each other across a hostile battlefield, Umbebe considered as he appraised them. But not now. Now they were brothers and sisters, united within the Order of Planetary Renewal. True believers, all of them.

Some had been with him from the start, others had been recruited more recently. But all could be trusted, Umbebe was sure of that. He had a sixth sense for such things.

They were at a disused military airfield, which was to be the staging ground for the next phase of Umbebe's strategy. The travel had not agreed with him, and his condition was getting steadily worse. He was in a great deal of pain now, almost constantly. And yet he didn't let it trouble him. Why would he? There wasn't long left for any of them anyway.

He had nearly forty soldiers in this personal attack force, all elite commandos. There would be other elements in the background too, a further sixty men and women with military experience to deal with logistics and security, but the soldiers in front of him now would be the spearhead.

The main attack force would come in four sections of eight commandos, with another section in reserve. Umbebe had rented land further south where the team had been rehearsing the attack for weeks. They had been at this airfield for the past two weeks, training and acclimatizing to the altitude and freezing temperatures. As Umbebe walked up and down their lines, he could see that they were ready.

'My brothers and sisters,' he intoned, 'true believers. The time has almost come for us to make the supreme sacrifice. You are all experts in your field, selected and trained to be the best. And you are.' He nodded his head to them. 'It is time now to use those skills to achieve our ultimate aim. The rebirth of our planet!'

Umbebe could see that some of the commandos wanted to cheer but were held in check by military discipline.

'You will have to kill,' he continued. 'We will all have to kill. And, likewise, we will all have to die. But we do so knowing it is for a better world! A new world, free of human vice, industry, pollution; a world where nature will once more reign supreme, allowing the green lung to fill again, to breathe once more.'

Symbolically, he breathed in deeply. 'Ah, to breathe air that is clean and fresh. This is what we give to the world. Mankind will be driven from the planet but, if fate decrees it, we will rise again, perhaps wiser than we are today. But that,' he said, raising his arms skyward, 'is not in our hands. What will be, will be. Our sole duty is to purge this diseased earth, to wipe the slate clean so that life can start anew and afresh. This is our divine responsibility, and I thank you, my brothers and sisters, for joining me on this crusade.'

His hand went to his chest, his head bowed, and the hundred men and women gathered on the airfield did the same. After a few moments of quiet reflection, Umbebe raised his head to address the crowd one final time. 'Our mission is sacred, let us never forget that. We will die so that the earth may live!'

He raised one fist high into the air in a gesture of defiance, letting out an animal roar that pierced the cold blue sky beyond.

And, despite the pain in his stomach, he smiled with undiluted joy when his chosen people raised their own fists in return, letting out their own screams of joy, pride, exultation and defiance.

Yes, he thought to himself, *they are ready*.

Now all he needed were the codes.

Anderson stood at the edge of the river, seething with anger. The dogs had lost the trail.

They had followed the scent for over twenty miles, right into the forest, tracking the fugitives through the trees and undergrowth. But then they'd got to the river – a wide, fast-running monster – and the dogs had come to a dead halt.

Durham and Murray hadn't trekked along the riverbank, that much Anderson could be sure. But had they swum to the other side? With the water as fast as it was, he wasn't sure if the pair could have made it. Still, he reasoned, adrenalin was a powerful thing. He'd send a team across with the dogs to check the other bank just to be sure.

Another possibility was that they'd tried to swim across and been swept downstream. Where did the river go? Anderson checked the map he carried, saw quickly that it led to a waterfall a couple of miles further down. Could they have survived if they'd gone over the side? He just didn't know.

Quickly, he organized his search teams into two groups; one would search this bank downstream and try and pick up the scent in case they'd managed to get to shore, either before or after the waterfall, while the other would try and get across the river to do the same on the other side.

Until he had evidence to the contrary, Anderson had to assume that they were still alive. Certainly, no bodies had been reported having washed up anywhere recently.

'Colonel!' came an excited voice from behind him, and Anderson turned to see one of his men racing from the trees. 'We've found evidence of a gunfight in the forest!'

'What?' Anderson asked with sudden interest.

'We've got casings for various different weapons, handguns and rifles, as well as shotgun shells. Damage to trees and foliage too, in keeping with a firefight. Well, a one-way firefight anyway,' the soldier continued. 'This early it's hard to tell, but it looks like the gunfire was just going one way.'

'Anything else?' Anderson asked.

The soldier nodded. 'We've got some blood in a small clearing, and some sort of man-made hole in the ground, with a tarp sheet to one side.'

'What's inside?' Anderson asked.

'Nothing,' the soldier replied. 'It's empty.'

Anderson thought for a moment before giving his orders. 'OK, here's what I want to see happen. We've got a gang of armed people in these woods, and I want them found. That blood's not from our targets or the dogs would have picked it up, so that means one of their party is injured. If we can find them, they can tell us what happened.' He quickly assigned men to the task, and they raced off back into the woods, along with two dogs to follow the blood trail.

He looked out across the river, glinting in the midday sun. With dogs on both sides, and possible eyewitness testimony, he hadn't lost them yet. There was still hope.

Dr Niall Breisner looked at the telephone with trepidation. It was time to make the call.

A large part of him didn't want to do it. The ramifications of his actions were starting to plague him, and he had all but stopped watching the news. The strange animal phenomena, the riots, the mounting chaos were bad enough; but he couldn't stomach any more reports about that little island, swallowed up whole by the ocean. It was just too much to bear.

But this was what he had agreed to, and neither Tomkin nor Jeffries had ever lied to him. General Tomkin had laid it out for him as plain as day, the first time they'd met. His plans were crystal clear. The technological, scientific challenge had been a tremendous lure, Breisner had to admit. Was such a thing possible? Breisner had believed so, and he had wanted to be proved right. His ego had demanded satisfaction.

And what was the result of his years of secretive, covert efforts? The endless months of research, analysis, experimentation, all covered up from the majority of the base's scientific staff? The fear of discovery, the pain and guilt of Colonel Anderson's ruthless prosecution of anyone who came too close? The end result, Breisner was loath to admit, was nothing like he had anticipated. He had dreamt of champagne celebration and pride and joy at a job well done, a job everyone thought impossible but which he alone had had the ability to see through to completion.

But now? Now, whenever the pride of success entered his heart for even a second, guilt expunged it in an instant. What had he been thinking? Spectrum Nine was a monster, no sane person should ever have conceived it.

But it was *his* monster, Breisner thought as he toyed with the telephone handset on his desk. Didn't he deserve some reward for his work, the decades spent in this Arctic hellhole, separated from his family and loved ones?

He deserved *something* at least, and the five million bonus promised by Tomkin in his next pay packet would go a certain way to assuage the guilt. Not all the way, but it would be a good start. He could forget about peer adulation or professional recognition; none of his peers even knew about the project. No, instead of awards and prizes, cold, hard cash would have to do.

But still, he found it hard to dial the number. It was too late to turn back, he knew that, but his mind baulked at this final step. He shook his head, downed the contents of the glass in front of him, and dialled the number for General Tomkin.

'David,' he said with false cheer, 'Spectrum Nine is ready.' He breathed out slowly, trying to regulate his heart rate. 'Your weapon is now fully operational.'

7

WHEN ALYSSA AND Jack arrived at the huge concrete bunker which served as the eastern entrance to the Department of Defence headquarters, they were both awed by the sheer scale of the building beyond.

Alyssa had read about it often, but seeing it in the flesh was something else altogether. She looked at the double steel access doors, with metal detectors and armed guards, and wondered, not for the first time, how they could possibly get away with their plan.

They had already passed through two external cordons to get this far – once at the entrance to the parking lot, and again at the perimeter of the actual building. Both times their identities had aroused no suspicion. But the further they got into the belly of the beast, the less confident Alyssa felt. She wondered how well Jack had hacked into the Beltway system. Would they begin to suspect something and contact the DoD? Maybe they were performing a routine check of employees and would come across Dave Jenkins and Elaine McDowell – Jack and Alyssa's current assumed identities – and wonder why nobody at Beltway had ever heard of them.

Ahead of her, a steady stream of workers filtered

through the security checkpoint. She looked past the queue and saw a man in a blue military uniform waving from the doorway, ushering them forward.

Well, she thought as she and Jack walked past the incoming workers, *it's too late to back out now*.

Five minutes later, they were being led down one of the complex's long corridors by their escort, who had introduced himself as Sergeant Adam Fielding. This pleasant young man was a private aide of Lieutenant Colonel Evan Ward, the man in charge of the Cyber Warfare Division, who had placed the call to Beltway.

The only hold-up at the concrete bunker entrance was when the security guards had to wait for the computer to print off their internal passes. They wore these ID cards now and this, combined with the presence of Sergeant Fielding, made them feel almost as if they really did belong here. Alyssa had been worried about people recognizing them from the news, but their simple disguises of glasses and dyed hair seemed to do the trick. Nobody was paying much attention to them anyway – hardly surprising really, Alyssa reflected, in an organization that employed thirty thousand people.

'We're pretty much on a war footing at the moment,' Fielding told his guests. 'With things as they are, word has come down to increase our threat level to only one stage removed from all-out war. I don't blame them,' he continued, and Alyssa presumed he meant the federal government. 'Things are getting crazy out there, and the military is already having to step in. It's not just in this country either.'

Fielding led them round two more corners, stopped at a bank of elevators and pressed a button. 'There have been plenty of attacks on our people abroad too. With all this talk of global destruction, a lot of groups – not just terrorists, but normal citizens too – feel it's their last chance to make a mark, and we're the target, yet again. The President just ordered two carrier groups out to southern Asia, and another to the Gulf.'

The elevator doors opened and Fielding stepped in. 'It's unbelievable, it really is. I mean, is it our fault this is happening? Of course not. But do we have to step in yet again to pick up the pieces, make sure the world remains stable? You bet we do.' He sighed. 'Anyway, that's why people around here aren't exactly a barrel of laughs at the moment.'

The doors opened again, and Alyssa realized she hadn't even felt the elevator move. Fielding strode out towards another long corridor, and Alyssa and Jack hurried to keep up.

'What do you guys make of it all?' Fielding asked, breaking a smile. 'Do you think we're all goners?'

'People have been saying the same for years,' Jack said. 'I don't suppose now's any more likely than any other time.'

Fielding grunted, and Alyssa wasn't sure if it was supposed to have been a laugh.

'But on the other hand,' Jack went on, 'it's probably gonna be true one day, right? Why not today?'

Fielding grunted again and turned away, increasing his pace. The man wasn't laughing this time.

* * *

310

'I'm not telling you pigs anything,' the grizzled old man said to Anderson, before spitting on the colonel's shoes.

Anderson responded in an instant, backhanding the man across the face. A stream of phlegmy blood shot out of the man's mouth, along with two teeth. The man sagged for a moment with the impact and then burst forward, straining for all he was worth against the two soldiers who held him.

There had been a nasty gunfight when they had found the survivalists. Six of the group's members were killed, along with two of Anderson's own men. When Anderson entered the camp, he was surprised to see that there were children there; and the surprise had turned to shock when he discovered that the children, too, were armed.

Durham and Murray must have stumbled upon the group and been hunted through the forest.

But who the hell were these people? He'd ordered his men to search the camp for anything that could identify them. In the meantime, he wanted to know what had happened to Murray and Durham.

He turned back to the old man. 'These people are terrorists! They want to destroy this country. I thought you were patriots.'

But the old man just regarded Anderson with hatred and spat again. 'You big government pukes are the only ones who want to destroy this country,' he said vehemently.

Anderson resisted the urge to hit the man again and looked over to where another member of the survival group was receiving medical attention for his maimed eyes. He had refused help at first, and Anderson's men had had to use drugs to subdue him. Durham or Murray must have gouged them, Anderson felt sure. He couldn't help but be impressed by their will to survive.

'Look at your friend,' Anderson said. 'I doubt he'll ever see again. He'll be completely blind, and I know one of the people we're after did it to him. Don't you want to help us catch them?'

The man shook his head. 'We thought they was government pukes like you at first,' he said, then smiled, the broken teeth making his face look grotesque. 'But they ain't with you, I know that much now. And the enemy of my enemy is my friend.'

Anderson looked at the man a moment longer before anger got the better of him, and he punched the captive square on the jaw, knocking him out cold. He watched with satisfaction as the body sagged into the arms of his men before turning away.

'Colonel, we've found something!' a voice called and a soldier came running across with a clear plastic bag full of documents and keys.

It didn't take long to match the various IDs to their captives and the dead bodies, apart from some of the children who may have been too young to have any. The problem was, two of the adults present had no documents. A man and a woman.

Anderson sighed. Two sets of ID were missing, and you didn't have to be a genius to figure out who'd taken them. *Damn.* But if he could find out who the two people were, he'd know what names Murray and Durham were using.

He told his men to take the fingerprints of the two with

no ID and send them off for analysis. The problem was, how long would it take?

He called for the pair to be brought forward, straining against their plastic flexicuffs. Torture wasn't his favourite thing in the world, but it was sometimes a necessary tool of his trade.

8

Colonel Ward stood and extended a large hand. 'Mr Jenkins,' he said courteously, shaking Jack's hand. 'Ms McDowell,' he said next, shaking her hand and inclining his head towards her. 'Thanks for coming out here so quickly. We've got a real ball-buster of a virus here – begging your pardon, ma'am – and we're struggling with it, to be frank.'

Jack nodded. 'OK,' he said. 'What we need is an office where we can get some privacy, four fully networked computers, and a vat-load of strong black coffee.'

Ward smiled, pleased with Jack's confidence. 'You've got it,' he answered.

Within a few minutes, Jack and Alyssa were in a corner office. Three more computers were carried in to sit on the desk beside the room's original unit, and the coffee came moments later.

The only fly in the ointment was Ward, who sat down in the room with them. Alyssa turned to him, smiling.

'Colonel, thank you for the office. But we really must insist that we are left alone. Some of the code work we use is proprietary information, and Beltway has a legal obligation not to reveal anything which has copyright or other intellectual property ramifications.'

'You think I'm gonna steal your algorithms?' Ward asked unbelievingly.

'We're a private contractor,' Jack chipped in, 'a business. We rely on being the best in the field, and we've got to be careful. I'm sure you appreciate that.'

'And I've got the security of the whole damned country to worry about. Surely you can appreciate *that*?' Ward responded icily.

'I do, but our hands are tied,' Alyssa said. 'Company procedure.'

'Well, maybe I'll just call up your boss and tell him I'm switching our preferred contractor to Armordyne Systems,' Ward responded.

Alyssa looked nervously at Jack. If Ward called anyone at Beltway, it could cause all manner of problems. They simply couldn't take the risk. But how were they going to access the system and find out anything with Ward watching their every move?

'OK, OK,' Jack said, holding up his hands. 'You've just got to understand, it goes against procedure.'

'I don't give a damn what procedure it goes against, I'm staying in the room and that's all there is to it.' Crossing his arms, Ward sat back in his seat.

'OK,' Jack said again, taking a sip from his coffee cup and turning back round to face the computer, cracking the knuckles of both hands as he did so. 'Let's see what we've got here.'

* * *

Alyssa's nerves were starting to grate. She was trying to talk to Ward, to get him involved in a conversation so that his attention was off Jack and the computers, but it was proving difficult.

Ward was watching Jack carefully, which meant that he had to go through the protocol to find and eradicate the virus rather than try and identify which computer terminal in the building had been used to sign off on Spectrum Nine. He would be able to stop the virus; after all, he was the one who had embedded it in the first place. But Alyssa could tell he was trying to string it out, maybe in the hope that Ward would have to leave the room to deal with something else, or even just to use the bathroom.

Alyssa was also wondering how long it would take before Ward asked her what her role was here; so far, she hadn't touched a computer. How could she? Her level of understanding was far below Ward's own, and it would be pretty obvious as soon as she tried that she had no idea what she was doing.

Finally Ward stood up to go to the bathroom, but he got one of his colleagues to cover the room in his absence. Alyssa watched Ward through the dark glass of the office windows to make sure he actually did head for the bathroom; part of her had worried that he was going to make a call to Beltway anyway.

They were going to have to do something, that was for sure. But what? Alyssa checked the time. Three thirty-five in the afternoon. She thought for a few moments. Ward hadn't left the room for over an hour, and presumably wouldn't now be needing another rest break for some considerable time. During that hour, nobody had disturbed them, which indicated that Ward had asked to be left alone, probably delegating his other duties temporarily to a junior officer. Any change in shifts would be on the hour or the half-hour, which gave them until four o'clock. Twenty-five minutes.

Alyssa rose from her chair and went to the window to lower the blinds. The other man looked up at her, eyebrows raised. 'The noise bothering you?' he asked.

Alyssa nodded her head. 'Yeah, Dave likes it a little more quiet than this usually,' she answered.

The man shrugged his shoulders. 'Figures,' he said. 'You can hardly hear yourself think out there on the best of days.'

Alyssa smiled, hoping that when Ward returned, he wouldn't immediately notice that the windows had been covered. He might not, she reasoned, as the room was still well-lit, and not dramatically quieter.

Moments later, Ward re-entered the room. 'OK, Corporal,' he said, 'thanks for that, you're relieved.'

The corporal left, and Ward sat back down in his seat, seemingly unaware that the interior of the office could no longer be seen from the outside.

Alyssa waited until Ward's attention was on Jack, watching as he leant forward in his chair to peer at the monitors, asking how he was progressing. Jack saw Alyssa moving, and started to involve the colonel in an intense discussion of what he was doing, and how far he had to go, capturing the man's attention completely.

Having manoeuvred herself directly behind Ward's

chair, Alyssa hefted her own collapsible steel chair above her head and swung it down as hard as she could on top of the colonel's skull.

Ward looked dazed, his eyes focusing and unfocusing for what seemed like minutes but was probably under two seconds, while Alyssa wondered if she'd hit him hard enough. She readied the chair to hit him again but then his eyes turned upwards, closed completely, and he toppled unconscious to the carpeted floor.

As Alyssa went to bind and gag him, she looked up at Jack who was staring at her in open-mouthed surprise. 'OK, Jack,' she said, checking her watch, 'you've got eighteen minutes.'

9

'DAVID NATHANIEL JENKINS and Elaine Jolene McNulty,' Anderson repeated to himself as he wiped his hands clean on an old rag, now stained red with blood.

The bodies of the real Jenkins and McNulty hung before him from a tree, pools of blood beneath their feet. They were still alive, but only by a hair's breadth. They were tough sons-of-bitches, but Anderson had still managed to break them ahead of the fingerprint lab.

'Cut them down and get them medical attention,' he called to one of his corporals.

Anderson flipped open his cellphone and called Tomkin. 'Sir, it's Anderson. We have reason to believe the fugitives may still be at large. We've tracked them to a river but we've not found any bodies, so we have to assume they are still alive. Also, they may have acquired identification which they could be presently using.'

He read out the names of the man and woman, along with other details he had gleaned from them – dates and places of birth, home addresses, car registrations. He knew he didn't have to tell Tomkin what to do with the information. The general would instantly activate every resource to track the fugitives.

'Leave it with me,' the general's gruff voice responded. 'I'll be in touch.'

'Yes, sir,' Anderson said.

His radio blipped. He pushed the button to receive. 'Anderson here, over.'

'Sir,' the digitally-enhanced voice came back, crystal clear, 'we're on the far bank a mile downstream from the waterfall. We've got tracks. The dogs are ready to follow, over.'

'Good,' Anderson replied. 'I'm going to stay here to clear up what we've found, but I'll send the other patrol to your side, over.'

'Yes, sir. Over and out.'

Anderson replaced the radio on his belt and smiled. Durham and Murray wouldn't get much further, he was sure.

James Rushton banged against the steel door again and again. It seemed as if he had been banging against the cold, hard surface all afternoon; and, when he thought about it, he supposed he had.

He looked at his hands, and saw they were deep purple with bruising. But dammit! Here he was, locked up without charge and unable to see a lawyer. He knew that somewhere else in the building Harry Envers was also an unwilling prisoner, unable to use his right to legal advice. The damn city mayor! It was entirely unconstitutional, but Rushton was beginning to understand that this was becoming an issue of less and less importance. The city – hell, the whole country and maybe even the entire world

– was changing. Events were out of control and had gathered a momentum of their own.

Rushton had assumed he would be tortured, or at least subjected to tactical interrogation, but he had been left alone. He thought that that was probably because the government's limited resources were being stretched to breaking point. They had achieved their aim by locking him up anyway; he was away from his beloved newspaper and couldn't get a word out to anyone about anything.

This was why he had been trying to get someone to come to his cell all afternoon; if he could tell someone – *anyone* – what he knew, questions might start to get asked in the right places. It was something to hope for, at any rate.

He wondered what had happened to Alyssa and Jack Murray. Were they still alive? He hoped so.

He approached the door to bang again, but thought better of it. He'd break his hands if he wasn't careful, and what good was it doing anyway? It was working off his frustration, but that was about it.

He turned to the other side of his cell and stood on the iron bed to look out of the small, barred window. He knew where he was, at least – the city's historic political prison, on the other side of the government plaza from the mayor's office. It had once housed dissenters and protesters, coming into its own during the civil war years ago. It was open now only as a museum, but Rushton saw that the cells were as practical as ever they had been; there was no way to escape.

He peered through the window to the plaza, six storeys

below. He'd tried to attract attention, but the citizens who still dared to be out and about were keeping themselves to themselves and wouldn't have looked up towards his window even if they had heard him.

He was about to lie back on his bed to nurse his aching hands when he saw a curious sight down in the plaza. Whereas most people walked with their heads bowed, ignoring everything around them in the hope that the situation would just go away if they pretended it didn't exist, a group now rounded the corner with an air of confidence that was in stark contrast to this attitude.

The group were dressed in clean white robes and were wearing what appeared to be gold armbands, but it was the way they carried themselves that made them conspicuous: proud, confident, their bearing that of soldiers on parade.

Their clothes reminded him of that man on television the other night, Oswald Umbebe, the 'high priest' of – what was it? – the Order of Planetary Renewal. Rushton had been seeing more and more of these characters over the past few days, the order really seemed to be speaking to people, and men and women were signing up in droves. A part of him could see why. If people were going to die – as millions clearly thought they were – then it was easier if they believed it was for a purpose.

But what were they doing now? Rushton held on to the window bars with his bruised hands and pulled his head nearer to get a better look. They were spreading out around the plaza, ringing it in a huge circle. How many were there? Rushton tried to count them, and thought it must be at least fifty, all dressed in identical white tunics. They made quite a sight.

They knelt together on the concrete paving and started to chant. Rushton strained to hear but he was too far away. He wondered how long it would be before soldiers came to move them along. This sort of mass prayer was now regarded as an illegal demonstration, and the robed figures were liable to be arrested if they didn't disband soon.

And then, as a crowd started to gather and people began to record the event on cameras and cellphones, one of the group stood and walked to the middle of the circle of devotees. He pulled what looked like a tin from under his robe, and started to empty the contents over his head, dousing himself in some sort of liquid.

Rushton gasped as the man then lit a match, realizing that it must have been gasoline that he had poured over himself. And then, before Rushton could fully comprehend what he was watching, the man touched the match to his head and his body went up in flames.

Rushton looked on in horror as the man stood there, engulfed in fire; time seemed to stand still as first his robes and then his body visibly melted away until he finally fell, first to his knees, and then to his hands, until all that remained was a burnt, charred corpse.

Rushton was stunned. The man had never even screamed.

And then Rushton, even after nearly four decades of reporting from all corners of the globe, looked on in utter astonishment at what happened next. As if called to action by the man in the middle, each of the other robed followers produced their own cans and poured the contents over themselves before lighting matches and setting themselves on fire. Within seconds there were fifty flaming, burning bodies writhing on the plaza. Some didn't have the self-discipline of the first man, and screamed. Rushton could hear their agonized cries through the thick glass of his sixth-floor cell.

Some of the onlookers left, appalled at what they were seeing; others carried on filming, and Rushton knew, media ban or no media ban, these images would be all across the world within minutes.

He watched for the remaining minutes that it took for the men and women to burn to death, the soldiers, police and fire officers who raced to the scene with extinguishers and blankets simply too late. All that was left were charred remains and gold armbands scattered across the plaza.

Rushton knew it was impossible but he was sure he could smell the horrific stench of charred human meat, even all the way up here in his cell.

His face pale, shaken to his core, Rushton staggered off the bed and just made it to the toilet in the corner of his cell before he threw up.

What were they thinking? he sobbed into the toilet bowl. *What were they thinking?*

10

'COME ON,' ALYSSA said, looking over at Jack as she waited nervously by the office door.

'I'm going as fast as I can,' Jack told her. 'Leave me alone.'

Alyssa didn't say another word, knowing he was right; her nagging him wouldn't help anything. She turned back to the windows, peeking through the slats of the blinds. The sprawling complex of offices and cubicles outside was a seething mass of humanity, but nobody appeared to be paying any attention to their own small office.

Alyssa checked her watch. Just seven minutes to four. Her heart rate increased automatically. They had seven minutes to get out of here. It was true that nothing might happen at four, but she didn't want to take the chance. It was a time many people left for the day, and Ward might be expected to be somewhere else.

Come on, she urged Jack again, silently this time.

'OK,' Jack said instants later, 'I've got it. The computer is located in the office of General David Tomkin, which is . . .'

His voice trailed off, and Alyssa realized he was trying to memorize the route. 'Why are you checking where it is?' Alyssa asked. 'I thought all the information was here?'

Jack shook his head, still studying the screen. 'I'm afraid not. I said this system was secure. What we need is on this general's personal computer, possibly nowhere else. This system just told me who the computer belonged to and where we can find it, that's all.'

'So now we need to break into a general's office?' she asked, aghast. Jack hadn't explained that to her. 'And what do we do about *him*?' she said, pointing at Ward, who was starting to drift back to consciousness.

'I didn't ask you to smash him over the head with a steel chair, Alyssa,' Jack said.

'Well, excuse me for coming up with a plan,' Alyssa shot back.

'You call assaulting a senior military officer in the head-quarters of the Department of Defence a plan?' Jack asked, eyebrows raised.

Before Alyssa could respond, Jack held up one hand to stop her and picked up a telephone handset with the other. He checked the screen again, and dialled a number.

'Is that General Tomkin's office?' he asked. 'Is he in?' There was a pause on the other end of the line, and Alyssa checked her watch. Four minutes to four.

'OK, not to worry,' Jack continued. 'This is Colonel Ward, head of cyber security, clearance access code delta two four nine alpha tango three four nine. You're probably aware of the virus that's been going through our systems, and we've traced it to General Tomkin's computer. I'm going to need access to his office for two contractors we have here from Beltway Security Systems, David Jenkins and Elaine McDowell. They have full authorization from my department.'

There was another pause, then Jack spoke again. 'Thank you, ma'am,' he said. 'They will be there in five minutes.'

He replaced the receiver and looked at Alyssa. 'It seems that whoever this General Tomkin is, he's just left. Flying off somewhere, apparently. But that means his office is wide open.' Jack stood and grabbed his jacket from the back of his chair. 'Come on,' he said. 'Let's get out of here.'

'And him?' Alyssa asked, pointing at Ward.

'I'm sure you'll think of something,' Jack said.

Tomkin smiled at the people he passed in the long corridors, something he rarely did. Breisner's phone call was the reason. The news that Spectrum Nine was ready produced the same feeling as a parent had on the day of their child's birth. It was relief and pure joy, albeit mixed with subconscious tinges of fear and anxiety. But after so long, so many years of toil, it was ready.

Tomkin thought back to the time he had spent in the military, fighting his country's enemies all over the world in one form or another. He'd been badly injured, and had lost many of his closest friends. Now he was one step further down the path of ensuring that this would happen no more. Not for his country the mindless infantry struggle, or even the more impersonal clash of armoured vehicles or air strikes. No, not any more. Soon it would all be over, the enemy killed, with no more loss of life on his own side. It was a wonderful thought for a career military man.

A helicopter was waiting for him just outside the

building, which would whisk him to a military airfield a few miles away. From there, he would get on board a personal jet and fly directly to the HIRP base to take over the operation himself.

Yes, he thought as he walked down another long corridor towards the waiting helicopter, *the world is just about to get one hell of a lot better*.

After leaving the office, Alyssa had explained to the nearest person that Ward wanted privacy to deal with some sensitive information that had been lost due to the virus.

In the meantime, Jack asked for an escort to General Tomkin's office, repeating the line about the virus having originated there. Alyssa had been impressed by Jack's confidence; with an escort, they would be able to pass through security checks with no problem, as long as her own story about Ward was believed and nobody went into the office.

And so it was that within the promised five minutes, they arrived at the desk of Tomkin's secretary. Jack and Alyssa thanked their escort, who made his way back to the CWD.

'Now, how can I help you guys?' the secretary – a blue-suited air force man, back ramrod straight and hair cut short – asked pleasantly.

Jack handed over a sheet of paper. 'I believe Colonel Ward called about our visit,' he said.

Alyssa glanced at the paper, which seemed to be some sort of official work order, and was impressed that Jack had managed to produce such a document so quickly.

The man studied the sheet of paper then looked up at them. 'OK,' he said, and rose from his desk, heading for the door to Tomkin's inner office, unlocking it with a key attached to his leather belt. 'Here you go.'

Alyssa was amazed when he just opened the door and ushered them in. 'I've got a load of work on,' he said, 'so I'll be just out here if you need me, OK?'

Alyssa and Jack thanked him and entered the office, Alyssa thinking that the man, though very pleasant, could do with a talk from Colonel Ward about security. She pushed the door closed behind her.

Jack was already at the general's desk. 'Damn,' he breathed. 'General Tomkin's the Chairman of the Joint Chiefs.'

Alyssa gasped. The name had been familiar but she hadn't been able to place it.

'That's pretty high,' she said. 'I wonder if it goes any higher.'

Jack turned the computer on. 'Well, let's have a look, shall we?'

11

Colonel Anderson waited in the forest clearing, hearing the noise of the helicopter still some way out.

Tomkin had put the names out everywhere, and results were already coming in. The general wasn't playing an active part himself now as he was about to leave for HIRP to take control of the Spectrum Nine deployment, but he had informed his sources to liaise directly with Anderson.

The fugitives had been traced to a mall not too far from here, where they had hired a car with the stolen ID. Traffic cameras had shown that they were headed towards the capital, but Anderson was now waiting for further updates on the exact location of the vehicle. He knew that when he had the car, he would have the fugitives.

His men had gone from store to store in the mall, trying to piece together what they had bought, if anything. The information that came back indicated that they may have changed their appearance with glasses and hair dye, and they might even have adjusted the pictures on the photo IDs. His men were still there making inquiries, but Anderson had no doubt where they were headed; it had to be the capital.

He shook his head in disbelief. Rather than try and

escape, they still wanted to continue with their investigation. They were determined, he'd give them that much.

Anderson looked up and saw the chopper hovering above the treeline. If Durham and Murray were heading for the capital – and they might even be there by now – then that was where he was going too.

The chopper began to descend, and Anderson nodded to his men – his six best, chosen to accompany him on what he hoped would be the last phase of the chase. They started to move with him towards the landing zone.

His cellphone vibrated in his pocket, and he backed off to take the call.

He strained to hear what he was being told over the screaming of the helicopter rotors. He made out, 'Fleece jackets . . . Embroidered . . . Beltway Security Systems . . .'

An icy premonition hit him, and he gestured at the chopper pilot, who cut power to the engines, slowing the rotor blades and quietening the deafening noise.

Anderson turned away and dialled another number. 'It's Anderson,' he said urgently. 'I want you to put me through to Beltway Security Systems. Immediately.'

Secretary of Defence John Jeffries couldn't comprehend what was going on, he really couldn't.

Spectrum Nine was ready, and Tomkin was on his way to take charge, and that was one thing to be grateful for, but the news coming in from around the country was simply horrific.

Who the hell are the Order of Planetary Renewal? the President had asked just a short time ago. None of the people in the room had been able to answer him. Not the intelligence chiefs, not the Secretary of State, none of his key political or military aides. The closest anyone got was to recognize that the order's 'high priest' had been on television some nights before.

As Jeffries had watched the footage, shown around the world already on social media sites but compiled into one long video by the President's staff, he had almost been sick. There had been scenes in every major city in the country of white-robed priests and priestesses setting themselves on fire. It was a coordinated effort, the self-immolations occurring at exactly the same time everywhere. The groups of suicidal followers ranged from thirty in number all the way up to over one hundred, in more than two hundred cities. The number of victims was currently estimated at somewhere over twelve thousand.

The number made Jeffries go weak at the knees. And the mayhem that had resulted was almost beyond comprehension.

Amazed and emboldened by what they had seen, citizens all over the country were rising up in arms, ignoring curfews and breaking through security lines. The country was now in a state of dire emergency, if not quite civil war – and the President had been very clear about the distinction. But it seemed like a civil war to Jeffries; he had had to order the full might of the military to step in to deal with the citizens of his own country. It made him feel sick all over again.

When Tomkin had first approached him with his plan, Jeffries had never suspected it would result in the deaths of *any* of his fellow-countrymen. It was the enemy who were supposed to die, not his own neighbours. The situation was clearly completely out of hand now, beyond any form of control. It had taken on a life of its own, and there didn't seem to be anything that could be done to stop it. What had this Order of Planetary Renewal been thinking? What kind of evil cult could convince twelve thousand people to kill themselves? And not just kill themselves, but kill themselves in one of the most agonizing ways possible?

Tomkin's absence from the meeting today was noticed. Where was he? Engaged on a private matter, Jeffries had said, all too aware that, given the current situation, it just didn't ring true.

Jeffries sagged into his leather armchair. He prayed that Spectrum Nine worked as promised. That was their only hope now.

'I don't believe it,' Jack breathed. Alyssa came close, peering over his shoulder at the computer screen.

'What have you found?' Alyssa asked.

'Everything,' he said. 'It's all here. All of it. All the way from initial discussions, strategy, plans, schematics, results of research, names of all involved personnel, we've got *everything*.'

'How high does it go?' Alyssa asked anxiously. 'Is the President involved?'

'No,' Jack said, 'not the President. The Secretary of Defence is in this up to his neck, but I don't think it goes any higher.'

'Can we copy this information?' Alyssa asked.

'I'm already doing it,' Jack pointed to a flash drive he'd

put into the unit, having found some spares in Tomkin's desk drawer. 'But there's something else too,' he said.

'What?' Alyssa asked, sitting down next to him.

'The list of targets. Casualty estimates.'

'Show me,' Alyssa said, and Jack brought up the information.

Alyssa's eyes went wide as she read.

She had thought that Spectrum Nine would be a highly targeted weapon – at worst, a flood taking out a coastal naval base, or a small earthquake destroying armaments factories or missile silos. Not this. It was clear that Tomkin wanted to use Spectrum Nine to its fullest extent, and the targets were whole *countries*, including entire civilian populations. With horror, Alyssa read what amounted to a battle plan for total genocide. Volcano eruptions and earthquakes would be used to destroy most of northern and central Asia, taking out their own country's main military and economic competitor in one fell swoop. Sandstorms, floods and earthquakes would be used to decimate much of the Middle East, purging it of its terrorist infrastructure once and for all. Meanwhile, other disasters would befall their neighbours south of the border, forever clearing up the problem with drug lords and leftist guerrillas.

The scale of the destruction Tomkin had planned was beyond comprehension. 'Casualty estimate . . . *One point two billion men, women and children*,' Alyssa said, collapsing back in her chair.

Jack shook his head. 'Those aren't casualty estimates, Alyssa,' he told her. 'They're fatalities.' He turned to look at her. 'Those people are all going to die.'

12

THE MEN AND women checked and rechecked their equipment as they waited for the helicopters to land. The order had been given, and the attack was about to commence.

Oswald Umbebe also checked his equipment as he waited. People were surprised, given his condition, that he was going to accompany them on the assault, but he wouldn't miss it for the world. If he was killed, what difference would it make anyway? But he had to be there. Besides, he had been a child soldier once upon a time, back in the seething jungles of his youth, and such work was something he would never forget. It was in his very blood.

He still didn't have the codes but he had a couple of options open to him on that score. The important thing at the moment was to take advantage of the current chaos and rioting, and attack while the facility was vulnerable. His faithful followers had performed their recent test superbly, sacrificing themselves for the greater good. He knew the effect the simultaneous bodily sacrifice of twelve thousand people would have; it wasn't just emergency services that would be stretched, but the entire machinery of government as well, including the military. The troops guarding the target up in the snow-covered mountains would have been reduced to a minimum.

Umbebe had wept as he had watched the footage of their brave act, tormented that he had asked them to do such a thing. But he knew, ultimately, that it was worthwhile. If everyone was going to die in a short while anyway, then surely they had only missed out on their last few hours. And their sacrifice would not be in vain.

Evan Ward awoke slowly, his faculties returning to him one small step at a time.

He had seen the two figures leave his office several minutes before but had not registered any more than that. Who they were, he had no idea. In his dazed state, he had only vaguely recognized that they were people.

But as his conscious mind started to reassert itself, recent events came flooding back to him. His eyes popped fully open, and he surged upwards from his chair, but found that he was tied securely. He tried to scream out, to call for help, to raise the alarm, but those damn fake technicians – terrorists? he asked himself in horror – had gagged him, and all that came out was a muffled rumble.

Damn them! What were they up to? It was clear they had wanted access to the computer systems. But why?

Suddenly, it occurred to Ward that they might even have been the ones who planted the virus in the first place. How could he have been so stupid? But he had checked their details on the Beltway database. Maybe they planted the details in the Beltway system – unless Beltway itself was some sort of terrorist/criminal/enemy government front?

He wasn't going to get any answers while he was strapped to this chair, that was for sure. He looked towards the door, estimated the distance. About six feet; not too far.

The chair wasn't fixed, and luckily the two intruders hadn't known enough about securing a captive to tie his legs and feet properly – the soles of both his feet were in contact with the ground. Ward himself would have strapped a prisoner's lower legs tight to the chair legs so that no more than the tips of the toes were in contact with the floor, making manoeuvring much more difficult.

Ignoring the pain that wracked his head and upper body – he knew he was concussed, and feared he may even have damaged some vertebrae – he started to shuffle his body, using the traction of his feet and a powerful twisting of his shoulders.

Slowly but surely, he worked his way to the door, its window covered by the blind. He tried to use his head to push down the metal handle but couldn't get the angle right. He shuffled on the chair some more but still couldn't do it.

He repositioned himself one more time, steeled his nerve, and smashed his head straight through the door's window into the main CWD control room.

'Somebody get over here and help me!' he shouted. 'Now!' Shards of glass stuck out of his head, blood flowing freely.

People raced over to him and carefully levered his head out of the shattered window. Even before he was fully untied from the chair, Ward was shouting orders. 'Alert security! Immediately! Those two Beltway technicians were imposters, we need to find them!'

Ward was standing now, shaking glass from his uniform and wiping blood from his face. 'Did anyone see them after they left here?' he demanded.

'Yes, sir,' a staff sergeant said sheepishly. 'I escorted them to General Tomkin's office.'

'General Tomkin?' Ward asked incredulously. This idiot had *escorted* them to the office of the *Chairman of the Joint Chiefs*? 'I'll deal with you later, Sergeant,' he said, pushing past him and reaching for his phone.

'Call for you, sir,' a female officer shouted to him from across the room. 'Colonel Anderson. He says it's urgent.'

It better be, Ward growled silently as he strode across the control room.

'Colonel Ward,' Anderson said, airborne in the helicopter with his men now, en route to DoD headquarters, 'we have a situation. I have reason to believe that a man and a woman posing as employees of Beltway Security Systems may have gained access to your offices under false pretences and—'

'That's right,' Ward barked, cutting Anderson off. 'One of them smashed my damn head open with a steel chair. Now you better tell me who the hell these people are.'

When Anderson had called Beltway and discoved they had a David Jenkins and Elaine McDowell on their books, who nobody seemed to know, he immediately called DoD headquarters to ask about unusual activity, and found that their computer systems were suffering from a virus.

If it hadn't been the DoD, the obvious target, Anderson would have made some more calls – there were plenty of other options in the capital – but his gut instinct had been proved right. And this call to the Cyber Warfare Division had just confirmed it. But what did they hope to achieve?

'They're terrorists,' Anderson told Ward. 'Highly dangerous. We don't know what they're planning but it is absolutely vital that they are captured immediately. We cannot afford to take any chances with these people. Do you have any idea where they are now?'

Anderson heard Ward clear his throat, and knew the news was not going to be good. 'I've just received word that they have been escorted to the office of General Tomkin.'

Anderson was speechless. *No*. It couldn't be. Tomkin's computer held *everything*.

Umbebe could see the target with his own eyes now. Access was relatively easy; helicopters had inserted them just five miles out, and 4x4 vehicles had taken them the rest of the way through forested roads. External security hadn't worried Umbebe in the slightest; it had all been taken care of.

The four frontline eight-man teams had encircled the target from its three approachable, guarded sides. A mile back from the complex's rear, the land fell away in a jagged cliff, and Umbebe knew there was no point in wasting men and resources by approaching from that direction. It would be suicide, and while he had no problem with that if it served a higher purpose, there was something abjectly wrong with pointless self-sacrifice.

The four teams would attack first, followed by the secondary section if resistance proved firmer than expected. If not, the secondary team would remain outside the target area in order to repel counter-attacks – not that any was likely to come in time.

Umbebe checked his watch. It was time. He withdrew his radio and thumbed the transmit button. 'Units Alpha, Bravo, Charlie and Delta, you are to proceed on three . . . two . . . one . . . go!'

Umbebe watched through his night-vision binoculars as the sky lit up around him, the four initial assault elements erupting into action simultaneously.

Umbebe would enter the site once it was fully secure. He would transmit a final message to the world. And then all the prophecies of his order would come true at last.

13

WHEN WARD HAD finished with Anderson, he'd called the security centre and been reassured to find that they had already activated emergency plans. The building was going into lockdown, external communications had been severed, and twenty armed military police officers were on their way to General Tomkin's office.

Ward was now racing down the corridors towards the office himself. His phone rang and he answered it without slowing his pace. 'Ward,' he said.

'Sir, this is security. We've reached the general's office but the subjects have gone.'

'Gone?' Ward asked, slowing.

'Yes, sir. The secretary saw them leave just a few minutes ago.'

'Dammit!' Ward swore, coming to a complete halt. 'So where are they now?'

'We don't know, sir,' came the reply. 'But we're in the process of locking down all exits. They won't get away.'

Ward stood in the corridor, shaking his head. The security officer's confidence was sadly misplaced, Ward knew. They were only in the process of locking down the exits? And the subjects had left the office several minutes ago?

He sighed. They could be anywhere by now.

General David Tomkin sat in the luxurious executive helicopter, peering out of the windows as the pilot started to spool up the rotor blades, readying the engines for take-off.

The helicopter landing pad was situated in the massive courtyard that occupied the centre of the DoD complex, an otherwise green space where employees came for some peaceful reflection. Tomkin had always thought it rather unfortunate that it should also be the site chosen for the helipad, the near deafening noise of the regular arrivals and departures in diametrical opposition to the stated aims of the courtyard.

But at least it was convenient, Tomkin reflected. It was a hell of a lot better than driving across town, anyway.

From the high pitch of the engines, Tomkin knew the helicopter was about to take off, and he settled down to relax for the flight. As he did so, he pulled his cellphone out of his pocket, surprised when he saw there were six missed calls, four from Anderson and two from DoD security. *What the hell?*

He must have missed the phone ringing due to the noise of the helicopter. He moved his thumb to the keypad to call Anderson, when he saw two uniformed generals running across the courtyard towards his helicopter.

Damn, how urgent was this? *Two* generals? He sighed,

and put his phone away, calling for the pilot not to take off. He reached forward to open the door when he saw another helicopter coming in to land, dangerously close to his own. This second chopper wasn't even going for the helipad but was tearing up the neatly trimmed lawn to the side. What the hell was going on?

Tomkin levered the door open to let the two generals come aboard.

He saw their faces then; furtive, scared, looking with horror at the other chopper. A man and a woman. *No*. It couldn't be.

Alyssa Durham pulled a handgun from underneath her uniform and aimed it at Tomkin's heart. 'Let's get out of here, General. Now.'

From his own helicopter Anderson saw the two uniformed officers approach Tomkin's chopper and cursed. He could see from here that the uniforms were ill-fitting. Couldn't Tomkin see that too?

But Anderson knew what had happened – during a search of the general's office, two empty suit hangers had been found in the wardrobe. And they weren't leaving via one of the protected exits; theoretically, in the courtyard they were still inside the building. It was no surprise they hadn't been caught.

But what was their plan now? And what were they going to do with Tomkin? There was a 9mm pistol missing from the gun cabinet in Tomkin's office too, a fact that definitely boded ill for the general.

Anderson couldn't let that happen, and he wrenched the chopper door open before it had even fully set down on the lawn.

'I suppose I should have recognized my own uniforms,' Tomkin said with a self-deprecating sigh, as the helicopter lifted off into the air. 'The gun's not loaded, by the way.'

'Good try,' Alyssa replied immediately. 'But even if I hadn't checked it – which I have – there's no way we'd be flying now if it was empty.'

Tomkin smiled. 'Good,' he said, as if rewarding a clever student. 'You're two very impressive people, I'll give you that. But what now? What are you going to do with me?'

'I'm going to make you an offer,' Alyssa replied, as Jack watched the courtyard below. 'We have enough evidence to bury you, John Jeffries, and everyone else associated with this sick project. Call it off, and we'll not go public with it.'

'And if I refuse?' Tomkin asked with amusement.

'Then I'll kill you,' Alyssa said with a straight face. 'One life for many.'

Alyssa heard Jack gasp, and then she felt the chopper lurch as if it had been hit by a huge blunt instrument, or as if it had been weighed down on one side suddenly.

'Jack,' Alyssa said, 'what is it?'

'Anderson,' Jack said in utter disbelief.

Tomkin's chopper was already in the air when Anderson made the jump, just managing to catch hold of one of the long metal skids that ran down underneath both sides of the chopper.

His legs dangling freely in the air below as the chopper increased its altitude, the DoD headquarters smaller and smaller beneath him, Anderson forced himself to concentrate, pulling himself upwards with all his strength until his body lay against the skid.

Now all he had to do was get into the aircraft.

All three passengers jumped out of the way of the door as Anderson started firing into the metal skin of the helicopter.

Alyssa tried to keep control of what she was doing, but the impact of the pistol rounds was terrifying and before she knew it, Anderson had pulled the door open and squeezed himself through into the cabin.

Keeping his pistol up and aimed, he shut the door behind him, blocking out the shrieking wind and allowing the pilot to stabilize the aircraft.

Tomkin managed to keep his focus better than Alyssa. His military training and years of operational experience had not been totally lost during his years behind a desk. He used the distraction of Anderson's entry to snatch the gun from Alyssa's grasp. In the same fluid action he spun her round, his arm round her neck in a choke hold as he pressed the steel barrel against her temple.

'Who's got the flash drive?' Tomkin asked. When there was no reply, he drove the barrel further into Alyssa's temple, tightening his hold round her neck. 'If you don't tell me, we'll just shoot you both and search your dead bodies.'

Alyssa saw Anderson raise an eyebrow, and realized in horror that he evidently thought that this was a better idea than asking them. She had to barter for time somehow, before they were both killed.

'We've both got drives,' she said quickly, to gain precious seconds. Maybe they could distract one of them and get one of the guns back.

But who was she kidding? These were both special forces officers, trained to kill like Jack was trained to use computers. It was what they did for a living. She sagged further into Tomkin's grasp, a feeling of hopelessness pervading her.

Tomkin pushed Alyssa roughly across the leather-lined cabin, and she landed on a couch next to Jack. 'Give them to us,' Tomkin said, his gun still trained on her.

Alyssa looked at Jack and shrugged her shoulders. What else could they do? 'We don't just have the evidence on the drives,' Jack said with more confidence than Alyssa could muster.

'I don't believe him,' Anderson said to Tomkin.

Tomkin nodded. 'I don't believe you either,' he said to Jack. 'So you better show us those drives before you get yourselves shot.'

Jack held up his hands, palms out. 'It's true, I swear. I encoded it with the virus, back in your office. The evidence is living there now, trapped in the DoD system. Unless you permanently sever your computers from the outside world, the evidence will be on the web the moment the system goes back online.'

Alyssa saw Tomkin and Anderson exchange uneasy

glances, clearly unsure if Jack was telling the truth. Like herself, they probably didn't even know if such a thing was possible. She assumed it wasn't, though, because Jack hadn't done what he was saying. But it was a great bluff simply because it could be true.

The cabin was tense for several long, drawn-out seconds. Tomkin and Anderson exchanged looks again, clearly wanting to discuss the matter but unwilling to do so in front of them.

Alyssa could feel beads of sweat running down her forehead. Anderson clearly wanted to shoot them, but what about Tomkin?

The heavy silence was broken by the shrill ringtone of Tomkin's phone, and Alyssa was convinced Anderson's finger was a half-pound's pressure away from firing at the sound of it.

Keeping his gun steady and his eyes on Alyssa, Tomkin reached into his pocket and answered the call. 'Tomkin,' he said, before listening with what appeared to be mounting horror. 'Are you sure?' he asked, clearly stunned. 'How? . . . When? . . . OK. Colonel Anderson and I are on our way up there right now. I'll take control of the situation when we get there. What assets do we have nearby? . . . You're joking? . . . OK. Keep me posted.'

Tomkin hung up, shaken to his core but his gun still up and aimed.

'Sir?' Anderson asked, concerned. 'What's going on?'

Tomkin didn't respond.

'Sir?' Anderson repeated.

'I'm sorry,' he said. 'It looks like the HIRP base has been

347

penetrated. Taken over.' He shook his head in disbelief, and Alyssa thought she could almost see tears in his eyes. 'The unthinkable has happened,' he announced. 'Spectrum Nine has fallen into the hands of the enemy.'

PART FIVE

PART FIVE

1

UMBEBE LOOKED GRAVELY into the camcorder held by one of his loyal followers, ensconced now in the main control room of the Ionospheric Research Array. The video of his speech – as well as a visual tour of the captured facility to prove his words – would be put out on the web, and would be picked up by news agencies around the world in seconds. Within the hour, Umbebe was confident that almost every man, woman and child on the globe would know about it.

The assault had gone perfectly, and his team of crack international commandos had met little resistance. The head of base security, Colonel Anderson, wasn't even there to help organize a cohesive defence, and so the facility fell with ease – almost as if it was meant to be, Umbebe had mused as he received the word from his team leaders that the complex was secure.

But now was the time for his final message to the world, and he settled himself. His entire life had led him to this single point, and he truly believed that it was his destiny. What he wanted to achieve today was no less than the desire of the universe itself.

'Extinction,' Umbebe intoned in his deeply melodious

voice, 'is inevitable. It always has been, ever since the dawn of time. It is the very nature of things.

'There have been seven such extinction events over the course of our planet's history, great upheavals which have resulted in catastrophic loss of life. My own order has charted these events with scientific rigour over the past thousand years, and we have discerned a pattern amidst the apparent chaos. It shows that the world is a living organism, expanding and contracting. Sometimes life on this planet explodes and we are faced with a multitude of new and incredibly diverse species; at other times, life is expunged. Think of it like a lung. What happens if air keeps filling the lung? It cannot expand forever, and without contraction, the organism will die.

'This is what is happening on our planet. We are continually expanding, with no checks and balances. We are going to kill the organism before long.

'Believe me, my brothers and sisters around the world, we are about to enter a very necessary period of contraction. Just as our order's scientists have predicted, our time here on earth is at an end. We have pushed it out as far as we can with our technological perversion of the environment, but we cannot let it continue any longer. The time has come for the great sacrifice, which we must make together.

'This broadcast comes to you from a government installation known as the High-frequency Ionospheric Research Project, based up near the Arctic Circle. The communications and navigation technology it purports to research is merely a cover. The real purpose of this facility is something called Spectrum Nine.

'Spectrum Nine is what has been causing the strange phenomena you have been experiencing in recent weeks, aberrant behaviour across the natural world. Even the moving statue was but a side effect of the weapon's testing process. It is a weapon of truly epic proportions. Evidence of its power is came a few days ago when that small island was completely destroyed.'

Umbebe paused, to let his words sink in. 'Yes, brothers and sisters, Spectrum Nine destroyed that island. And it can do much more than that. By manipulating sound waves within the recently discovered, so-called ninth spectrum, whoever controls the weapon can control the weather. And whoever controls the weather can create disaster.' Umbebe raised his arms to the camera, hands wide open as if he was conjuring the disasters himself. 'Earthquakes, tidal waves, typhoons, volcanic explosions, floods, storms, death and destruction on an unimaginable scale – Spectrum Nine can create it all.

'And now, my brothers and sisters, the weapon is in the hands of the Order of Planetary Renewal. We attacked the facility earlier today, and have complete control of the entire system. Some of you may wonder what we are after; in other words, what do we want? What will make us refrain from using the device? My answer to you all is, *nothing*. There is nothing that will stop us. We did not capture the weapon to negotiate. We captured the weapon in order to use it. And use it we will.

'We will unleash Spectrum Nine, and the result will be the annihilation of life on earth as we presently know it. This must now be accepted as cold, hard fact.

'I make this broadcast not to terrify, but to inform. There is no going back, nothing that can be done to save you. What happens after the weapon has been unleashed is up to fate. Will humanity survive, perhaps in small isolated pockets? It is possible, of course. Unlikely, but possible. Who knows how the planet will restructure itself after its cleansing? But cleanse it we must,' Umbebe said forcefully. 'And we, the true faithful of the Order of Planetary Renewal, are proud to be the instrument of the universe's will.

'I give you notice so that you may ready yourselves. The road will not be easy, but accept it you must. Six hours from now, the world as you know it will come to an end.'

The four passengers watched Umbebe's video together in the helicopter's cabin, their differences momentarily forgotten.

It was Anderson who recovered his composure first. 'It doesn't matter any more anyway,' he said. 'We might as well kill them now. Two less witnesses when this comes to court.' He raised his gun towards Alyssa and Jack.

'He's right in a way,' Tomkin agreed. 'Whatever evidence you have on you is moot now anyway. Our involvement will be front-page news by tomorrow. So fewer witnesses are a good thing.'

'If there *is* a tomorrow,' Jack shot back. 'What was the answer when you asked about available assets on the phone earlier?' Jack saw the look on Tomkin's face and nodded his head. 'Exactly. There *are* no assets available, because everyone's tied up with the civil unrest. So why don't you tell us your plans for recapturing the base?'

'Watch your tongue, Murray,' snapped Anderson.

'They're not going to use the weapon,' Tomkin said. 'Terrorists don't follow through with threats like that. They want to negotiate, despite their words. They want something. People always do.'

'You must be crazy,' Alyssa said. 'Did you hear the man? He's probably been the one instigating the riots right from the start. His people have been everywhere since this whole thing began. And you don't think he's going to use it? I've read the plans,' she said accusingly, fixing Tomkin with an icy stare. 'If *you* were going to use it, why won't they?'

'We were going to use it selectively,' Tomkin said instantly. 'Our enemies would die, and we would win. What does he win if he destroys the whole world? He'd die too. What would it get him?'

'Can't you see?' Alyssa said. 'He believes what he's doing is right. And whether he's insane or not, he now has control of the world's most powerful weapon. So what can we do to stop him?'

'Tactical missile strike,' Anderson said, his attention at last turning away from Alyssa and Jack to grasp the enormity of the situation. 'We take the base out completely.'

Tomkin shook his head. 'Can you imagine the chaos erupting around the President right now?' he asked. '*What is this weapon? Why didn't I know about it?* I mean, it'll be hours before it's even confirmed that there *is* such a weapon. And then authorizing such a strike, on our own soil, would take even longer. We have thousands of our own citizens there! The President would have to be one hundred per cent convinced that the threat was real. The problem is that there is no precedent for this, no protocol for him to follow. And even if an order *was* given in time, there are other complications. HIRP is probably the world's most isolated research base. Submarines are out of range, our carrier fleets have been diverted to Asia and the Middle East, and it would take hours to arm and fuel our long-range bombers.'

'Do we have any special operations forces in the area?' Anderson asked.

'None. Most of them are preparing for deployment to those same countries where the carrier groups are headed. In fact, many have got their feet covertly on the ground for reconnaissance already. There's no way we can pull them back in time to launch an operation on the other side of the world.'

'Other countries?' Anderson persisted.

'I'm not sure. Most are involved in their own civil crises, some are providing disaster relief and others are joining our own troops in the wrong part of the world. And it would take forever to sort through the red tape for such an operation, even if there were forces available.' Tomkin squared his shoulders, seeming to come to a conclusion. 'Colonel,' he said, 'have you got men on that chopper back at the DoD?'

Anderson nodded. 'Yes, sir, six of my best.'

Tomkin nodded. 'Get them rerouted to the air base, have them meet us there. We've got a plane ready and fuelled, with a flight plan filed. We're going to spend the next few minutes calling all our contacts here in the city. Anybody trained, we want them with us. The plane will hold sixty, so let's see what we can do. We started this thing, and it's our responsibility to finish it. Let's call in all our favours and get that plane filled.' Tomkin looked at Anderson. 'Colonel, you know that base better than anyone. With you leading the party, we might have a chance of retaking it.'

'Sir,' Anderson protested, 'we have no idea how many people they have, where they're posted, what kind of weapons we'll be facing, and we're only going to have a one-hour window to launch the counter-attack when we get there.'

Tomkin just stared at him. 'What other options do we have?'

Anderson looked out through the window at the blue, clear sky. Eventually, he made a decision. 'I can get some men rounded up,' he confirmed. 'We can plan and rehearse on the plane while we're flying. We can get all the schematics of the base, I can identify likely points for the enemy to be stationed. We'll look at worst-case scenarios and take it from there.'

Tomkin inclined his head, glad to have Anderson back on board.

'But I'll need something else too,' Anderson said stiffly, and Alyssa wondered what it was. Surely he wasn't going to ask for permission to shoot them, was he?

'What's that, Colonel?' Tomkin asked.

Anderson nodded at Jack. 'I'll need Murray with me, sir,' he said. 'He knows the base security systems better than anybody. With him, we just might succeed.'

357

2

THE FLIGHT NORTH was long but over all too quickly for Alyssa.

After the decision had been made to launch a counter-attack, Tomkin and Anderson had been on their phones all the way to the airport, contacting everyone they knew in the area. By the time the plane was ready to take off half an hour later, it was nearly full with fifty-four grim-faced soldiers, and a cargo-hold full of arms.

Alyssa was on board too, although held separately. She was being taken as insurance, in a way. Jack appeared keen to help but Anderson, ever suspicious, decided that he might need a bit more inducement. Alyssa was there-fore being taken along as a hostage.

She spent the flight looking across the plane at Jack, locked in conversation with Anderson. It was clear that, despite the circumstances, he was in his element, lecturing the colonel and the other team leaders on HIRP's security protocols. For a lot of the journey, Jack was also entering information on to a powerful laptop computer, and Alyssa wondered if he was able to access the security systems remotely. Was he already creating the conditions that would enable the shock troops to get close to the base without being seen? She remembered how he had created that invisible corridor, unwatched by security cameras, when they had climbed the roof of the main control building and they had first kissed; only days ago, but it seemed a lifetime.

She was sorry – so achingly sorry – that she couldn't spend the hours of the flight together with Jack. They had been through so much together in such a short time; the intensity of their experience was like nothing she had felt in her life before. Other experiences had been intensely bad – the long, drawn-out and painful death of her husband, the shocking, all-too-sudden death of her daughter – but this had been intensely good, despite everything. It had all been worth it, to find Jack.

And as she watched him across the plane for hours – as the soldiers ripped out chairs to give themselves room to rehearse their team procedures, as they gathered around a mock-up scale model of the base, as they cleaned and prepared their personal equipment – she knew in her heart of hearts how she felt.

She was in love with Jack Murray.

'Alyssa,' Jack breathed softly, her head buried in the warm skin of his neck. 'I'm sorry. I'm so sorry.' He held her hands, kissed them. 'I have to go.'

Tears welled up in her eyes, although she tried to stop them. 'I know,' she whispered weakly. 'I know.'

Jack would be accompanying the preliminary assault party, leading them into the base with Anderson. He had apparently already adjusted part of the system remotely, but the closer he got, the more he would be able to do. As Anderson had hoped, he would be able to make them invisible.

When the aircraft landed, Alyssa was surprised by Tomkin's humanity when he allowed them a few brief moments together before Jack left. Tomkin, too old now for such an assault, would remain with Alyssa to keep an eye on her.

She knew she was unlikely to ever see Jack again, which made these last few moments so especially painful.

She pulled him close, looking into his deep blue eyes. 'But I want you to know, whatever happens . . . I love you.'

And with that, she kissed him once on the lips and turned back inside the aircraft, not waiting to hear his answer.

It would have been too painful to bear.

During the flight, Anderson had been in touch with the director of Allenburg Airport. Upon landing, the entire team and their equipment were transferred to helicopters, which landed in hidden clearings in the forest just outside the base perimeter.

A control tent was set up in one of the clearings, where Tomkin took command of the radio communications equipment, enabling him to give direction from afar.

Alyssa was secured to a chair, and the soldiers received their final mission briefings and disappeared into the forest like silent wraiths, Jack right next to Colonel Anderson.

Alyssa's face burned in the cold night air. All she could do now was sit and listen to the counter-attack as it unfolded live over the radio.

3

THE SOUNDS OF violence that penetrated the cool mountain air were horrific.

Over the radio, Alyssa heard the screams of dying men alongside gunshots, explosions, and the shriek of tortured metal. Some of the same noises came to them through the surrounding trees too, echoing strangely. She heard the shouts of men issuing orders, fire commands, positions. She heard Colonel Anderson shouting at Jack, telling him to get the cameras sorted, how they were walking into a trap, an ambush . . .

Tomkin listened too, helplessly. He tried to issue orders over the radio, but to no avail. It was too hard to keep track of what was happening; there were too many people who had never worked with each other, following section leaders they had never met, putting into action a battle plan created on the run, against a completely unknown enemy force. It had been a recipe for disaster right from the start. But it had been all they had, and the first few minutes — after the teams had reached the perimeter and entered the base without sounding the alarm — looked positive. It seemed the electronic surveillance was on their side, and they might have some sort of chance.

Then the explosions had sounded, and Alyssa had seen the night sky light up through the trees. But it was too early to be their own troops, and Alyssa and Tomkin both realized that the teams had been compromised.

The firefight that subsequently broke out was terrifying in its intensity, and Alyssa shook with horror as she thought about Jack, there in the middle of it all without even a simple pistol to defend himself.

'Come on, Jack!' she heard Anderson shout over the live network. 'Get that computer over here now!'

As he waited – presumably for Jack to get to him – Anderson reported back to Tomkin. 'We've been ambushed, sir,' he said desperately. 'We've already lost most of our men. They must have known we were coming.' He breathed heavily, and gunfire momentarily interrupted the transmission. 'But I've made it as far as the radar array. I've still got two men and Jack with me. I— Jack! Jack!' Anderson called, his report forgotten.

Alyssa's heart stopped as explosions and gunfire drowned out Anderson's screams, leaving only silence at the other end of the radio.

'I'm going,' Alyssa said.

Tomkin shook his head. 'It's out of the question. They've been defeated. We've lost them. The best thing we can do now is find some place to take cover. Even if they do use the weapon, this is going to be the last place to go, so we've got time. And what are you going to do anyway? Fifty men have just failed.'

Alyssa stood her ground, adamant. 'I've got to go,' she

said. 'I know he's in there. I know he's still alive.'

'Murray?' Tomkin asked in disbelief. 'Not a chance. He didn't even have a gun.' He looked at Alyssa. 'I'm sorry, but that's just the way it is.'

'Look, General,' Alyssa said. 'You give up if you want to. What do you care now what I do? Just untie me and let me try.'

Tomkin sat back and considered her words, then leant forward and cut her restraints. 'You're right,' he said. 'It doesn't matter to me what you do. I've got more important things to worry about.'

Alyssa inclined her head in thanks, about to race into the woods, but Tomkin put a hand to her chest to stop her. 'But please,' he said, holding a pistol out towards her, 'at least take my gun.'

Twenty minutes later, Alyssa wondered what the hell she was doing.

She had remembered the cliff from her previous visit, how she had been told that it was all but unclimbable, and how guards didn't even bother to patrol that section of the fence line.

She knew that the assault teams had not chosen this route but tried to enter from the three flat sides. She wasn't surprised – time was of the essence, and such a climb could only be made by an expert. They couldn't have taken the chance of losing people before they'd even made it to the base. But she had decided it was worth a shot, and she'd raced through the forest that encircled the facility, following the trails down in a wide, sloping arc to the foot of the cliff.

She gazed up at it now with foreboding. It looked treacherous as hell. She rotated her head, her neck clicking, then shook her entire body, getting the blood pumping, the adrenalin flowing. She knew adrenalin would be her friend on the cliff face.

But she found it hard to move, hard to take those first few tentative steps. Scenes from the past flashed before her eyes – falling in the tractor from the top of the cliff just a few days before; another cliff, the one she had been climbing that day long ago, in other mountains; her race up the ladder to the chair lift cables; Anna's death scream filling the valley.

She snapped out of it, forcing herself to look at her watch. Just half an hour to go before Spectrum Nine would be switched on. For a horrifying second, she vividly recalled the radar array blasting that beam of concentrated energy up into the sky just a few short days before, a reversed bolt of lightning that had presaged the destruction of an entire island and many thousands of people.

And then she set off up the sheer, icy rock surface, her face set in grim determination.

4

FOR THE NEXT twenty minutes, Alyssa climbed like she had never climbed before. Barely daring to breathe for fear the passage of air would push her off the treacherous surface, she traced her hands along the icy rock to pick out tiny fissures, small imperfections in the wall which would have been unnoticeable to most other people. On any other occasion they may well have been unnoticeable to her; but tonight, she was filled with a startling clarity of vision. Indeed, it was as if her very fingers could see, and her feet too. She was almost becoming one with the cliff face, as if she had climbed it every day of her life, she knew it so well.

As she climbed higher and higher, she barely noticed the cold wind that whipped at her and threatened to rip her off the rock wall; she was unaware when the first signs of frostbite started to attack her shredded fingertips. All she could see was the wall, disappearing beneath her as she devoured it step by step.

Jack, she repeated in her head like a mantra. *Jack*.

Before she realized what she had done she was at the top, pulling herself onto the rocky precipice.

She paused only momentarily to get her breath, her mind focused entirely now on getting to the base. Getting to Jack. Together, she was sure they could stop this thing.

Keeping low, she crept along the grass of the cliff top towards the seven-foot-high barbed-wire fence. The radar array was directly on the other side. She looked at her watch again; less than ten minutes to go.

She checked that her pistol was secure in her belt and raced towards the fence; there was no time for anything more subtle. She leapt high as she reached it, hands reaching out for the top. She grasped the barbed wire, ignoring the pain which shot through her cold-numbed hands, and pulled herself up and over.

The barbs caught in her stomach as she pulled herself across, cutting through her jacket and lacerating her flesh. One of the barbs caught deeply, and she moaned, pushing herself back to free it, blood running down into her trousers as she dropped heavily to the ground on the other side, her hands ripped to shreds.

Undeterred, she moved on, legs pumping as she skirted the inner wire fences of the huge radars, heading for the site's main control room.

She could make out roving patrols of guards, and kept close to the shadows to avoid them. If they had night-vision goggles, her tactics might still be foiled, but none of the guards seemed interested in looking in her direction. They would have been briefed that the cliff-side area was impassable, and would keep their attention focused on the other side.

As she moved down past the rows of giant radars, she

felt the ground shake as a powerful humming sound started to emanate from the array.

She increased her pace, her head down low, watching with horror as the vanes at the tops of the radar posts started to buzz with electricity. *No*, she thought. *Please no*.

Sounds of gunfire erupted from over the hill, towards the central control room at the front entrance. Glad that some of the good guys were still alive at least, she watched as the remaining guards moved to help their comrades, and took her chance, sprinting the remaining distance to the now unprotected cabin that housed the radar array's command centre.

She had to step over a mangled, dead body on her way in and paused for a moment, shocked as she recognized Colonel Anderson, half of his face blown away. But where was Jack? Had he managed to escape? Had he made it inside, only to be killed?

Pulling Tomkin's pistol from her belt, her frozen, ripped hands struggling to get a grip on it, she threw the doors open and entered the nerve centre.

5

In front of her lay the complex machinery of the radar array's control room, completely empty except for dead bodies. She gasped as she recognized Niall Breisner and Martin King among them.

Then a door opened at the far end and a man came through.

Their eyes met, and in that split second the man began to raise his assault rifle. But Alyssa's gun was already up, and she fired once, twice, hitting the soldier in the chest; she watched in horror as he slumped to the floor, knowing he was dead.

She had never killed anyone before, but she knew she had to quell the feelings of sick, fierce guilt that burned through her; there was no time for it.

She raced for the door the man had come through and pulled it open, wondering where it led, and if anyone had heard the shots. As she pushed through the doorway, she noticed it was a small room, like a pressure chamber. And, like a pressure chamber, there was a hatch in the floor.

She bent down and hauled the hatch open. An access tunnel, with a ladder attached to its side, descended deep into the bowels of the earth. Outside, she heard the hum and vibration as more and more radar units powered up. Steeling herself, she entered the vertical tunnel, knowing it might be the last thing she ever did.

6

AT THE BOTTOM of the ladder Alyssa paused, breathing hard, one bleeding hand gripped round her gun, the other on the handle of the lower access hatch.

Summoning all her self-control, all of her considerable willpower, she pulled the door open and strode out into the brightly lit room, pistol raised in front of her.

The room was large, much like a nuclear bunker hidden deep underground. She ignored the people around the room, her eyes fixed on the man behind the computer console.

She recognized him from the television: Oswald Umbebe, the high priest of the OPR. If she could kill him, there might still be a chance.

Maybe Jack was still alive somewhere in the grounds, and when this whole thing was finished, he would be found and saved. But for now, Alyssa could only see Umbebe.

The large, impressive man turned in his chair to look at her, and for a moment she was frozen by the look of utter calm in his eyes. It was the look of a man who knew he couldn't be stopped.

And then she noticed a shadow move on the tiled floor beside her feet, and knew with a sickening feeling that someone was standing right behind her.

7

'Jack!' Alyssa cried. 'You're OK!' She opened her arms, so happy to see him in one piece that she all but forgot about Umbebe sitting in the chair behind her, hands on the controls of Spectrum Nine. How had Jack done it? But it didn't matter, he was here, and together they could—

She froze. Jack was holding a gun and he was pointing it at her. 'Jack?'

'Alyssa . . .' he said softly, almost regretfully, and, although his eyes looked sad, the gun never wavered from her chest.

'Jack works for me,' Umbebe's deep baritone broke in from behind, and Alyssa's head snapped towards him, disbelief across her face.

'You're a liar!' she screamed at him, her own gun raised once more. 'Tell me he's wrong,' she said to Jack pleadingly.

'Tell her, Jack,' the deep voice commanded.

'Drop the gun, Alyssa,' he said sadly. 'It's true.'

'Jack,' she said weakly. 'I don't understand . . .'

'I work for Umbebe,' Jack said. 'I'm a believer.'

Alyssa's mind seemed to buckle, along with her body.

'I've been with Oswald since I was a boy,' Jack explained.

'My parents died, I had nothing, I was bounced from one orphange to another. Then he found me, took me in, gave me a home, taught me about the world, the universe. What he says, what the order believes in – what *I* believe in – it's true.'

'But why did you help me?' Alyssa asked, so bewildered she did not notice the bustling activity in the operations room around her.

'What choice did I have?' Jack responded. 'I'd been in place for years, feeding Oswald information. I'd found out about Spectrum Nine when it was still in its infancy, and Oswald saw the potential right away.' He shook his head. 'I was supposed to be here when the attack took place, help them by sabotaging the security systems. It was only sheer chance that I ended up back here anyway.' Jack smiled wryly. 'Anderson brought me here himself, and he never realized that instead of helping, I was feeding information to the order.

'I was also supposed to get the access codes from the secure computers here. But when Anderson saw me with you, the plan changed. I had to escape with you, or else I might have been killed, and then I couldn't have helped at all. After we split up, when we escaped from the motel, I managed to let Oswald know what was happening, and he told me to keep trying to get the codes. But I'd already decided to do that anyway.'

'Is that why you came to meet me in the station café?' Alyssa asked.

'Yes,' Jack replied levelly. 'I knew you had information from the base on that flash drive, and I wanted to see if the codes were on there. But that wasn't the only reason. I know you won't believe me, but I wanted to see you again. I knew the world was going to be destroyed anyway, and I wanted to spend my last few hours with you.'

Alyssa tried to ignore this last statement. 'So you weren't trying to get the information out to the media at all?'

Jack shook his head. 'No, I was never trying to get the information out, I just wanted the codes. As it happens, the codes weren't on the disk anyway. That's why I came up with the plan to break into the DoD.'

'But what were the chances of that being successful?' Alyssa asked. 'We did it, but the odds were against us. What if you hadn't got the codes?'

'The back-up plan was for Oswald's men to torture Breisner and King until they gave them up,' Jack said. 'But that would have taken time so it was never the preferred method. Oswald would have found a way to work the system one way or another. My way was just a lot cleaner. And besides, it was worth risking my life for. We're all going to die anyway, remember?'

'Why didn't you just meet up with Umbebe and join the team? Get the codes here at the base like you'd originally planned?'

'Oswald had already left; he was with the assault team up here where they were making their final preparations. I'd spent too long escaping from up here, and it would have taken forever to get back. And with everyone looking for me, there was no way I could have travelled by plane. And I meant what I said earlier,' he said seriously. 'I wanted to spend my last few hours with you.'

Alyssa shook her head. 'But you were never helping me to get evidence.'

'No,' Jack admitted. 'I hacked into Tomkin's computer to get the codes for Spectrum Nine. But I knew you wouldn't have long to live anyway, so I thought I may as well let you have the evidence, at least give you hope in your final hours.' He paused, looked straight into her eyes. 'You mean a lot to me.'

Alyssa's mind spun. Who was this man in front of her? Not the man she'd thought he was, that much was certain, and the betrayal hit her like a spike through her heart. And yet, under the pressure of the chase, when their lives were at stake, she had genuinely felt that Jack loved her; she had felt it.

'Jack,' she pleaded, 'don't let him do this. This isn't you. He's manipulated you, used you, don't you see? We can't let the world end this way. Who are we to decide?'

'No,' he said, 'it's not we who decide. It's the universe itself. It's written in the stars, Alyssa, don't you understand? It's inevitable.'

'He's right,' Umbebe's voice boomed. 'The codes have been inputted, and there is no time left. It's all over. Embrace it, Ms Durham. It is our destiny.'

'It doesn't have to be,' she said, her eyes still fixed on Jack, her mind made up. It was the only thing left that she could do. 'Please don't try and stop me.'

'No!' Jack said as she turned and raised her gun towards Umbebe.

Alyssa saw the look of surprise on Umbebe's face as the barrel tracked towards his face.

'Damn it, Alyssa, don't do it!' Jack shouted.

Umbebe's hands came up in front of him in an instinctive gesture of protection, but Alyssa didn't hesitate. Her finger depressed the trigger of Tomkin's gun, and three shots hit Umbebe in the stomach, shaking him violently in his chair. His eyes went wide with shock and pain and, even more terribly, the fear of defeat and failure – before closing in death.

But Alyssa never saw the eyes close, and would never know what would happen to the world, as Jack unloaded his pistol into the back of her head, his anguished cries the last thing she ever heard.

8

JACK SAGGED, THE impact of the last thirty seconds overwhelming him. He stared at Alyssa's dead body on the floor, blood spilling across the tiles.

The truth was, he really had loved her, the first time he had genuinely felt the emotion for another human being; at least since his father, who had first taught him about the nature and purpose of life and death.

But he loved the planet more, and in his heart of hearts he knew Umbebe was right. The maths, the science, it was all perfect; the earth was due to be cleansed according to the great cosmic programme, and only human technology stood in its way. Flood warning systems, early earthquake detection, weapons which could knock incoming meteorites out of their trajectory with the earth – what chance did nature have? And so it was *right*, so absolutely *right*, to have the earth's ritual cleansing brought about by the same technology that was protecting it from natural destruction.

Umbebe's plan had been perfect. It was just a shame Alyssa had had to become involved, a shame he had let his feelings develop the way they had.

Jack walked forward, stepping over Alyssa's body. He

bent towards Umbebe and pulled him out of his chair, toppling him to the floor next to Alyssa.

His mentor had wanted to initiate the destruction of the earth, but his chance had gone.

Jack sat down in the chair and cracked his fingers. He would just have to do it himself.

9

James Rushton felt the ground shaking beneath him.

For hours now, he had heard the constant blare of car engines, horns and sirens in the streets outside. He had seen the people who worked in this building fleeing across the plaza, though nobody ever came to unlock his cell door.

And so he felt the tremors, and watched through his cell window as buildings started to fall, and the entire plaza disappeared into a giant crater as the earth ate it up whole.

He had only seconds to register the fact that he was witnessing one of the most powerful earthquakes the world had ever seen, titanic forces of nature wreaking utter destruction.

And he watched in mute fascination as the walls of his own cell collapsed, the floor giving way just as the ceiling above him disintegrated and his body was lost forever amidst three million tons of rubble.

It was what he deserved, John Jeffries realized as he stared out across the wide city boulevard. He and his colleagues had meddled with powers they shouldn't have, and this was the result.

The President and most other members of the cabinet

had been moved to secure bunkers, but Jeffries had refused. He knew the futility of such a gesture, because he knew the power of the weapon.

It was over for him almost before it began. The colossal wall of water from the tsunami moved towards him down the avenue, swallowing building after building, carrying cars, people and broken brickwork in its titanic wall.

And then it hit him, and for a glorious moment he was a part of that wall. And then he was gone, and the tidal wave continued on its unconscious mission to destroy every single thing in its path.

The snowstorm was increasing in intensity. General David Tomkin shivered as he backed away into the small cave.

He had fled the camp area with food, weapons and supplies, wandering the forest for as long as he could before he had to find shelter, somewhere to hole up until this whole damn thing was over.

But as he retreated into the cave, he realized it was already over. Snow simply didn't fall like this naturally, and he had to respect whoever was controlling the device, for they must know that by covering the area with such a deep, impenetrable layer of snow, they would be ultimately killing themselves too.

He looked on in dismay as the snow drifted up past the entrance to his cave, so unnaturally thick and cloying that he knew he would never escape, never again set foot outside, never again breathe fresh air.

He shook his head sadly and sat down on the bags of supplies he had dragged through the forest.

Humming a tune to himself, he started to load the shotgun he had brought with him from the camp, knowing now that there would be no chance to hunt with it like he had intended. Not in this life, at any rate.

And then, saying a prayer for the salvation of his soul, he put the shotgun's double barrels in his mouth and pulled the trigger.

10

JACK SIGHED AS he sat back in the chair, eyes dark, his body collapsing. He had been sitting alone in the small room for two days now, controlling the end of the world from his computer station. It had been too much for the other technicians down there, and they had all fled eventually, ultimately unwilling to commit to the final responsibility.

And now it was all over.

Across the world, devastation was raging. Earthquakes, tidal waves, volcanic eruptions; all had been sent to destroy the earth, by his own hand.

The base itself lay under a field of snow some twenty metres deep.

So much destruction, in so short a time. But, he thought with satisfaction, the world would endure. It would be reborn to start anew, afresh. He wondered what sort of world it would be.

He had read somewhere once that such wide-scale disasters might even cause a so-called 'polar shift', the entire crust of the earth shifting round the molten lava of the magma layer beneath like the skin of an orange pulled round the fruit.

What would the world look like when it was finished?

He shook his head, dazed from his vigil at the computer. He would never know.

He looked across the blood-slick floor at Oswald Umbebe, his father figure for so many years.

And next to him, the body of Alyssa Durham, so lovely even in death. She was such a driven woman, surely she would have understood his own single-minded determination.

A tear came to his eye as he realized he would never know.

The days dragged on and Jack's food and water supplies finally ran out; he was also struggling to breathe. The pressure of the snow, or some other, unknown force – he had long ago lost contact with the outside world – had caused the internal air-conditioning system to malfunction.

With a feeling he could only identify as relief, he understood that he would asphyxiate before he died of starvation or thirst.

As the last of the oxygen left the control room and the lights started to dim, Jack thought again of what the new world would be like.

He looked at the body of Alyssa, dead by his own hand. Would there be love in this new world, as she had displayed?

He hoped so.

And then the lights went out completely, and Jack's last painful breaths took place in the pitch black of space; the same, he told himself, as eternal creation.

And then . . . nothing.

EPILOGUE

THE MACHINERY HUMMED beneath Egypt's unforgiving desert sun, operated by a specialist team called in by Clive Burnett.

Indeed, Burnett had been forced to call all manner of people in to help him with his find in the Valley of the Kings. He had even had to inform Egypt's Supreme Council of Antiquities, who had – for the first time in Burnett's long experience – agreed that they needed outside help.

And so an international team had descended on the fabled valley – computer technicians, biologists, metallurgists, experts in all manner of different dating techniques, radar communications specialists, anthropologists, and even linguists. Every science which could be represented was there, waiting for their turn to explore the treasures hidden beneath the sand.

This morning's visiting party, Burnett noted as he waited at the bottom of the access tunnel, were the linguists. It would be interesting to find out if they could decipher anything. But first, there was the tour.

'Good morning, ladies and gentlemen,' he said brightly, excited as always by what he was going to show them. 'If you'd like to step this way, we'll enter what we've established is some sort of reinforced control room for the radar field that's being revealed by our archaeologists back on the surface.'

As the linguists entered the room, they looked around with excitement. The room was a mass of incredibly complex machinery, reaching from one wall to another. The visitors were struck by how similar the computer systems looked to what they were familiar with themselves. But their amazement soon turned to horror as they saw the bloodstains that covered the floor.

'What happened here?' one of the visitors asked.

'There appears to have been some sort of shoot-out,' Burnett said. 'This room hadn't been disturbed since the incident happened, it was a completely closed environment. When we realized this, we pulled out immediately and waited until we could secure the bodies, knowing that the oxygen could destroy the organic matter. But we managed to save the bodies – which share almost one hundred per cent of our own DNA, by the way – and figure out what happened.

'There were three bodies, two men and a woman. As far as we can make out, the woman shot one of the men, who sat in this chair here,' he indicated with his finger. 'Someone, most likely the second man, then shot the woman in the head from behind, pulled the man out of his chair and took his place behind the console, where he later died of a combination of starvation and lack of oxygen.'

'But what *happened* here?' another of the linguists asked, while some of the others tried to read the strange words inscribed on some of the machines around the room.

'As far as we have been able to ascertain, this whole room was the command centre for some sort of sonic weapon. These computers are full of files, full of information, and our specialists have managed to get them operational again, with power from the generators back up top. But we're going to need your help to decipher what we have.'

'Is it true?' a woman asked. 'About what happened?'

Burnett nodded, knowing that the story was already working its way out from the enclosed research site, and would probably soon be hitting the world media anyway.

'We believe so, yes. But let me show you,' he said, heading towards one of the computers. He switched it on, and the visitors again marvelled at how similar it was to what they themselves used.

'Although we can't yet read their language, we can still learn a lot from their maps.' He pulled one of the maps up on to the screen as he spoke, showing a world which looked familiar, yet somehow different.

'It's shifted,' one of the scientists commented eventually.

'Yes,' Burnett confirmed. 'A catastrophic string of disasters – possibly caused by the technology in this room – produced a polar shift, resulting in cataclysmic climate change and mass extinction. The map of the world was changed irreversibly.'

He gestured around the room. 'This chamber, indeed Egypt itself, used to lie within the Arctic Circle. And what appears to have been the major civilization of the time had its main cities further down the eastern coast of modern-day Africa. The capital appears to have been located somewhere around present-day Dar es Salaam in Tanzania, with another major city a few hundred miles below, in what we now know as Mozambique.'

'Like Washington and New York,' one of the linguists said, struggling to take it all in.

'But when did all this happen?' the woman asked, clearly shaken.

'From our initial investigations, we have reason to believe that the people in this room died just over two point four million years ago.'

The shock hit the linguists like a physical body blow, writ clear across every one of their faces. Burnett didn't blame them; he could scarcely believe it himself.

'But that means . . .' one of the men stammered.

'Yes,' Burnett answered the unfinished question. 'It means we are not the first.'

And if that's true, Burnett did not add, *then it also means we probably won't be the last.*

Origin

J.T. Brannan

For Millennia it has lain there undiscovered. Now the time has come . . .

Research scientist Evelyn Edwards always knew the Antarctic held deep secrets, yet the discovery of a 40,000-year-old body buried under the icecaps surpasses even her wildest expectations. But just as her team begins extracting the body the dream turns into a horrific nightmare as they are targeted for death by someone who wants to keep this secret buried. Evelyn barely escapes with her life . . .

On the run, alone and desperate, she turns to her ex-husband Matt Adams, a former member of an elite government unit, for help. Soon, they find themselves caught up in a frantic race against time, which takes them from Area 51 to the Large Hadron Collider in Geneva, as they try to uncover the biggest conspiracy of all time before it's too late for everyone . . .

If mankind thought it knew its origins, the time has come to think again because its every belief is about to be challenged . . .

978 0 7553 9684 9

headline